# Player's Ruse

ALSO BY
## HILARI BELL

*The Knight and Rogue Novels*
The Last Knight
Rogue's Home


The Prophecy
The Wizard Test
The Goblin Wood
A Matter of Profit

# Player's Ruse

### A **Knight** AND **Rogue** NOVEL

## HILARI BELL

**HARPER**
TEEN
*An Imprint of* HarperCollins*Publishers*

HarperTeen is an imprint of HarperCollins Publishers.

Player's Ruse
Copyright © 2010 by Hilari Bell

Library of Congress Cataloging-in-Publication Data
Bell, Hilari.
    Player's ruse : a knight and rogue novel / Hilari Bell. — 1st ed.
        p.      cm. — (Knight and rogue)
    Summary: In alternate chapters, eighteen-year-old Sir Michael Sevenson,
an anachronistic knight errant, and seventeen-year-old Fisk, his street-wise
squire, relate their journey to Huckerston, a port town where dangerous ban-
dits are raiding merchant ships.
    ISBN 978-0-06-082509-6 (trade bdg.)
    [1. Knights and knighthood—Fiction.   2. Fantasy.]   I. Title.
PZ7.B38894Pl   2010                                          2008046905
[Fic]—dc22                                                          CIP
                                                                    AC

Typography by Joel Tippie
12   13   14      LP/RRDH      10   9   8   7   6   5   4   3
❖
First Edition

*To the Denver Science Fiction Writers' Guild—*
*We had a great run, guys, and I miss you.*

# Player's Ruse

# CHAPTER 1
## Fisk

**H**ave you ever noticed that your friends get you into more trouble than your enemies ever could? But this time it wasn't Michael's fault. He was as surprised as I when we approached our lodging on that lazy summer evening and found trouble waiting, right on the doorstep.

We'd spent the day fishing. Michael had insisted that any man approaching his twentieth birthday, city born or not, should know how to fish. When that didn't motivate me, he added that if he caught them all, I would have to clean them. I wasn't as good a fisherman—or as lucky—as he was, but we'd caught three goodish river cod between us, and Michael carried them, dangling from a string.

The town of Litton was too small for cobbled streets, and our footsteps were raising dust on the rutted track when the familiar stink of the leather-works reached my nose. Our lodging, in one of the narrow wooden houses that lined the narrow street, was too close to the tannery for either of our taste—or anyone else's—which was why it was so cheap. But it was only a few streets from the rough tavern where Michael worked—as a bouncer, of all things. It was also near enough to the edge of town that Michael could ride past the fields to the woodlands to exercise Chant and Tipple and do a bit of hunting to supplement our meager income, since I made even less for fine sewing, copying, and letter writing than he did as a bouncer. But Litton was the first town we'd entered in over a year that hadn't thrown Michael out as soon as the sheriff found out about the tattoos on his wrists, so we'd lingered here all spring and into early Berryon, the first month of summer.

Looking at the crowd surrounding our angry land-lady, I had a feeling our welcome wasn't going to last much longer.

Then Mrs. Inger, who was standing on the stoop before her door, caught sight of us and shifted her massive form to one side. The glare she shot at us from under the ruffle of her cap could have felled an ox, but I barely noticed it, for her movement had revealed the girl who sat behind her.

A cloud of rose-gold hair had come loose from the knot that slipped down her neck, framing a face of heartbreaking beauty, smudged and weary as it was. I'd probably have stopped dead in my tracks, as Michael had, except that I'd seen her before. At Michael's home, when his father began the long, tangled idiocy that led to his being unredeemed today.

Michael's jaw dropped. He looked remarkably like one of our unfortunate fish, but he did have some excuse. He was in love with the girl.

Rosamund followed Mrs. Inger's gaze and saw us too. "Brother!" She sprang up from the battered trunk she'd been seated on and darted down the steps and through the crowd. The fine silk of her full skirts was grubbier than her face, and the lace on her wide white collar was torn. "Oh, Brother dear, I'm so glad you've come."

Neither Michael nor I was her brother.

And Michael, almost as poor an actor as this lovely nitwit, was already shaking his head in denial.

"Rosa!" I took two long strides and intercepted her embrace, gripping her shoulders and giving her a small warning shake. It was a good thing the crowd couldn't see *her* face just then. "What under two moons are you doing here? Where's your escort?"

"Ah," said Rosamund. "I . . . um . . ."

My own sisters were lost to me, but you never lose the knack. I scowled and went on in my best brotherly tones. "Does Father know where you are? You ninny! They'll be frantic."

"But I had to." Even wailing, her voice was sweet. "He has half a dozen suitors lined up for me, and I want to marry . . ."

She suddenly realized that the crowd around the doorstep had fallen silent, and a wild-rose flush bloomed in her cheeks.

I controlled my appreciative expression before it went too far for brotherhood, but it was a near thing.

Michael's jaw had closed. The glare he sent me as I threw a fraternal arm around the girl's shoulders almost matched Mrs. Inger's.

"Well, for mercy's sake don't tell the whole street." I hauled her back to the house and maneuvered her up the front steps.

"You asked," she protested, sounding so miffed, it came out quite sisterly.

"Fine, tell me later. Mrs. Inger, I thank you for welcoming my sister, but could she go upstairs now? She's had a long journey."

A stocky, middle-aged fellow I hadn't noticed before snorted. "Is that so, Master Fisk? If she's your sister, how come she has a noble's accent and you don't?"

This drew a murmur from our audience, who hadn't noticed that small detail, curse the fellow. It wasn't as big a crowd as I'd first thought, just a dozen lads from the leather shop and a few farm girls with baskets on their arms. After four months in Litton, Michael and I knew most of them, but Michael's become wary of mobs. He lingered at the fringes of the crowd, managing, for once, to be inconspicuous. Not too hard, with Rosamund around.

"You don't look much like her, Squire," Mrs. Inger said suspiciously. "That's a fact."

Curse the cranky old besom, too. Rosamund and Michael were some sort of third or fourth cousins, but neither my curly, medium brown hair and stocky, medium tall body, nor Michael's taller, leaner form and straight, light brown hair bore the least resemblance to Rosamund's dainty fairness. In fact, no one . . . "No one looks like her." I shrugged, with just the right degree of rueful pride. I've had a lot of practice lying my way out of difficult situations.

"She's really my stepsister. Her mother was of a Gifted line, but she and Rosa weren't. When her father died, their noble kin . . ." I shook my head sadly, evoking a murmur of outraged sympathy at the thought of a noble family so ruthless and dastardly that they'd cast off this lovely girl, just because she hadn't been born with the Gift for sensing magic.

In fact, nobles are usually no more or less ruth-less and dastardly than most folk. But no one in this rough, working-class crowd had my experience with gulling the wealthy, and they were firmly on my side when I turned to the stocky man.

"And what business is it of yours, anyway, Master . . ."

"He's been following me," Rosamund put in angrily. "The horrid man. I had to—"

"Quidge," the man interrupted. He had thinning sandy hair, and his manner was unobtrusive, but he neither yielded nor stiffened to defy the antagonism of the rabble. "Oliver Quidge. I'm a warrant officer, hired by this girl's uncle—"

"Her uncle?" I decided to interrupt, before he told too much of the truth. "Why would he send a bounty hunter for Rosa, after all these years? Or let me guess— he learned she grew up pretty."

Even Mrs. Inger looked angry at that, and Quidge's gaze slid to the growling crowd before he went on. "I was hired by her uncle, who's cared for her since her parents died—as you well know. It's Master Sevenson here is her cousin, and you, Master Fisk, are no kin at all."

"You wretched creature," said Rosamund, putting her arm around my waist. "Fisk and I grew up together just as he says, and no one here is going to believe your nasty lies for one minute. Will you?"

She looked at the crowd and widened her clear, aquamarine eyes. Her lashes were just dark enough to set them off properly, and they subverted every man under ninety. There was a time when they'd have had the same effect on me, but a con man, which had been my profession before I joined up with Michael, learns to see people as they are.

Quidge had the sense to know when he was beaten, though his eyes narrowed in annoyance. "Very well, Mistress, you win this round. I'll just take your uncle's letter to Lord Roger. I doubt he'll be as gullible as this lot, who don't even realize that you're calling your 'brother' by his last name."

"If your name was Nonopherian, you'd go by your last name too," I said, before the dismay on Rosamund's ingenuous face could give us away. I was usually called Squire here in Litton, thanks to Michael's ridiculous persistence in introducing us as knight errant and squire to everyone we met. Several tanners snickered, and Quidge shrugged in grudging defeat. He took himself down the steps without another word, paying no heed to the hostile stares.

"A hard man." Michael had quietly climbed the steps.

"I'm afraid so. Come up to our rooms, Rosa, and

tell me what this is about."

I whisked her past Mrs. Inger's threat to raise the rent if she stayed, and hustled her up the stairs to the two dingy rooms that Michael and I shared. He picked up her trunk and followed.

Rosamund settled herself on one of the unmatched straight chairs that served our all-purpose table, looking like a wildflower in a turnip bin. The lowering sun lit her hair with soft fire; we'd left the shutters open since these attic rooms collected heat and we had nothing worth stealing. She gave me a beaming smile. "Thank you, Master Fisk. That was very quick of you. I hadn't intended to lie, you understand"—she cast a rueful glance at Michael—"but your landlady refused to let me in. She said no women were allowed except family, and I knew that wretched little man would be along in moments, so I—"

"What are you doing here, Rosamund?" Michael's voice was quiet, even firm, but the glow in his eyes as he looked at the girl made me flinch.

I'd realized how Michael felt when I'd seen him with Rosamund before and written it off as calf-love. Painful while it lasted, but no real problem since the wench was safely stuck under the care of her guardian, Michael's father, in the last place in the realm Michael was likely to go.

"That's what I started to tell you," she went on now. "Michael, the most wonderful thing—I'm in love!"

Now that same foolish glow lit her face, and Michael's smile flattened. "Who are you in love with? Come on, Rosamund—Father isn't greedy. If he's at all suitable—"

"Rudy *is* suitable." Her eyes actually flashed. I thought that only happened in ballads. "He's the handsomest, kindest, most honorable—"

"Not suitable at all, I take it?" I put enough sarcasm into it to sting, and she frowned and lapsed into silence, one hand picking at the lace on her cuff.

"Out with it, Rose." Michael's voice was very gentle— only someone who knew him well could have heard the pain beneath. "What does this Rudy do?"

She sighed. "He's a traveling player. In a perfectly respectable troupe with excellent references, and my money is mine anyway so I don't see why it matters that he doesn't have any, and my own grandmother was a miner's daughter so I really don't see why your father made that silly speech about vagabond rogues and fortune hunters, for he *isn't*."

"I see why," I said. And she was going to entangle *us* in this farce? Wait a minute . . . "Mistress Rosamund, how did you find us?"

"That was easy," she said smugly. "Kathy told me

where you were. The hard part will be finding Rudy, for Uncle intercepted all his letters."

Michael's eyes met mine, and a ghost of a smile touched his lips. "You see, Fisk? 'Tis what comes of breaking the rules."

When Michael was declared unredeemed and cast off by his family, his father had forbidden his brothers and his young sister to write to him. So Mistress Kathryn, with typical ingenuity, started writing to me.

Michael, honorable fool that he is, refused to respond to the bedraggled, long-traveled letters that caught up with us periodically—less out of respect for his father's wishes than for fear of getting Kathy into trouble. I had no such scruples, for fifteen—sixteen now—is old enough to make your own choices and take your lumps if they turn out badly. Besides, she was a lively correspondent. When we settled in Litton, it had seemed quite harmless to pass on our address.

Michael turned back to his cousin. "Rosamund, you must see that Father has a point. Gifted, wealthy—you could wed as high as you choose—"

Indeed, the Gift for sensing magic in the plants and animals that have it is so highly prized that it can raise a butcher's granddaughter to baroness—*if* it breeds true. For the sensing Gift only passes through the female line.

"I don't choose high," said Rosamund, her fine jaw firming in a way that looked downright mulish. "I choose Rudy. And you're in no position to lecture anyone about unsuitable choices, Michael-the-knight-errant-Sevenson."

This stopped Michael in mid speech. Knights errant were more than half myth even when there were such things, and that was over two centuries ago. To choose it as a profession was an act of lunacy, though he'd done it, at least in part, to defy his father. To actually make it work, even in the haphazard fashion Michael had managed, was so insane that when I wasn't cursing him for it, I had come to see a bizarre beauty in the thing. But mostly I cursed him.

Especially when Rosamund went on, "Michael, Kathy says you help people. Well, I need your help. Master Makejoye—he runs the troupe Rudy works with—he took them south, into other fiefdoms, out of Uncle Roland's reach. I thought I could find them on my own, but then Uncle sent that man after me, and now . . . Will you help me?"

Those aquamarine eyes would have melted a stronger man than Michael, even if he wasn't in love with her. In fact, Michael being Michael, he'd probably have said yes even if she was a total stranger and plain as a boot. The only thing that surprised me was that he hesitated nearly two seconds before saying firmly,

"Yes. We'll find this Makejoye's troupe and help you get there. My word on it."

"Ah, Michael, may I talk to you for a moment?"

"Certainly, Fisk." He was gazing at the delighted gratitude on Rosamund's face, his smile so fondly dolt-ish as to make anyone want to whack him.

"In private, Noble Sir."

That roused him, for these days I only call him Noble Sir when he's being particularly idiotic.

He told Rosamund to make herself comfortable, dropped the string of fish he still carried into the water bucket, and followed me into our small bed-room. I closed the door firmly behind us.

"Michael, setting aside the fact that Quidge is even now hunting up Lord Roger to talk him into ordering his deputies to pick the girl up, and aside from the fact that, as an unredeemed man, you're in no position to offer anyone protection, and even aside from the fact that those players could be anywhere in the realm by now, are you sure this is the right thing to do—for her?"

"Yes, I am." The assurance in his voice caught me by surprise, and he held up a hand to silence my protest. "Oh, not that she should actually wed this handsome player—that's naught but the foolishness of first love."

He should recognize it. I managed not to say it aloud.

"But Father's going about this all wrong, Fisk. He should have let her go with that troupe, along with a suitable chaperone, and spend six months living in a camp and trudging down dusty roads, having to perform day in, day out when you're tired, or have a headache, or just don't want to. In a few weeks—two months at the most—she'll have fallen out of love with this Rudy and be longing to go home."

This made so much sense that it silenced me for several seconds. "But what if she doesn't change her mind?"

"If the hardships of a vagabond life don't deter her, then she truly loves the fellow, and to compel her to wed another would be deeply wrong. But a player's life isn't so different from our own, and Rosamund is . . . ah . . ."

"Spoiled?"

"Gently reared. Eighteen is old enough to make her own choices. If she can cope with such a life, then mayhap . . . 'Twould mean she feels deeply."

And it might mean that she wasn't so hopelessly beyond the reach of an unredeemed fourth son after all. He intended to court her himself. I tried not to wince visibly, for like Quidge, I know when I'm beaten.

Michael was opening the door when I made my final point. "All right, but I don't know what we're going to do for money. We'll have to—"

"Oh, money won't be a problem," said Rosamund helpfully. She'd taken advantage of our absence to wash her face and pin up her hair, but she still looked tired, and I felt an unwilling sympathy. It took courage for a sheltered rich girl to set off on her own, though in these peaceful times there wasn't much danger. As long as she kept away from the worse parts of the towns she passed through. And didn't flash a lot of money. Or come across someone who thought to try her uncle the baron for ransom.

She opened her trunk and dug into a tangle of lacy white linen. "I knew I'd need money to travel, so I brought my jewelry." A smaller chest emerged from her undergarments, locked with one of those dainty, flimsy padlocks that women think are cute, not realizing they can be broken with a twist of the fingers. She no doubt kept the key . . . yes, she was pulling the chain out of her bodice now, which even I found distracting. Michael swallowed audibly.

Then she opened the box, revealing a tangle of gold and silver, with gems flashing amidst them, and *I* swallowed. Though I hope it wasn't audible. "Mistress Rosamund, you haven't *shown* that to anyone, have you?"

"Of course not." She looked indignant, and for a

moment I hoped I actually had insulted her intelligence, but she went on, "Well, only when I had to
sell a piece, but I knew the shop people would be
honest."

I propped a chair under the doorknob even as I
spoke. "Did you sell anything in Litton?" It was a
miracle she'd made it this far—truly the Gods must
take pity on drunkards and fools. They certainly do
nothing for the rest of us.

"No, I haven't sold a piece for . . . three days I think.
Why?"

Color slowly returned to Michael's face. "Rosamund,
mayhap you should let Fisk look after that for you. He's
good with money, and would likely get a better price
for the jewels than either you or I."

In three days anyone who was going to come after
her probably would have, but I wedged the chair hard
against the door anyway.

"If you like." Rosamund shrugged, watching my
antics with some surprise. "But you see, money won't
be a problem. In fact, I can pay you for taking me to
Rudy, so it all works out."

"We don't want your money," said Michael
predictably.

"Speak for yourself," I said.

Rosamund and I exchanged a smile, and I knew

that whatever Michael said, some of her funds would find their way into our coffers.

I decided hiding the jewels under our unwashed clothes was probably safest, and I also took the precaution of transferring them to a plain cloth bag and replacing the jewel box in Rosamund's trunk as a decoy.

Then we all went down to the kitchen to watch Michael prepare the fish. I chopped a few vegetables for him, and Rosamund told us about her adventures on the road, including the appearance of Master Quidge shortly after she'd passed out of her uncle's fiefdom.

"It makes sense," said Michael thoughtfully, poking the sizzling fish with a fork. "He couldn't know whose fiefs she'd be traveling through, and he's offended some of his neighbors. As a bounty hunter, Quidge is accustomed to crossing the fiefdom boundaries and taking the unwilling back to justice. He'd know how to go about it."

We glanced at each other wondering why he hadn't succeeded with Rosamund, and she caught the look.

"Oh, he tried several times, but I met some of the nicest people and they wouldn't let him take me. All I had to do was scream." Her lips twitched, and Michael and I both grinned.

"How disconcerting for Master Quidge," said Michael.

"He was quite put out." Rosamund was grinning too. "And now I have you to look after me, so that's that."

"We shall," Michael promised, and lost himself in her thanks so completely that I was the one who saved the fish from burning.

Infatuation had its advantages—for me. Michael gave up his cot to the chit while all I had to forfeit was a blanket. Scant hardship in this weather.

I'd braced the chair under the door again, but I really wasn't expecting a disturbance and fell asleep with no more than the usual gloom of a man about to embark on yet another adventure.

The pounding on the door woke us, but the booming voice demanding that Mrs. Inger open to Lord Roger's deputies must have roused the whole street.

Michael had been sleeping on the floor—now his eyes met mine and he shot out of his blankets.

"What's going on?" Rosamund asked sleepily.

"Get dressed!" Michael hissed. "We have only a few minutes."

"A bit more than that." Though I didn't waste time climbing out of my bed either. "Mrs. Inger will delay them for a while. And here I thought I'd never be grateful to the vicious, old . . . There, you see?"

Mrs. Inger's voice, demanding to know how they dared raise such a commotion at this hour, was louder than the deputy's. But she didn't much like Michael and me, and I'd no illusions she'd delay them for long.

Michael and I dressed in seconds, then stuffed our things, and some of Rosamund's, higgledy-piggledy into our saddlebags. I took an extra second to make sure the jewels were stowed safely.

"I thought you said Lord Roger's home was several days' ride off," Rosamund whispered. She'd taken little more time with her clothes than Michael and I.

She was pulling on her shoes as Michael replied, "Quidge must have found him visiting nearby. 'Tis the only way the deputies could become involved so quickly—unless Fisk has been up to something I don't know about?"

Ordinarily I'd have replied smartly, but Mrs. Inger had stopped shouting, and that was a bad sign. They'd do no harm to Rosamund, or to me, for I'd broken no laws. But unredeemed men have no legal rights, and those who harm them face no penalty. Most folk take a dim view of the unredeemed, especially law keepers.

Rosamund stood and started for the door.

"No, this way." Michael guided her into our bed-room, where I threw the shutters wide. A man whose name was not Jack Bannister had taught me to always find several exits from any room I stayed in, and in two years as an unredeemed man Michael had picked up the habit.

Rosamund's jaw dropped. "But we're on the second floor."

"'Tis not a problem." Michael swung through the window as he spoke and stood, holding out his hands to his cousin. "The kitchen roof is right here, and you can walk it all the way to the tannery behind us. Our horses are stabled there. Come on—I've got you."

I braced a second chair under the bedroom door. The chairs themselves would slow the law only a few seconds, but if they broke the first one, they'd have to fight Mrs. Inger to deal with the second.

Rosamund went out the window willingly, and I marked in her favor that she hadn't protested leaving half her clothing behind. I picked up our saddlebags and stepped out onto the slippery wooden shingles, closing the shutters behind me. Every second it took them to figure out where we'd gone was to our advantage.

Both moons were up, the Creature Moon near full though the Green Moon was waning, and the cool, gusty breeze was just strong enough to make you fear it might knock you off balance without actually doing it. I was walking a bit slower than I'd intended, but I soon caught up with the others anyway. I cast a hunted glance at our windows, but the shutter seams were still dark. Mrs. Inger was doing better than I'd hoped.

Rosamund slipped and Michael caught her, smothering her small shriek against his chest. He didn't look like he intended to let go of her any sooner than he had to; a sudden memory of how I'd felt when Lucy, skidding on an icy step, had fallen into my arms made my throat tighten in sympathy.

I sidled past them and went on toward the stables. There are many things that hurt worse than the loss of your first love, except when it's actually happening—then nothing hurts worse. Lucy left me for a butcher's apprentice who still had pimples, though he also had a stable job and a respected position in the community—or so I'd thought. I've since wondered if Jack didn't pay her off. Either way I was well out of it, but at the time . . . The pain of losing my first love had long since faded, and I hardly even thought of her now. But at the time . . . Poor Michael.

Making my way over the roofs to the stable took most of my attention, for I had to go from our kitchen roof onto the fence that separated the two properties, and then grab the tannery's eaves and swing myself up. Michael and Rosamund could drop to the ground there and make their way out through the narrow gap between the building's back wall and the fence. As for me, I scuttled along the roof peak and through the stable loft window with a swiftness that made me realize I'd not yet lost my touch as a burglar.

The horses were dozing, but Chant whuffed and pricked up his ears when I climbed down the ladder. Soft as it was, his snort woke Trouble, who ran to the foot of the ladder wagging his ropy tail and making the hoarse gasps that are all the bark he has. Only Michael would adopt a mute guard dog, though tonight his silence proved useful. I gave his short, brindled coat a pat when I reached the ground, and his frisking calmed a little.

Michael was forever telling him to guard things. I didn't think the irresponsible cur could guard his own bones, much less two fairly valuable horses. But Mrs. Inger had the same policy toward dogs in her house that she did toward women, and if he was out in the stables, he wasn't trying to wiggle into my bed. Yet another pleasure to look forward to, in the days to come.

I saddled Tipple first, so she'd have time to release the breath she took when I pulled up her girth. Chanticleer, trained by Michael's father as a tourney horse before a weakened tendon forced his early retirement, has no such bad habits. He and Michael had competed in several tourneys in the last year, and made it to the final rounds before they were defeated—thereby winning nothing but bruises and losing our entry fee.

I patted his long gray neck, then moved on to pull up Tipple's girth. She turned her absurdly spotted head and gave me a reproachful look as I gathered up the reins and led both horses from the big stall that had been their home for the last few months.

Tipple appeared more resigned than anything else, but Chant came behind me so eagerly that he ran into my back when I stopped dead at the sight of the man in the doorway.

"Leaving a bit early, aren't you, Squire?"

Most of the leather workers were good-enough folk. So was Ribb, usually, though hotheads are never my favorite people, and especially not *now*.

"Why should you care when we leave? We paid in advance. What are you doing up at this hour, anyway?"

"I got a girl, over on Baker's Row. At least, I *used* to have one." His eyes glinted with frustrated fury. This was my night to be cursed with thwarted lovers. "Seems to me, Master Fisk, that it's a bit suspicious, you creeping out in the middle of the night. You and your unredeemed friend. Seems to me a civic-minded man ought to stop you."

He picked up a stirring pole as he spoke—almost two yards of stout oak—and planted his feet firmly.

Trouble frisked, begging him to throw the big stick. He liked the tanners for the scent of their leather britches and aprons, though tonight Ribb wore only a shirt and vest above his britches.

His upper arms were thick with muscle, but as any card sharper knows, knife beats stick, unless the stick is handled far better than a tanner was likely to. Carrying a knife in my boot was another habit I'd picked up from Jack.

Ribb was spoiling for a fight to assuage his romantic frustration. Michael probably would have obliged him. But a fight would be noisy, time-consuming, and cursed painful if that stick connected. And I'm not Michael.

I reached down, slowly and carefully, and pulled out my purse. "How much is your civic duty worth, Ribb?"

I try to be practical about these things, for with Michael around someone has to be. I had a sinking feeling we were going to need practicality in the weeks to come. And besides, Rosamund was paying.

## CHAPTER 2

# Michael

Since I don't share Fisk's addiction to towns, I had done a lot of riding and hunting in the forest around Litton. My knowledge of the countryside permitted us to depart Lord Roger's fiefdom without encountering the obnoxious Master Quidge, and we saw no sign of pursuit as we traveled from the wooded hills where Litton lay, across the rolling plains to Crowly.

Only the High Liege's writ runs across borders, hence the existence of bounty hunters like Master Quidge. They're generally hard men, for kidnapping a criminal out of someone else's fief can be considered a criminal act, if the local lord chooses to regard it so. In the case of serious lawbreakers they usually don't, being sensibly glad to see the last of them. In the case of a fair and innocent girl such as Rose . . . I almost felt sorry for Master Quidge. And since there was a better than even chance that Father would have offended any baron whose fief we passed through, we were able to turn our attention to finding Master Makejoye's troupe.

Crowly was the largest town in the region and thus a likely place for a troupe of players to seek work. I watched over Rose carefully there, for 'twould be easier to kidnap someone out of a bustling, teeming city than from the countryside.

A few days' efficient inquiry, conducted by Fisk, failed to turn up any mention of Makejoye's troupe, but Crowly did have an office of the Players' and Performers' Guild. Inquiring there produced copies of all the contracts Master Makejoye had signed—some of them up to nine months in the future. I hadn't known that players filed their contracts with the guild, though the clerk assured us 'twas common, as it gave a troupe recourse should some lord or township summon them many weary miles and then decide their services weren't needed.

Master Makejoye's contracts showed him traveling slowly south along the coast. Judging by the dates, we should be able to catch up to him in . . .

"Huckerston? Where under two moons is Huckerston?" Fisk sounded indignant at the thought of more travel, for our soft life of the last few months had spoiled him a trifle.

But my heart rejoiced at taking to the road once more, even if I no longer carried Rose perched on my saddlebow. Much as I had enjoyed that experience, we had purchased a mount for Rosamund as soon as we reached a town large enough to have its own horse market. I worried about Chant's weak leg carrying double, and Tipple was too small to carry more than one for any distance. Rose had named the little gold mare Honey, which I thought a fine name despite Fisk's sardonic comments.

"Huckerston's here, Mistress." The clerk pointed helpfully to a large map of the realm. He was smiling at Rosamund, even though it was Fisk who'd asked. The Players' Guild's offices were small but well appointed, and sunlight streamed though the diamond-shaped windowpanes. Fisk, Rose, and I all crowded forward to see. "It's the only deep-water port on Keelsbane Bay, which is why it's stranded there, all by itself."

I had heard of Keelsbane Bay, for sailors tell tales of its fearsome rocks and the sudden, violent storms that sweep up the western coast to the hazard of passing ships.

"Hmm. I'd guess 'tis a three-week ride, but if Master Makejoye keeps his schedule, we should be able to catch him there. What say you, Fisk?"

"*If* he keeps to his schedule," said Fisk. "What are the chances your father has offered a reward for Rosa's return? A big reward?"

"Ha!" Rose snorted. "'Tis unlikely to be more than I'm already paying, you unprincipled rogue."

I had to smile. It wasn't only for her beauty that I loved Rosamund—indeed, I was fond of her when she was a scruffy urchin of ten—'twas for the sharpness of her wit and her gentle manner. She had taken Fisk's measure some days ago, and Fisk teased her as if she were indeed his sister.

I was relieved to see no sign he was falling in love with her, as that would have been altogether too much of a tangle. Half the men we encountered seemed to do so at first sight, as it was.

"Don't concern yourself, Mistress," said the clerk, puffing out his chest. "No troupe will break a contract if they can avoid it. A reputation for being unreliable can be the end of you in this business."

There was a deal more pointless conversation, but the end of it was that we set off for Huckerston the next morning.

The land changed slowly as we made our way south; the grass turned brown and the trees shortened to what looked to me like overgrown bushes. We were drawing near to the great desert that comprised the southern tip of the realm. I knew a stirring of hope that one day I might see it, though 'twould not be soon, for Huckerston was far short of it, and Master Makejoye's route skirted its desolate borders.

The country had become very dry. Talking to the farm folk, I learned that any crop they planted had to be both storm and drought resistant, and that they were forced to import most of their grains, which was why bread was more expensive here.

'Twas obvious what they exported; three quarters of the fields we passed were filled with huge, dusty grape leaves, though the grapes they sheltered were still green and hard. Their wine, purchased at the inns where we stopped, was quite good. Even the dust in this southern country was different, its color ranging from the softest gold to a dark orange-red, most strange to my green-accustomed eyes. It coated our clothes and made mud on our sweaty faces. There were times I couldn't have identified True's real color, he became so coated with it.

For the most part, our journey was uneventful, marred only by one incident when a chambermaid, entering unexpectedly, caught sight of the tattoos on my wrists that mark me unredeemed. The innkeeper suddenly found that his wife had told us the wrong price—a room for the night would be far beyond our means.

Rose, bless her tender heart, was indignant on my behalf. Fisk pointed out that it could have been worse, but it seldom is. I have found that being outside the law's protection is less a matter of lynch mobs out for blood (though I've encountered that, too) than of more subtle cheats and insults. I have yet to meet any-one who was minded to assault me just because they'd face no legal penalty. But the number of people will-ing to cheat me out of a day's wages was higher than I liked, and the number of folk who simply wanted nothing to do with me higher still.

In this case it meant no more inconvenience than a night in camp—of which we'd already had several when we'd failed to reach a town before dark. The trees were too low to provide actual shelter, but clustered in a grove around our fire, they lessened the solitary feel-ing of the night. I'd been asleep for some hours when Fisk whispered, "Michael! Michael, wake up!"

"Um?" I wasn't really awake, but his next words sent my eyes snapping open.

"There's a snake in my bed."

"What?" I sat up. "Are you sure?"

"It's long and round and lying against my left ankle. Sometimes it wiggles."

"Don't move." I scrambled out of my blankets, glad that in Rose's presence I'd worn both shirt and britches to bed.

Fisk glared at me, moving no more than his eyes. Indeed, I doubted he'd so much as twitched since he'd detected the snake's presence, for his sense of self-preservation is remarkably sound.

The rough ground beneath my feet reminded me that boots might be useful dealing with a snake, and I donned them.

"What's going on?" Rose murmured sleepily.

"There's a snake in bed with Fisk," I said calmly.

"A snake!" She didn't actually shriek, but she sat up swiftly, a dim white shape in the light of the setting Creature Moon. A shapely shape, I couldn't help but notice.

There wasn't much light to deal with something as small and fast as a snake might be. I went around to the left side of Fisk's bedroll and looked down at him, wondering how to extract the thing. I'd heard of this happening, but I'd never personally encountered it.

"Suppose it's poisonous?" Fisk whispered. He was breathing rather fast.

"Then we'll take you to a doctor. Adults very seldom die of snakebite." If I lifted the blankets, and Fisk held still, it should just slither away. If startled enough to strike, it should strike at the blankets. Or at me. Or it might move further up Fisk's body, clinging to its warmth.

"Here." Rosamund handed me the long stick we'd used as a fire poker. Then she hurried off to perch on a nearby rock, safely out of reach of retreating snakes. She was splendidly levelheaded in emergencies.

"Good thinking, Rose." I turned to Fisk. "I'm going to pull your blankets off with this stick. If it's startled, the snake will strike at the stick or the blankets, as long as you're holding still."

"Suppose it's magica?" Fisk whispered.

"Then I'll be able to see it better," I murmured back, soft enough to keep Rose from hearing. The Gods that gift plants and animals with magic do not give it to humans. Through a foolish set of circumstances, and the viciousness of one Lady Ceciel, I had come to possess the ability to see magic as a visible light—and perhaps other abilities as well. I fought down the familiar chill this thought brought with it.

"Suppose it's a magica poisonous snake?" Fisk whispered. "Magica poison. I could die in seconds."

I considered this a moment. "Suppose 'tis not." I hooked the stick under the edge of Fisk's blankets and pulled them slowly back. No glowing magica serpent met my gaze, but there was something lying against Fisk's ankle, long and pale. It twitched. Ready to leap back if it struck, I bent closer.

Then I laughed. The lump in the blankets past Fisk's feet, which I'd not noticed in the urgency of the moment, rose and swayed back and forth. True is a sound sleeper, but not that sound. The "snake" began beating the ground in a familiar, friendly rhythm.

Fisk's outraged roar sent True scooting from under the blankets. Fisk shot to his feet, swearing, and hurled his pillow at the dog.

True caught and shook it. His slightly startled expression proclaimed he thought it an odd time to play, but if that was what Fisk wanted, he was willing. He shook the pillow again, and frisked out of reach of Fisk's snatch.

I strolled over to Rose, who now sat upon the rock. "I'm sorry we woke you for this."

"I'm not." She watched Fisk chase True about the camp. His threats were imaginative enough to make her giggle.

"I've told Fisk over and over that if he doesn't want the dog in bed with him, he has only to tell him so firmly and mean it. Instead, he makes a great production of the matter. I'm not sure which of them enjoys it more."

"Well, he's not going to get his pillow back that way," said Rose.

"He knows it. When he tires of the game, he'll resort to bribery, and we'll all be able to get back to bed."

She let me carry her to her bedroll, which spared her bare feet and delighted me. Soon Fisk and True settled down and the night became quiet. But I lay listening to Rose's soft breathing, and it was some time before I slept.

I had fallen in love with Rosamund almost a year before I quarreled with my father and took up knight errantry. I'd always known that she didn't love me, at least not the way that I loved her. My dream was to accomplish some deed courageous enough to win her. Even in my practical moments, I thought I'd have some years to win her affections, since the marriage of an heiress is a time-consuming process and she was still young. But now my time appeared to be up; if I was to win her heart away from this player, I had to do it soon. And in this matter, failure would be unbearable.

We were all glad to reach the coast, with its fresh, constant breezes. Looking over the water, I understood how Keelsbane Bay came by its name, for never have I seen a coastline so rocky. Jagged, dark stones broke the shining surface for a quarter of a mile out, and occasional rifts of foam out farther warned of more rocks lurking below. At low tide this coast was impassable—at high 'twould be a nightmare of hidden hazards. No wonder sensible shipmasters gave it wide berth.

This had its effect on the countryside; there were no towns besides Huckerston for the length of the bay, and even the farming and fishing villages were small and precarious.

Our good luck finally broke half a day's ride out of Huckerston. I don't mean that someone else saw my tattoos. I've learned to keep my shirtsleeves down, even in the warmest weather. 'Twas the weather that failed us, though we'd warning enough—you could see the clouds sweeping in over the sea for miles. The thunderheads' bellies were near black, and the fringe of lightning flashing at the storm's leading edge sent us scurrying in search of shelter.

Unfortunately, shelter was scant, and the storm rolled in apace. The wind began to whip, and the thunder's constant grumble was ominously louder when I located a shallow overhang that a small stream had cut into the bluff. 'Twas barely deep enough to give cover to a horse, but long enough to hold all three of them; we led them in and inserted ourselves between them.

Fisk held Tipple and Chant, leaving Honey to me, for I've the Gift of animal handling, and unlike the others she was nervous of storms.

This was a storm to make anyone fearful. In the scant lull between thunderclaps the drum of approaching rain sounded like an infantry charge. The temperature dropped as if winter had come upon us overnight, and 'twould have been as dark as night if not for the lightning.

Gift or no, I had my hands full with Honey—so much so that the temptation to try to use that other Gift, or curse, that Lady Ceciel's potions had left me stirred once more.

Anyone we call Gifted has the reliable ability to detect magic in those plants and animals that possess it, but only by touch. With that Gift come a host of lesser talents, also called Gifts, which function oddly and unreliably though they can be trained to usefulness. None of these Gifts are magic themselves, for the only humans close enough to the Furred God's realm to possess magic are the simple ones. And even in them 'tis so unnatural that those who possess it never live to adulthood.

Lady Ceciel was a brilliant herbalist, obsessed with the desire to give magic to normal folk. Seeking to bring her to justice for her husband's murder, I had fallen into her hands. I'd been an indebted man then, with no legal rights or recourse, so she'd seized on me as a subject for her experiments. At the time, as she forced her noisome potions down my throat, I'd thought 'twas only my magic-sensing Gift that changed. When I'd begun to *see* magic, as a visible aura around the plants and creatures that possessed it, that was horrifying enough.

Months later, in the midst of a desperate attempt to save a burning building, I discovered she had succeeded beyond her wildest hopes, for magic had risen in me to enhance the water I was dashing on the flames.

'Twas Fisk who brought me to see that for all its freakishness, 'twas not a cause for despair, but I had sworn never to use it, in the hopes that it might someday vanish as strangely as it had come.

No new manifestations had occurred in over a year, and for the most part I ignored it. I had even become accustomed to seeing that bizarre glow in the magica ink in the tattoos on my wrists. But there were times, as now, when I used my normal Gifts and felt it stir in answer. The chill of fear that touched me made the cold of the storm seem trivial. I squelched the uncoiling serpent of power firmly, and sought once more to forget about it.

I was aided in this by the way Rose buried her face against my back and clung to me, and further distracted by True, who was trying to bury his whole body in her skirts. True appears to be a cross between a hound and one of the large, lean breeds built for running, and he's not a small dog—he all but pushed both of us out into the wet.

After a time the storm's first fury lessened, but the rain settled into a steady downpour that showed no sign of abating. We'd been using our winter cloaks as part of our bedrolls, and it took some time to extract them. The tight-woven wool would shed even this downpour for a time. Unfortunately the road, formerly dusty and firm, was now a river of mud so slippery that I'd swear it was laced with goose grease.

The horses managed well despite the occasional skidding hoof and the way True darted beneath their feet, but I worried for Chant's weak leg if he should slip. We could go no faster in safety, and I judged we were still several hours from our destination when water began to soak through my cloak at the shoulders.

So when I saw a great fire, leaping on a ragged hillock that crowned one of the sea cliffs, my first thought was of shelter. And yet . . .

Fisk followed my gaze. "What could be burning

on top of that lump? Did the lightning set a tree on fire?"

"Not in this rain," I said. "Lightning fires start slow. In a sheltered bit of wood one might smolder for some time—in any exposed place the rain would put it out."

We'd all stopped now, squinting at the top of the distant outcrop, the rain pattering on our faces. We couldn't see the source of the blaze, for the road had wandered inland and a ridge of rock concealed it. But the fire was so large that tips of flame leapt above it, and the back of my neck prickled.

There was something very wrong about that fire. No Gift but that of sensing magic is truly reliable, as I've proved often enough, but never before had my Gift of warning spoken so strongly as it did then. Had I been a dog, I'd have flattened my ears and tail and growled—indeed, the impulse to do so was so strong, I glanced at True, to see if he was doing it.

Not being Gifted, he was trying to find a dry spot beneath one of the low bush-trees that lined the road. True's short coat served him well in warmer weather, but in the cold or wet he was easily chilled.

"Mayhap some shepherd built a hut up there," said Rose.

"But why would he build such a big fire?" Fisk objected. "Why would anyone build— Wait, maybe the shepherd's hut caught fire. In which case he'll soon be heading for town to get help. I hope he's not the type to steal horses."

My brows knit. Could that be what I found so wrong? Was someone trapped by the blaze, needing our help?

No. The moment the thought occurred, I knew 'twas not what caused the sense of wrongness pulsing through my mind. I gazed at the fire, trying to pin down my elusive instincts, until Fisk cleared his throat, and I looked up to find both my companions staring at me.

"Nodded off?" my squire asked tartly.

My lips twitched despite my unease, but still . . . "Mayhap Fisk and I should investigate," I said. "Wait here, Rosamund. 'Tis less than a quarter mile off. It shouldn't take long."

Fisk grimaced. "Even if it is some shepherd's hut, what could we do? He almost certainly got out, and if he didn't, he's dead. He's probably on the road ahead of us."

*Wrongness. Wrongness. Wrongness.* It wasn't that. But Fisk knows all too well how capricious these warnings can be.

"The horses will be chilled," said Rose, "if we wait much longer."

A cold droplet trickled down my spine. We were all chilled, though Rose was too brave to complain on her own account. And Fisk was right: Whatever was wrong, 'twas unlikely I could fix it.

But as we rode past the ridge, and on toward Huckerston, I kept turning back to gaze at the flames till a bend in the road took them out of sight.

The sense of warning passed in time, as such things do, and we reached the town walls before darkness fell. The rain had lightened to a drizzle by then, though 'twas too late to give much aid to our sodden clothing.

Most towns in this tranquil time have outgrown the defensive walls that ringed them before the first High Liege united the warring barons and brought peace to the realm at large. I wondered why Huckerston hadn't. There was obviously no local law against it, for several inns and taverns had spread onto the main road outside the big, old gate, but there was no suburb of workshops and warehouses, which are usually the first buildings to move outward, leaving the older parts of the cities to the rich and the poor.

Our first concern was to find an inn as soon as might be. The ones outside the gate looked expensive enough to draw a yelp of protest from Fisk, before he remembered that Rose was paying.

Even had we paid, I'd not have quibbled, for we were chilled to the bone and weary too. Unfortunately, we weren't the only ones. All the inns on the main road were filled with storm-stayed travelers. The host of the first house gave us directions to an inn in town called the Slippery Wheel. He said 'twas unlikely to be full, for 'twas more tavern than inn and few knew to seek rooms there. He added that 'twas respectable enough for the lady and that the host would take good care of us if we said Dell Potter had sent us. So we gathered ourselves for the last leg of the journey and clattered through the gates and onto the cobbled streets of Huckerston.

Even in the dim light I could tell 'twas different from the towns I was accustomed to, for all the buildings were built of brick, in the same reds, oranges, and golds of the dusty roads. The better buildings were roofed with arched tiles, often of a different shade than the brick that made up the walls. I had never seen this before, and watching the rain pour off those roofs in torrents, I wondered how expensive it might be.

The common buildings were roofed in the familiar thatch, which dripped mournfully. At least the city had installed a modern system of street drains, and a good one too, judging by the way the flooding water rushed through the grates.

They didn't have streetlamps, and the old-fashioned torches that lined Huckerston's streets shed no light now. But most of the windows we passed were of the new, thin glass, and as folk lit their lamps and candles, they provided enough light for us to make our way to the Slippery Wheel.

'Twas a slow night for the tavern, and the host himself came out to assure us that Joe Potter would take good care of us, just as Dell had promised.

"Kin of yours, is he?" Fisk asked.

I wondered myself, though aside from the snowy apron of his trade this lean, bald man bore no resemblance to Master Dell. Now he laughed, and I heard a touch of real amusement behind his professional cheer.

"I can't blame you for thinking it, sir, but every fifth man in this town's named Potter, and most of us no kin to each other at all. But come in, and we'll get you settled in front of the taproom fire while we heat up a bath for the lady."

It sounded like a fine idea to me. I left it to Fisk to take Rose inside and bargain over room rates, while I helped the groom lead the horses around to the stable and tipped a bit extra to see they were given plenty of oats and well rubbed down. There was a lad there who seemed quite taken with True, so I paid him a silver ha' to see the shivering dog dried and bedded down. The lad swore he could get beef scraps from the kitchen, so I finally abandoned our furred comrades and went to seek warmth myself.

True to his word, and mayhap his business acumen, our host had led Rose and Fisk to the roaring fire in the taproom and was conducting negotiations there. Except for a small man standing behind the bar, whose pale hair stuck out in awkward tufts, only two elderly men shared the room with us, sitting at a table near the windows with a scatter of cards between them.

I shed my water-laden cloak and wended my way between the benches to the hearth. The fire was generous for such a sparse crowd, and Fisk stepped aside as I approached. I all but walked into the blaze, though I had to back off when steam started rising from my clothes. Not too far off, for the heat was delightful. Rose's face was already losing that pinched look that comes of being too cold, and she pulled her hair loose so it could dry.

They'd settled on a price for rooms, baths were heating, and we could go up as soon as the girl had warmed the beds. Though 'tis seldom a thing I trouble myself with, there's something to be said for ready money.

Then Rose asked, with a shy intensity that brought Master Potter to attention faster than a lord's order, if there was a troupe of players in town.

Yes, indeed there was. Come in two days ago, and Lord Fabian had hired them to perform in the town square on Skinday. The crier'd been announcing it all day, and everyone was looking forward to it. They'd likely save their best tricks for private performances, the rogues. But they had to make a living too, didn't they now?

I'd lost track of whether today was Furday or Finday, but either way, Skinday would be several days hence.

Potter didn't know the name of the troupe master, but 'twas unlikely two would visit this isolated town, and Rose's face glowed brighter than the firelight on her flowing hair.

Her joy in her player's nearness was enough to strike gloom to anyone's heart, but the ruddy light reminded me . . .

"Master Potter, do you know if there's a shepherd's hut or some such thing, built on a rise atop the bluffs? 'Twould be mayhap an hour's ride west in good weather, though it took us nearly two."

"On the bluffs?" Potter's voice still held its practiced heartiness, but the geniality seeped from his expression, leaving it hard and intent. The foreboding I'd felt at the sight of the flames returned to me. "I don't know of anything built there, sir. Why do you ask?"

The two card players had turned to watch us, and the woolly-headed tapster forgot the glass he was drying.

I replied with more caution than I'd intended. "We saw a great fire, burn—"

The tapster dropped the glass. Rose jumped at the crash, looking as bewildered as I felt, but without my apprehension that for once my untrustworthy Gifts had spoken true.

"You saw a fire on the cliffs and you didn't report it?" Potter's voice was sharp now.

"I knew of no reason I should, for we are stran—"

He'd already turned away. "Tippy, run for the sheriff. He might still catch the motherless bastards, if nothing else. Tell him to bring two extra horses—theirs are done in."

He had to shout the last of his instructions, for the tapster had taken off at a run, not even stopping to snatch up a cloak.

"What's wrong, Master Potter?" Fisk asked. "What was that fire?"

"Ah, I'm sorry I spoke so sharp to you. New in town, there's no way you could know. We've wreckers here."

My breath hissed in, and Fisk's lips tightened.

Rose looked from one of us to the other in confusion. "Wreckers?"

"You'd not know, Rose, for they only do their wicked work on rocky coastlines, such as this one." And Rose, like me, had been raised inland. But I'd met and spoken with sailors since, and even crewed a ship myself, and I'd heard their tales. I should have guessed. . . .

'Twas Fisk who continued. "They're pirates, of a sort. They light a couple of fires, like the one we saw, near a place a shipmaster expects to find harbor beacons. Only when he sails in, there is no harbor."

"But then the ship would hit the rocks." 'Twas more an anguished protest than a statement of disbelief. "They'd sink."

"Not for a time, Mistress," said Potter bitterly. "It takes days, sometimes, for a ship on the rocks to break apart. Though mostly it's just a few hours. They go out in small boats that can dodge the rocks and loot. And some of the cargo will float. But the passengers and crew can't."

Rose's lovely face looked cold again. "But the ships have small boats, too? And on the rocks, they'd be close enough to swim. . . ." Her voice trailed off at the sight of our grim faces.

"Some do make it to shore, Mistress, but they find

the wreckers waiting. If you gentlemen would care to change your clothes, I'll find some dry cloaks to cover 'em. The sheriff'll need your guidance. And you've no need to worry about horses, for—"

"We heard you tell the tapster," said Fisk. You could see that the idea of going out again held no appeal, but only resignation sounded in his voice.

For myself, I only hoped we'd be in time.

Lester Todd differed from the last sheriff I'd had significant dealings with, for he was tall and thin, and still had his straight, mouse-brown hair. With his long, lined face and an almost scholarly stoop to his shoulders, he couldn't have been more different from Sheriff Potter—if nothing else, he greeted us courteously. I had some hope of dealing well with him, as long as he didn't discover that I was unredeemed.

Even the drizzle was beginning to lift, though the odd shower pattered down from time to time. But if the rain had ceased, the mud was no better. After one of the twenty-some deputies' horses fell, and its rider broke a wrist and had to go back, we reduced our pace to a brisk trot, deeming it better to arrive late than not at all.

"Or without enough men to fight," Todd told us grimly. "Three years ago, when this started, I posted groups of three, then four and even five men along the headlands in the likely places. As far as I can tell, it didn't even slow them down. We'd find my deputies dead, along with the handful of sailors who made it to shore. Now I send out patrols in force, but the wreckers do most of their work in the storms, and in weather like this . . ." He shook his head. "We do our best. We patrolled this stretch of road this afternoon before the storm broke, and we'd just come back from the East Coast Road when Ebb Dorn came running in."

"It sounds like they know where you're riding—could you have a leak in your department?" This was fairly tactful for Fisk; he claims that sheriffs' departments leak gossip like an old bellows leaks air.

Todd shrugged. "Half the town can see which gate we ride out, and half the countryside sees us if we loop back through the fields. It's hard to conceal over twenty men and horses, Master Fisk."

" 'Tis amazing that you've so many volunteers," I put in soothingly, for we'd learned that most of the men who rode with us made their living in other professions.

But Fisk pressed on, "Can't you trace the loot back through its fence? In three years, surely some of it's surfaced. At least . . . Can you get cargo manifests for the ships they sink?"

"Yes," said Todd shortly. "Huckerston's a small city, in some ways, for the potteries and brick works are our only large manufacturers. But we're also the only deep-water port for dozens of leagues, and all the wine in the area ships out through us. Several of the major banks and insurance brokers have offices here. We usually have a ship's manifest before it arrives. But none of the goods have surfaced anywhere in Lord Fabian's fief, or that of any of his neighbors. And the reward's high enough now to tempt any fence to come forward."

"So either they're sitting on three years of highly identifiable loot," said Fisk, brows knitting, "or they're sending it off and fencing it elsewhere."

"The latter, I think." Todd wiped a fresh splatter of drops from his face. "They take only jewelry and other small valuables—things that could be hidden in some larger cargo and shipped out without the captain even knowing what he carried. We've tried to check that possibility as well, but we can't open every cask of wine or basket of crockery that leaves port. That's a very knowledgeable comment, Master Fisk. Tell me, what brings you and Master Sevenson to Huckerston?"

I believe he said it more because Fisk had annoyed him than from any true suspicion, but I answered quickly, before Fisk came up with some lie that would bring real suspicion on us when 'twas exposed.

"I'm a knight errant, Master Todd, in search of adventure and good deeds, and Fisk is my squire. We're escorting my cousin, who has come here to meet a friend."

Most folk laugh when I tell them this, a response to which I've become so accustomed, it no longer even pricks. Todd was one of the other sort—he drew back and examined me for signs of further, more dangerous insanity. I waited serenely.

"I hope your business prospers, Master Sevenson."

"It's Sir Michael, actually," said Fisk, in a tone of helpful sincerity that sprang from pure mischief.

"Yes, of course. If you'll excuse me . . ."

He urged his horse forward and was gone without further ado.

"Fisk . . ."

"You started it. I'd think that by now you'd have learned to *avoid* the interest of the local law."

"Is he questioning us now? My argument rests. Fisk, if we'd gone to investigate that fire when we first saw it—"

"We'd have met the same fate as the deputies the sheriff used to post," said Fisk grimly. "And no one would have known about this till it was far too late."

He was right, and my mind knew it. 'Twas my heart
that couldn't accept it, and my sinking dread deepened as we approached the headland where the fire
had been.

I rode forward to point it out to the sheriff as soon
as it came in sight, for the flames no longer burned.
Without Fisk's and my directions they'd never have
found it.

We had to backtrack several hundred yards to
reach the trail that led down the bluffs to the beach—
though calling it a trail was overly optimistic—'twas so
narrow, we had to leave the horses atop the cliff and
slither afoot down the muddy track, no more than a
ledge in spots, with an unnerving drop beneath. My
sword's unaccustomed, awkward weight was a cursed
nuisance, but 'twould do me little good in the roll on
Chant's saddle where I usually kept it. The irregular
light when the moons peeked through the clouds was
of little help, mayhap even a danger, for I kept trying
to see if there was a ship upon the rocks instead of
paying proper attention to my footing.

Fisk's mind dwelled on more practical matters. "No
wonder they take only small stuff—not even a mule
could carry much up this path. I wonder how many
ships they've sunk, to find they carried only cotton
bales, or lamp oil."

"Just two," said one of the deputies behind us. He was a young man, with a workman's leather britches and vest under his thick, rough coat. "Not that they didn't have bulky stuff aboard the others, too, but except for those two the bastards have never hit a ship that wasn't carrying something small and valuable. The bulkiest cargo they've taken was a load of dyes, and they pay almost as much as silver, by weight."

Fisk's brows knotted again. "But how could they learn what ships carry the kind of goods they're looking for? How many have they sunk, by the way?"

The deputy's eyes, like mine, were on the sea; he slipped and swore. "Eleven, so far. Some we didn't find till days after. But everybody knows which ships are due in. We're a port town." He shrugged. "As to how they know what's on the manifests—that's one of the things we can't figure out."

We saw nothing as we climbed down the cliffs. I began to hope, as we hurried over the slippery stones and water-hardened sand, that we might be in time. Or that they'd failed to bring their prey into the shore.

But then we rounded a jagged outcrop of rocks, splashing through the higher waves, and the men ahead of us cried out in anger and dismay.

Once past the rocks I could see the wreck myself, and 'twas no wonder we'd not seen it from the cliffs.

The ship had come within a few hundred yards of the shore and, on striking the rocks, had broken and rolled. Or mayhap the wreckers had sunk it. Only the round, dark curve of its hull showed above the waves, like a half-beached whale.

Even at this distance we could see bodies crumpled on the sand. Crabs were already scuttling about, plucking at clothing and flesh.

'Twas that which drew my unwilling feet forward, for I confess the ignoble part of my spirit wanted only to turn away. My useless sword jingled mockingly at my side. The least we could do for those poor souls was to carry their remains up to be identified, that their kin might be told.

I've seen violent death before, in the collapse of a mineshaft some years before Fisk and I met. But no matter how many times you've seen it, 'tis still griev-ous to gather the heavy, lifeless limbs. And now 'twas grievous to bind blankets over the empty faces, that they might be protected until transport up the cliffs could be arranged.

I've no idea what Fisk's experience with sudden death might have been, for though I believe I am as close to his heart as any person living, my squire has the habit of keeping his past to himself. Indeed, had his sisters not summoned him home the winter before last to settle a most troubling matter, I don't believe I'd know anything of his life at all. His brief visit home had ended badly. I sometimes wondered if he corresponded so happily with Kathy to make up for the fact that he wasn't answering his own sisters' letters. Fisk's reticence about his feelings had long since told me that someone had badly broken his trust, but I knew that badgering him would gain me nothing. I was content in his friendship, and time eventually mends all hurts.

As he worked beside me now, his expression bleak and hard, I was grateful for his company. We wrapped a blanket about a man in his middle twenties—scarce older than the two of us. Had he a wife or babes who would mourn him?

Fisk scrubbed his hands in the damp sand, for this time he had lifted the broken, blood-soaked head. "I hope they hang the bastards." His voice was vicious, for this was the fourth such skull we'd seen.

"'Twill not bring back the dead," I told him, though my heart agreed. "I only wish—"

"There! Look there!" 'Twas one of the deputies, pointing out to sea. Had it not been for his gesture, I'd have missed it. The scrap of wreckage slithering in the wave troughs was less than a yard square. In the shifting light only the sharpest of eyes could have caught the white flash of clinging human hands.

The cold waves slapped my calves as I ran into the sea; then I was swimming, growing cold and wet, my whole attention focused on the need to reach that makeshift raft. On the hope that one life might be salvaged.

The surf fought my progress, battering me back, but I pressed onward, and soon I seized the floating wood—the corner of a hatch—groped my way around it, and looked.

She was dead. I'd seen it often enough in the last hour to be certain even before I touched her icy skin, but I still scraped her sodden hair off her throat to feel for a pulse. I've heard tales of men who were certain someone was dead and proved to be quite wrong.

I found no pulse, and nothing but the rush of a sudden wave disturbed the damp spikes of her lashes. There were no bubbles in the water when it ran across her mouth. I had been right, alas.

But even so I couldn't leave her here.

The hatch cover she clung to was bigger than it looked from a distance, for much of it floated beneath the surface. But it did float, and rather than entangle myself with the girl's drifting skirts, I grabbed the corner and started swimming for the shore. The rough wood scraped my hands and wrists as the sea fought to keep its prize, but already others were swimming out to help me.

Three of us hauled the poor lass's raft to the shore. Fisk wasn't among those waiting in the shallows, for he cannot swim, or so he claims, and so had chosen to remain dry.

I half forgave him when he held out my cloak, which I had evidently dropped before going into the water. The cool breeze cut through my wet clothes as if they weren't even there. The other half of forgiveness came when I saw the sorrow on his face as he took in the expression on mine.

"Dead? Not surprising in this cold. You'd better wrap up, or you're likely to follow her. I wonder if there's anything left of the signal fire."

My first thought was that I'd rather freeze than warm myself at so villainous a fire, but that would be foolish. My teeth were beginning to chatter, and my fellow swimmers must be as cold as I, though one of them was alert and concerned enough to capture my hand as I pulled my cloak tighter.

"Here, you're bleeding. Let me—"

Had it not happened so fast, I'd not have let him. In my own defense I should say that my cuff buttons do not come off, for Fisk stitches them on with a heavy thread, and checks them for looseness whenever he washes my shirts. And at that point I was so numb with cold that I'd not realized that my sleeve had torn, and that blood from the scrape beneath it stained the pale fabric. And my mind still dwelled on the dead girl. So I think there's some excuse, whatever Fisk says, for me to be just a second too slow when the deputy took my hand and pulled the torn cloth aside to see the cut. Of course, that wasn't all he saw.

To my bizarrely enhanced sight, the two broken circles on my wrist glowed with eerie silver fire. They use magica ink so the tattoos cannot be scraped or burned away. The deputy would see only the thick, black lines, but that was enough. His grip clamped tight—tight enough to hurt. I met his eyes steadily, despite the shock and disgust that showed there, for I've had practice with this, too.

Indeed, I couldn't blame him. The most usual reason for a common man to bear the mark of a broken debt to the law is that he had killed someone and there were sufficient extenuating circumstances that the judicars didn't want to hang him. Since murder is a debt that can be paid only in life or blood, he goes "unredeemed," his debt forever unpaid.

The most common reason for a noble to bear those marks is that his family's power or money influenced the judicars on his behalf. The irony of that always hurt, for 'twas not to influence anyone in my *favor* that my father's power and wealth had gone. To do him justice, he truly believed that the life he'd tried to force me into was what was best for me. 'Tis seldom my father's plans fail, and as usual, the satisfaction of that thought lent me strength enough to stand, silent, in the deputy's grip.

"Sheriff! I think you'd better see this."

Todd had been examining the dead girl, but soon he stood before me, looking down at my wrist, his mouth tight with disdain.

I felt almost as resigned as Fisk looked, for I knew what would follow.

Sometimes, especially if they saw the flogging scars on my back, they made a speech. In fairness to my father, and myself, I should explain that those scars had nothing to do with him or the law, but were acquired in the course of a somewhat uncomfortable good deed. Whether they gave a speech or not, they ordered me out of town, sometimes out of their lord's fief entirely. One particularly sanctimonious son-of-a-bitch held me in lockup for two weeks. When his deputies escorted me to the border, the deputies of the next fiefdom met me there. I crossed four lords' holdings under such escort, before they released me onto the lands of someone whose neighbors didn't care to warn him.

But Todd surprised me. "I don't suppose it'd do much good to ask how you came by this?"

He meant that I'd not tell the truth. Remembering how complex the tale had become the last time I'd tried to explain that for all her faults, Lady Ceciel had not committed the murder of which she was accused, and that due to some obscure matters of inheritance and taxation her trial wasn't likely to be fair, and especially when I'd tried to explain why my father had set such terms on my redemption in the first place . . .

"Probably not." I pulled my wrist from Todd's grasp and wrapped my cloak about myself, for I was now very cold.

The sheriff's serious, scholarly gaze rested on my face for some time. Then his eyes went to the dead girl, and then past to the line of blanket-wrapped bodies at the base of the bluff. Surely he couldn't think I was involved with the wreckers? They'd been working on this coast for three years, and I'd just reached town. 'Twas—

"Don't leave Huckerston, Master Sevenson," Todd said curtly. "You and your friend are witnesses. I know you've told us what you saw, but other questions may arise."

My jaw dropped. "Don't *leave* town?"

"That's what I said. For now"—he was already

turning away—"I believe we can dispense with your assistance."

"Don't *lea—*"

"Yes, sir," said Fisk smoothly. "Come along, Michael— we're going." And he hustled me off, as is his practice when he thinks I'm about to do or say something that might cause us trouble.

"Well, that was a surprise," I said, still struggling with the concept of being ordered to stay somewhere.

"Don't worry," said Fisk. "I'm sure it'll work out just as badly in the end."

I laughed, which restored me somewhat. "At least we'll see those warm beds Joe Potter kept promising before dawn. Although . . ." I turned and looked back at the beach—at the dead. "Truly I had rather stay, and do what little I can. We should have gone to investigate, Fisk. We might have caught them in the act. Seen their faces."

Fisk snorted. "And I thought this *wasn't* my lucky day. Ignoring that fire was the best decision we ever made, Noble Sir."

"You don't mean that."

"Oh yes, I do. These people *kill* when they're crossed. I don't even care how large the reward is. I don't want to *know* how large it is. All we want is to stay out of their way, right? Michael, say yes. Please, say yes."

"Don't fret so. If the sheriff and his deputies haven't uncovered them in three years, 'tis not likely we could find them."

"I knew you wouldn't say yes," Fisk said gloomily.

Even as I laughed, I realized he was right. For all its unlikeness, if a chance to stop these monsters should come into my path, I would seize it with both hands. 'Twas the least a knight errant could do.

## CHAPTER 3
# Fisk

To my surprise we reached
our beds not merely before dawn, but in time to get a
bit of sleep. The only thing we passed on the road was
a pack of hunting dogs, no doubt brought in to track
the wreckers. Michael's face lit with hope when he
saw them, but if the dogs had failed on eleven previous occasions, I saw no reason to think they'd succeed
this time. With the sea right there, eluding dogs was
simple.

Back at the Slippery Wheel, I roused a groom to
let us in the back door and then see to the horses,
while I hustled Michael in to strip before the embers
of the taproom fire. It wasn't as if there was anyone
awake to see either nakedness or evidence of criminal
conviction, and two icy drenchings a day is too many.
But trying to stop Michael from swimming out to save

that girl would have been like trying to stop a hanging once the trap has fallen. Frankly, the determination on his face as he'd looked back at that beach worried me more than any chill.

Wrecking is a loathsome business—even Jack wouldn't touch it. In fact Jack, being a practical man, never committed any crime for which death was the penalty. *Dead men can't spend it, my boy.* A sensible policy, which I too had adopted.

In some ways Jack had been a terrible mentor, even for a new-fledged con man, but in some ways he'd been very good indeed. The moments when I wanted to see him again to thank him alternated with the moments when I wanted to see him again in order to kill him, but he'd taught me the survival skills I needed before he skinned out on me. Yes, he'd honed my skills personally—and I might yet be grateful. Trying to capture those wreckers was more likely to get us dead than any crime I could think of.

I tried to console myself, as I crept up the stairs for Michael's nightshirt and slippers, that the wreckers had successfully eluded the law so far. But Michael has a gift for attracting trouble. No, that's not accurate— that implies simple bad luck has something to do with the matter. Michael goes looking for trouble and invites it in. No wonder I felt so depressed.

* * *

Rosamund tapped on my door next morning at a perfectly ridiculous hour, halfway between breakfast and the mid-meal. I checked to be sure my nightshirt covered all it should and wrenched open the door to snarl at her, but she was bubbling with excitement.

She'd spent the morning *investigating*! It *was* Master Makejoye's troupe, and they were camped somewhere outside of town, which Rudy said they usually did to keep the street urchins from sneaking in to watch rehearsals. But Ebb the tapster, whose nickname was Tippy because he sometimes drank too much, said they were coming into town this morning to arrange for the scaffolding to be built in Crescent Square for their first performance. If we hurried, we could *catch* them, and if I didn't stop yawning, she was going to kick my ankle, so there!

I'd had time to become more or less inured to her beauty, and also had time to learn that she usually kept her threats, so I stopped yawning and promised I'd be down shortly. Then I closed the door and latched it.

I contemplated going back to bed, but she'd soon be pounding on the door if I tried it, and since I was awake anyway, I dressed and made my way down to breakfast.

Except for Michael and Rosamund the taproom was

empty, but sunlight streamed through the windows and they'd opened the door to admit the rain-fresh morning air.

I was unsurprised to see that Michael had beaten me downstairs. He's an early riser by nature and even has the gall to be cheerful about it. I couldn't endure good cheer just yet, so I went to the bar to cadge a cup of strong tea.

Ebb "Tippy" Dorn was younger than I'd guessed last night, for his small size and pale, flyaway hair gave him the air of an older man. Or maybe it was his timorous manner that gave an impression of age—he apologized twice for the lack of variety available for breakfast. It wasn't a meal they often served, the tavern not opening till midday.

I assured him, twice, that fried ham and hot porridge would suit me fine. By the time I finished a second cup of tea, I felt up to joining Michael, and even putting up with the way Rosamund was dancing from one foot to the other.

"Relax, Rosa. If they're coming in to arrange for scaffolding, they'll be there for hours. Even if they don't come, it won't be hard to find their camp."

"I know, I know—Michael said that too. But I haven't seen Rudy in months, and I just . . . You've never been in love, either of you. You don't know what it's like."

Michael's eyes fell to his plate, and he laid down his ham sandwich as if he'd suddenly lost his appetite. I was too hungry to succumb to sentiment, so I told Rosa she was right and went on with my breakfast. I had wondered a bit at the intensity of Michael's infatuation for Rosamund. It seemed to me that when she had claimed he was her brother, she'd been telling Mrs. Inger the truth—at least, the true state of her own heart. She was beautiful, of course, but after a while most men see beyond a woman's beauty, and Michael had known her all his life.

We were ready to go shortly, for Rosamund spent only half a minute settling her wide-brimmed straw hat and primping her reflection in the window before we set off. True love, indeed.

Huckerston was far more appealing in the sunlight than it had been last night, for the rain had washed the streets clean, and the mellow bricks glowed in the sun. Many of the buildings had thin, modern glass in their windows, and I deduced that there was a glassmaker in town. If ships started avoiding this port because of the wreckers, Huckerston would be in serious trouble. Crockery, glass, and most especially brick are too heavy to ship far overland. The reward must be . . . No. I didn't want to know.

The Slippery Wheel was just outside the market

square, and muddy roads hadn't stopped the farm carts that filled it. They had three colors of onions in these parts, not just the yellow to which I was accustomed, and the vivid summer vegetables were bright as bunting. Michael offered to buy Rosamund a slice of golden melon, but she was too impatient to stop.

The farmers told us that all the streets in this part of town led to the Narrows Bridge, and that Wide Road would take us straight to Crescent Square. A slight exaggeration—we found the river easily, but we had to ask the boatmen who poled long barges up and down where the bridge might be.

After that, Wide Road took us east. If you marked the size and quality of the buildings, it was easy to guess where to turn to reach the town's main square, though Michael regards such simple city navigation skills as a wondrous gift.

Crescent Square was crescent shaped, since its inner curve followed the river. Most of the guildhalls that surrounded it were fairly modest, except for the two buildings that perched on the crescent's horns, presiding over the top and bottom of the "square." The one we passed to reach the open cobbles was a mass of wings, abutments, and turrets, and the bricklayers had gone mad—every wall had bricks laid in a different pattern, so the wall where every few feet half a dozen bricks turned vertically met the wall where they marched in Vs like a herringbone knit, which met the wall where it ran into yet another pattern. The trowel and potter's wheel on the banner outside their door explained it, though I'm not sure anything could excuse it. Even Michael shook his head sadly as we passed.

The building dominating the other end of the cobbled arena was almost as ugly in a different way. Uncompromisingly rectangular, its gray stone slabs and narrow windows made it look like a squinting gargoyle among the more sedate buildings around it, and it seemed to wear a prickly, defensive air.

"'Twas the first Lord Waterweis's keep," Michael murmured. "'Tis the town hall now. The tapster told us the family still holds the town in fief, but the Potters' and Brickers' Guild is appealing the High Liege for independent township."

"I'll bet the current Lord Waterweis is out for their blood," I commented. If the High Liege granted the guild's appeal, the local lord stood to lose quite a bit. It was the kind of tension that makes a perfect setup for a con—a High Liege inspector open to bribes, a prospector who could reveal resources that would greatly benefit the town, carrying the Liege's decision to whichever side possessed the land they lay on . . .

I shrugged the possibilities aside, for I was no longer a con man. I was squire to a knight errant, here in the service of young love. Sometimes I really wonder about my sanity.

In the service of young love we started looking for players, which isn't as easy as it sounds. When they go about ordinary business, stripped of their paint, players look just like ordinary folk, and the square was full of them.

"See anyone you know?" I asked Rosamund.

She craned her slender neck to look over the crowd. "Not yet. Though I'm not sure about that man there." She pointed to a short, scruffy-looking fellow who appeared to be pacing off the open space. "That might be Master Barker, though he looks different without his costume."

The man paced a few more feet and nodded. He appeared to be talking to himself.

Rosamund's hand was tucked into Michael's arm. I suddenly felt impatient to get on with it. "Let's go ask him."

Michael scowled, but Rosamund nodded and pulled him over to the stranger.

"Excuse me, sir," she began sweetly. He turned to face her, and further inquiry became unnecessary—strangers meeting Rosamund are never stricken with dismay. His widened eyes swept over her in disbelief and then closed in a wince. Rosamund was oblivious.

"It is you! Oh, Master Barker, please, where is Rudy?"

Master Barker looked around for rescue and muttered under his breath. Rescue not appearing, he shrugged and gestured toward the old gray keep at the end of the square.

"Thank you so much." Rosamund pressed a kiss on his cheek and darted off. Michael and I exchanged bemused looks and followed.

Had we waited a few minutes, it would have been unnecessary to ask. As we approached the town hall, a young man shed his doublet and boots and climbed up the molding around the great door, agile as a squirrel. Several people stopped to stare, but he paid no heed, examining the decorative mantel. He appeared to be clinging to the smooth stone with only his bare toes. Having done some burglary myself, this impressed me more than any ropedancing act. None of the men below him seemed to make anything of it, though I noticed they stood positioned to catch him.

Rosamund came to a stop a few feet off, gazing up at the youth with a joyous pride that left no doubt that this was the noblest, handsomest, gentlest, etc. At least she had the sense not to call out and startle him.

He was handsome, I suppose, if you liked lean muscles and romantic dark curls, which women often do. He looked to be much the same age as Rosamund, which made him several years younger than Michael's twenty or my nineteen, and he was sensibly attending to business, for even the strongest toes can't hang on forever.

". . . I think we could attach the support beams here." His voice was deeper than I'd expected. "But we'll have to brace 'em all over. Putting up our own supports might be cheaper."

He slithered deftly down the carved stone and reached for his boots, smiling at a spatter of applause from the folk who'd stopped to watch. "Skinday, my friends, starting just before dusk." He began to make a sweeping bow, but then he saw Rosamund.

The smile froze on his face, but the incredulous joy that replaced it made smiling irrelevant. He *was* handsome, curse him. He dropped his boots and took the handful of strides that brought him to Rosamund. I thought he would kiss her, but instead he took her hand, as gently as someone capturing a bird. "Rose."

I felt Michael stir beside me. I couldn't completely interpret the expression on his face, but my heart flinched at it. When I turned back to the lovers,

Rosamund had snuggled into Rudy's side like a dipster going for an inside pocket.

The crowd clapped again, but neither of them noticed.

"Accursed," a rumbling voice murmured. If I'd not been standing at the base of the stair that led to the wide portico that fronted the town hall, I'd have missed it. Had the man's diction been less clear, I'd have missed it anyway. "What have I done to deserve being cursed with a cliché like this?"

The speaker was a man nearing the end of middle age. Big and heavy boned, with gray streaking through his dark red hair, he looked more like a dockhand or a bouncer than an actor.

"It is a bit hackneyed." I smiled at him, then dragged Michael out of his gloomy contemplation and up the steps. "Are you Master Makejoye? My name's Fisk, and this is Michael Sevenson, Rosamund's cousin. You've us to blame for bringing her here."

He ran big hands through his rumpled hair and glared at us. "I'm Hector Makejoye," he admitted. "And I *ought* to blame you! What under two moons do you think you're about? She can't marry him, he's fool enough not to settle for less, and her uncle will accuse us of kidnapping the wench and have the skin from all our backs—*if* we don't swing for it."

"You're wrong there, sir," said Michael quietly. "Rosamund would never permit such a thing. And whatever our differences, my father will believe me when I tell him you had nothing to do with it."

"I'll take you up on that offer, Michael Sevenson—by all means tell your father, as soon as you . . . Wait. We heard about you in Willowere. You're the one who's . . ."

"Unredeemed," said Michael. "But my father will accept my word despite that, for he knows me well." His expression was bleak, but his spine was stiff with stubborn pride.

"A knight errant." Makejoye's eyes brightened with interest. "I didn't believe that, when I first heard it. And *that's* not a story that's been done before. I don't suppose . . ."

"No!" Michael looked more horrified than when they had tattooed his wrists.

"But it would make a magnificent tale, Sir Michael. And we'd change the names. It's not as if—"

"Master Makejoye, you make a play of my life, and my father is the least thing you'll have to worry about." But his lips twitched as he spoke. I made a mental note to work with my employer on the convincing delivery of threats.

"Don't feel too bad," I told Makejoye. "Even if

you wrote it up, no one would accept it. It's too far-fetched."

Makejoye looked thoughtful. "You may be right. Suspension of disbelief goes only so far. But my first question stands: What possessed you to bring her here?"

"Because my father has gone about this matter wrongly," said Michael. "If he'd only allowed Rosamund to go with you . . ."

Barker and the other man who'd been with Makejoye drew near to listen to Michael's explanation. The second man was a bit over middle height and near skeleton thin, though he moved like he walked on springs. He had a long, mobile face, which at the moment reflected the same worry as the others. I noticed that all the actors wore their hair middling long, in a way that could pass for a peasant who needed a haircut, or a noble who'd gone just bit short—no doubt so they could take on any role that came to them.

Makejoye's expression became thoughtful as Michael spoke, though the thin man's dismay deepened and Barker looked glum throughout.

"There's something in what you say," Makejoye remarked when Michael had finished. "But—"

"Hector, have you gone mad?" the thin man interrupted. "We can't possibly take on a rich bas—"

"Ahem." Makejoye glared him down. "But as I was saying, we can't fight a man as powerful as your father, Sir Michael."

"But—" Michael began.

"But"—Master Makejoye clearly had some experience dealing with interruptions—"I'll tell you what we will do, for truly, I think you're right about the long-term solution to our problem." He looked at Rosamund and Rudy, who were gazing into each other's eyes. "Get over here, you lovebirds—this concerns you."

Rudy jumped, but Rosamund only smiled. They didn't let go of each other as they walked, and looking at Michael's carefully controlled expression, I foresaw trouble ahead.

"I'm going to propose a plan," said Makejoye.

"Really? How amazing," the thin man said. Barker snorted, and even Rudy grinned.

Makejoye assumed an air of lofty dignity and ignored them. "Mistress Rosamund may return to our camp and stay with us for as long as she will, *or* until—"

"Master Makejoye, thank you!" Rudy's handsome face glowed. "We will wed—"

"Oh no, you won't! She'll stay with us till her uncle claims her. I can't fight a man like Baron Sevenson, and I'm not going to try. That honor"—he bowed in

Michael's and my direction—"will go to Sir Michael and his squire."

"What?" I yelped. "We can't—"

"We'll handle it," said Michael. Rosamund cast him a glowing look.

I moaned, and the thin man gave me a smile that combined amusement and sympathy, though I think amusement came out on top.

"But if the baron retrieves her," Makejoye went on firmly, "she's going to be in the same state as when she came into my hands. By which I mean she's going to sleep in the women's wagon and my wife will chaperone her. And you two"—he gestured to us—"will serve as my witnesses to the baron that she was never alone with Rudy for more than a moment. So if anything happens, he can't go blaming us for it. Is that clear to all of you?"

So if she was pregnant now, the child was either Michael's or mine. Oh yes, perfectly clear.

Rudy was plainly indignant on Rosamund's behalf. Rosamund, the minx, looked disappointed. And Michael tried, not very successfully, to hide his satisfaction. I don't know how I looked—probably gloomy.

"Now, if you're joining our little troupe, you'll all have to earn your keep—we don't take passengers or cargo."

Makejoye was enjoying himself, probably because the dozen or so bystanders had given up any pretense of not listening and were frankly appreciating the performance.

"Can any of you act?" Makejoye went on.

Rosamund's "I should love to try" clashed with Michael's "No." I shrugged.

"Well, we'll give you an audition and see. You can be crowds if nothing else. Never hurts to have extras in the crowd scenes." But his gaze lingered thoughtfully on Rosamund's lovely face, and I knew she wasn't destined to be part of an anonymous crowd. "Can you juggle? Tumble? Throw knives? How about puppets? Dancing? Singing? Oh come, surely one of you can sing?"

Rosamund, as I'd learned on our journey, had a voice like a jay, and mine's not much better. Michael's voice is pleasant, but he doesn't like to sing in front of strangers. But I suspected that a large share of the menial chores would fall to those who didn't perform. "I can do card—"

Michael's boot-heel came down on my toe and I broke off, concealing my wince as I met Makejoye's gaze with a shrug and a smile. On second thought, it probably was better for one of us to retain some respectability in the sheriff's eyes.

"I fear we can do little in terms of performance," said Michael. "But I can look after your animals, hunt, and mayhap mend your wagons or tack. And Fisk can sew and embroider most finely."

"And I," put in one of the men who stood at the fringes of the crowd, "can put up your scaffolding if you'll spare me a moment to talk about it. For if you're Hector Makejoye, I believe we have an appointment?"

The audience laughed, and Master Makejoye bowed his admiration for the carpenter's timing. Observing the crew behind the carpenter, with timber and saws in hand, I murmured to Michael that I'd go back to the inn and get our gear and the menagerie, for I'd no desire to be drafted as a carpenter's assistant.

Michael chose to stay, so I was alone when I walked into the inn and Joe Potter hustled out of the taproom and caught my arm.

The hum of voices told me that luncheon here was popular, and it smelled good too, but one look at Potter's face told me we'd eat no more meals at the Slippery Wheel.

"Come upstairs, Master Fisk; I've something to say. Your *friend* isn't with you?"

"No," I said, glad that he wasn't. It hurts Michael to be thrown out like this. I'm pretty much indifferent to it.

"Good." Potter gave the taproom crowd a final glance and hauled me off—or tried to, for I twisted my arm out of his grip before he'd taken two steps. I don't mind being kicked out, but being manhandled is something else.

He glared, but since I followed him meekly up the stairs, he chose not to press the matter.

"Master Fisk, if I'd—"

"Only known," I recited with him.

Angry red stained his cheeks. "I'd never have let the three of you in, and that's a fact. This is a—"

"Respectable house," I chimed in again. "I don't see your problem, Master Potter. Did we slip out on the bill? No, we paid in advance. Have we caused any trouble? No. In fact—"

"No, and I'm not giving you a chance to cause trouble, either, 'cause—"

"The question won't arise," I told him. "Because we located Mistress Rosamund's friends, and we'll be staying with them. I've just come back to fetch our things."

"That's good, Master Fisk." He glared at me. "You do that." He turned and stalked off.

Just over twelve hours from one sheriff and deputy to the whole town knowing. And half those hours at night. That was fast for a town this size, even from the

sheriff's department. Maybe the sheriff, or one of his
deputies, had made a point of telling Potter since they
knew we were staying here. When they came to pick
up the horses we'd borrowed, no doubt. We were leaving, anyway, but I must admit I'd have liked a meal.

As it happened, I got it. As I lashed packs onto
Honey's saddle, Ebb Dorn crept up to me with a worn
canvas sack in his hand and such a furtive air about
him that I looked over my shoulder before I could
stop myself.

"I feel bad about this, Master Fisk." He too looked
about, but the grooms had been drafted to wait tables
and wash up, and we had the stable to ourselves.
"Especially for the lady."

Trouble pranced up and licked his hand, and he
gave the dog's head an awkward pat.

I smiled forgivingly—judging by Trouble's interest,
there was something edible in that bag. "It's not your
fault, Master Dorn, so—"

"But it is my fault. I was the one who heard"—his
voice dropped—"about your friend. That he's . . ."

"Unredeemed," I finished calmly. "But we were
leaving anyway, so it hardly matters."

"Well, that's good then." He summoned up a
timid smile. "But the least I can do is offer you some

sandwiches, to make up for any inconvenience Mistress Rosamund may have suffered."

I took the bag, thanked him sincerely, and watched him scurry back to the inn. Tapsters always know everything first.

I investigated the sack before I mounted Tipple and found it contained not only sandwiches but pickles as well, and enough of both that an inexpensive stop at one of the sausage carts in the market square would let me feed our newfound hosts as well.

The last thing I did was check the lead rope that secured Trouble's collar to Chanticleer's saddle. Michael claims he can control the brute in towns, unless he sees a cat. Or a pigeon, or a rat, or . . . I always double-check the leash.

Over luncheon, we learned a bit about Master Makejoye's troupe, both present and absent, including the women who'd remained in camp. We sat on the town hall's shady steps, for the sun was hot now, the morning's coolness only a memory. The scaffolding was rising behind us already; the scent of cut wood mingled pleasantly with that of sausage, though the hammering interrupted our conversation.

The thin man's name was Falon. He was their juggler and knife thrower, and he played villains, heroes' best friends, and assorted bit parts. "But it's villain that suits him best, isn't it, you rogue?"

Makejoye's voice held only friendship, and Falon's smile was open and easy, but there was something about him that reminded me of . . . me. I resolved not to let him learn where we kept Rosamund's jewels, which meant finding a new place to hide them from her and Michael as well. Which wasn't such a bad idea, now that I thought about it.

Master Edgar Barker and his wife, Edith, trained dogs, and performed with them as clowns. Which I might have guessed, for Trouble was practically sitting in the man's lap.

Rosamund sat almost that close to Rudy, who was the troupe's ropedancer and tumbler, and played—what else?—the hero.

"The dogs start off the show." Master Makejoye swallowed a bite of pickle. "I've planned it all out. We'll hire a lad to hold the wagon at the other end of the square, and the Barkers'll jump out, set up a bit, then whistle and the dogs leap out everywhere. They're little mites, not like your fine fellow, but they're smart beasts."

"Unlike our fine fellow," I murmured.

Master Barker snorted. "You're plenty smart, aren't you, boy? You tell him."

Trouble gazed at him adoringly and thumped his tail.

"Anyway, they'll do tricks all the way down the square," Makejoye went on. "While everyone's looking at them, we'll slip in, scramble into costume, and open the phosphor lamps. The dogs will run up onstage and through the curtains." He used a sausage to gesture at an opening in the tangle of scaffolding. "Then Edith and Edgar will climb up, looking for 'em, you see, and open the curtains, and there we are. The play starts off right then." He took a bite out of his pointer.

"It sounds well planned," said Michael politely.

"Tell me, pup, have you always been mute?" Barker asked Trouble.

"He was when we met him." Michael spoke for the dog, amusement dancing in his eyes. "But that was only winter before last."

"And you're four or five, aren't you?" Barker felt Trouble's throat with expert fingers. "I'm not finding any tumors, which is good. Speak!"

I jumped at the sudden command in his voice and was about to offer Trouble's excuses, for that was something we hadn't even tried to teach him—unlike come, sit, heel, and stay-out-of-my-bed. But to my astonishment, Trouble lifted his head and made the rasping gasp that is the best bark he can manage.

"Good boy." Barker fed him a bit of his sandwich. "My guess is you were born mute, poor pup. But at least they're taking good care of you, aren't they now?"

Trouble rasped again, his tail thumping harder.

"Thank you," said Michael—to both of them, as near as I could tell.

The carpenters finished their work shortly after we finished eating, and Falon and Rudy checked their measurements with a bit of knotted string to be sure the scenery panels would fit before Master Makejoye paid them off.

The players had walked into town, so we led the horses and walked beside them—except for Rosamund. It was Michael who insisted she ride, but Rudy, being an acrobat, beat him to Rosamund's side and won the right to lift her into Honey's saddle.

Makejoye watched the whole farce with narrowed eyes.

"You're thinking of casting her as heroine?" Falon asked softly. "Glory'll claw her eyes out. And then she'll go for you. You don't even know if she can act."

"But look at that face," Makejoye muttered. "I'll cut the heroine's dialogue down. And look at that little spotted mare—she's in costume already! Edgar, could you use that little mare in your dog act?"

The players' camp was set in a clearing in a grove

of small, shady trees. Bright costumes strewn across the laps of a group of women, seated on a circle of rickety-looking chairs, made a splash of color to one side. The players' wagons, wooden sided and canvas roofed, were bright with paint and gilding, appearing almost civilized against the darkness of the trees. Not as civilized as a cozy inn, mind, but better than the bedrolls that would be Michael's and my lot for the duration.

Rosamund clasped her hands. "'Tis charming! Oh, Rudy, this is so pretty!"

"I hope she thinks so tomorrow morning, when she's washing in cold stream water," I murmured.

"Really? I hope not," Michael murmured back.

The sewing women rose to their feet, the oldest catching a green velvet cape the youngest was working on before it fell to the grass. Their own skirts were drabber than the costumes they stitched, and the elder two wore white caps and aprons, as working women will. Another was bareheaded, but the youngest wore a broad-brimmed felt hat with pheasant feathers in the band.

It was the oldest who folded her arms and scowled, and no one could mistake her authority or her displeasure.

"Gwen, my dear." Makejoye strode into the clearing

with all the feigned confidence of a man trying to make something supremely foolish sound wise. "We have a new plan!"

Judging by Gwendolyn Makejoye's expression as she recognized Rosamund, she didn't think much of the plan so far. She looked as thin and sour as her husband was thick and juicy, but I had a hunch that being practical for two, perhaps even for eight, might sour anyone. And Makejoye's explanation, which was in full spate, didn't appear to change her mind.

It was easy to guess that the other capped and aproned woman was Edith Barker, for she started fussing over Trouble before she even glanced at the rest of us. "What's the matter with your voice, poor fellow?"

It was equally obvious, as she pushed back her hat to watch Rudy help Rosamund down from the saddle, which of the remaining women was Gloria Glorious. She looked like a woman who played heroines, pretty enough, with long blond hair and the slim grace of a tumbler and dancer. But her expression held none of a heroine's insipid innocence; the fury of a woman scorned is pale compared to the fury of a woman who has suddenly gone from leading lady to heroine's sister, best friend, and maid.

"Oh, dear." The voice was deep for a woman's, almost furry. I turned to glance at the fourth actress, and my glance became a stare. Her hair was a soft shade between brown and amber, and she evidently went without a hat often, for her face, throat, and the rich swell of her breasts were tinted with gold.

She was taller than I, Michael's height perhaps, and plump in a way that was very pleasing indeed. My eyes traveled down the curves of her body and back up, almost of their own accord. Her arms and hands, emerging from the fall of lace at her elbows, were round, soft, and dainty.

Her face, also round and soft, looked from Rudy and Rosamund to Gloria with a rueful amusement that spoke of intelligence as well as humor. Then she turned and met my eyes. Hers were the same golden brown as her hair, and I suddenly felt my face heat.

She looked even more amused. "Callista Boniface, Master . . . Fisk? Then from what Hector's saying, you must be Sir Michael. It sounds like you'll be joining us, for a time at least, and you're welcome. But for now"— her eyes turned to Gloria—"I'd better go and explain some facts of life to Glory before she demonstrates just what a bad actress she really is. If you'll excuse me?" She glided off, like a plump cougar, and I swallowed and turned to meet Michael's eyes.

"My," he murmured.

"My, indeed," I replied. "If she has that kind of

impact on an audience, it's a wonder men don't rush the stage."

Michael smiled, but his eyes slid to Rosamund. Rudy had taken her to inspect one of the wagons, and she was exclaiming over how delightful it was. Callista had intercepted Gloria and was trying to convince her to retract her claws. Gwendolyn Makejoye's glare had faded to exasperated resignation. It seemed we were in, and easier than I'd expect—

A chorus of yaps heralded the appearance of a pack of small, muddy dogs. They poured into camp, skidding to a stop as they saw *their* master and mistress fussing over a stranger. There was a second of eerie silence—then they charged.

It was the most honest display of emotion I'd seen yet.

Michael and the Barkers pulled the brawl apart and got the dogs properly introduced before anyone was bitten. Having talked his wife around, Makejoye went to the back of his wagon and pulled out a chest full of what looked to be half-bound books—though their bindings were loosely stitched, they had no covers. I was curious about the wagon, too.

He soon noticed me looking over his shoulder. "I'm just digging out a few scripts to give you three an audition. You know, I charged Lord Fabian for only an eight-player troupe. With three more players, we can raise the price of our next performance."

"Assuming any of us does well enough that you'll let us perform."

The wagon was roomier than I'd have thought, but every inch seemed to be filled with boxes, baskets, and some clever cabinets built into the wagon's wooden sides. It even had two small windows, though their panes were the old, thick, round ones, filled with bubbles and distortions. What it didn't have was beds, or any space to put them that I could see.

"Do you sleep in here?" I asked.

"Only in bad weather." Makejoye flipped pages on one of his scripts. "In the summer we sleep under the wagons for the most part; in winter . . . Ah, here we are. Come along, Master Fisk. The sooner I discover your talents, the longer I'll have to modify our play to incorporate them."

If he could get extra pay for extra players, I had no doubt he'd modify them, no matter how bad we were.

Makejoye assigned each of us a part and had us read the short scene, and he let us keep the scripts so we didn't have to memorize the lines. He declared the sunlit center of the small clearing to be the stage, and set the ladies' sewing chairs in front of it for half the audience. The other half, which included himself, Edgar Barker, and (tactfully) Gloria, stood as far away as they could and still see us through the trees, "Because the fellows in the back need to hear, too, you know."

The scene was fairly standard, with two men competing for the attention of a flirtatious girl. I've seen such scenes many times, though the dialogue in this one was witty enough to make me snicker as I read it.

Gwen Makejoye took on the role of stage manager, placing us in the positions she wanted like a housewife arranging furniture. She told us when to move, and where, and then stepped aside to join the rest of our audience and nodded to me to begin.

I pitched my voice to carry. "How pleasant to find you alone, my dear. Or as near alone as makes no difference. Do you . . ."

I suppose the audition could be described as a moderate disaster. It was hard to say whether Michael or Rosamund was more wooden, but at least Michael, after a few reminders, started talking for the farther members of the audience. After the fifth call of "louder, my girl" Rosamund's eyes began to fill, and Mistress Gwendolyn signaled her husband to stop trying.

I played my part as if it was a con—or not quite, for

the better part of pulling off a con is to sound natural. I tried to con them into believing I was an actor, and I must not have lost my touch, for after we'd finished, Makejoye gave me a speculative glance. "Have you done this before, Master Fisk?"

"Not exactly."

"Well, you'll do. There's room in the script for the hero to have a best friend—not so many soliloquies that way—and in the end he could bring the sheriff's men to the rescue . . . or . . . No, that'll work. As for you, my dear . . ." He threw a fatherly arm around Rosamund's shoulders. "No, don't cry, you looked lovely, and I'll show you a trick or two that'll have your voice traveling all the way to Huckerston! We've all day tomorrow to work together, you and Rudy and I."

Rosamund straightened her shoulders and blinked her eyes dry. "I'll work hard, Master Makejoye. I'll do anything to stay here."

"That's a good lass. And as for you, Sir—"

"Just Michael, please." His voice was full of resignation. "You can't say I didn't warn you."

Makejoye laughed. "So you did. And you're right, it's crowds for you, lad. Or at least . . . Can you fence?"

Falon brought out the stage swords, which looked real but to my considerable relief had edges blunter than a butter knife's. They stood me up against

Michael, despite my protests, and told me to try, so I lifted the awkward thing and blocked Michael's first, lazy-looking slash.

His sword whipped around mine, knocking it out of my hand with a force that made my wrist tingle. I made a great show of shaking my fingers and the others laughed. Michael went, good-naturedly, to fetch my sword.

Then they matched Rudy against Michael, saying he was the best swordsman among them. Rosamund clapped her hands in excitement, and both fencers looked at her and assumed identical, fatuous smiles.

Rudy took up a stance that looked better than Michael's to my untrained eye, and Michael's first blow was faster than the one he'd aimed at me. The resounding clang as Rudy parried made me glad the swords' edges were dull.

Rudy had obviously picked up a bit of training somewhere, but noblemen's sons are taught the sword in earnest. Rudy lasted all of twenty seconds before his sword followed mine into the bushes, and I thought he suppressed a wince as he tried to work the numbness out of his hand.

"Not bad," Makejoye commented. "In a choreographed fight, you'd do well together. I wonder if I could work in a brigand to attack the heroine's coach.

Then young Lord Gaspar could . . ."

Makejoye spent the rest of the day revising his scripts and I helped recopy them—not a massive task, since he rewrote only the pages he made changes on and then bound them in with the others, using an awl to pierce the paper.

It was a rather silly story, about a heroic young lord (whose name, by pure coincidence, bore some resemblance to that of the man who was paying for the piece) who falls in love with a beautiful peasant girl and is forbidden by his horrified parents to wed her. After many silly plots to separate them, which now included a brigand's attack . . .

"Let me guess—the girl is revealed to be noble, rich, and Gifted, and was being raised by the poor farmer for some tremendously silly reason?"

"Don't be so cynical, Master Fisk." Makejoye wagged an ink-stained finger. "If it was a tragedy, no one would watch. Her father was accused of conspiring to overthrow the High Liege and died in a flooding river trying to escape, so all his property was forfeit. Evidence turns up to prove he was innocent and it's really me—that is, the girl's villainous uncle—who was guilty. The father usually dies at sea fighting pirates, but with what's going on around here . . ." He shook his head sadly.

The copying got me out of helping with dinner preparation, and Edith Barker was an even better camp cook than Michael. I was amused to see Rosamund don an apron and chop vegetables, which she'd never done for Michael and me. She really was trying. It made me nervous for the meal.

But dinner, a leg of roast pig cooked up with vegetables, and soft fluffy biscuits, was as good as any inn might serve.

And the entertainment was better, for afterward Master Makejoye went into his wagon and came out with a viol case, which I hadn't noticed that morning.

Michael stiffened as Makejoye pulled the instrument free, and I looked at him curiously. The sun had set as we finished eating, and not having cooked, I knew I'd be called on to help wash the dishes as soon as the water heated. I was pleased at the prospect of some music to lighten the chore.

The viol looked perfectly ordinary, with lamp and firelight glowing on its varnished curves. Of course Michael's sight wasn't the same as mine, but surely a fiddle couldn't be—

Then Makejoye tucked it between his knees and drew the bow across the strings. The soft, pure notes may have started in my ears, but they didn't stop there—they vibrated in my throat, my belly, my bones. I hardly recognized the melody, though it was a country ballad I'd often heard. I'd just never lived it before.

Gwendolyn Makejoye raised her voice, giving words to the viol's speechless wail. I'd have thought a human voice, even one as clear and sweet as hers, would have been lost in the intensity of the viol's sound, but somehow it took her voice with it, giving it the same penetrating impact. Between the two . . .

I was trembling when the music finished, and my throat was tight. Rosamund had tears on her face, and Michael had to swallow twice before he could speak.

"How did you come by such a thing? A magica viol . . . I can't imagine the sacrifice that must have paid for it."

"It was enough, I suppose," said Makejoye softly. The others were going about their chores, far less shaken than the three of us. Exposure, no doubt, lessening the shock. But the echoes of the music touched all their faces. Even Gloria looked content.

"My grandfather was a fiddle maker," Makejoye went on. "My father played well enough, but he hadn't the knack with wood that Granda had. At the end of his life Granda's hands began to stiffen, and he realized he'd be making only one more viol. So he went to a Savant to get the wood, and he paid for it with just one finger—this one." He lifted his left forefinger and wiggled it. "He could never play again. He never played the instrument he made, but my da played it for him, before he died, and I play it for his memory. Neither of our girls cares much for music—and how that happened, between Gwen and me . . . but there, sometimes these things skip a generation. I've a young grandson who's showing talent, so I don't think Granda would feel his sacrifice was wasted."

"What in the world," I demanded, "are you doing on the road? You could play that for the High Liege's court—in the great theaters in Crown City or Tallowsport—and charge any fee you'd care to name!"

"So I will," said Makejoye. "When I'm ready to retire. But there's other crafts than music, and folk other than lords who care for such things. The deaf can hear this fiddle, can you imagine? It terrifies them at first, but then . . . Surely music, of all the arts, is made to share."

And share he did, all through the mellow evening. I suppose I washed the dishes, though I have no memory of it. The music still hummed in my bones as I drifted off to sleep. My last thought was to hope Makejoye hid the thing well. All Rosamund's jewels weren't worth half its price—though it might be hard to fence.

* * *

The next day Master Makejoye made good his promise to work with Rosamund—at first just with her, then in rehearsals that included all of us.

It wasn't a problem for me—despite Makejoye's praise of my delivery, my lines were few. Michael played a peasant, whose only dialogue was a constant repetition of "I dunno," and a brigand who spoke no lines at all. And Rosamund did make progress. By the day's end, you could hear her voice on the far side of the clearing almost half the time.

Skinday morning Makejoye stayed in camp with the women "to put just a bit more polish on your splendid performance, lass." The rest of us drove the prop wagon into town and nailed painted panels onto the scaffolding, transforming it into the semblance of two plaster-and-beam buildings with a forest between them. It looked out of place in this town of brick on brick.

"We realized that the moment we set eyes on the place," said Rudy ruefully. "But Hector says the different architecture will look exotic to these folk."

Once the panels were up, and the props and costume changes laid out in the dark, cramped "wings" of the stage, someone had to stay and watch them, along with the horse and wagon and the magica phosphor moss-lamps, whose brightness made night performances possible. In a dry region like this, those lamps, filled with living moss, were probably worth more than the horse. Since they already knew their parts, Rudy and Falon chose to stay, and Michael, Barker, and I walked back to camp.

I found myself unaccountably nervous as the day dragged on—unaccountably, because I'd only a handful of lines, and I've run cons where if I blew my role I'd end up indebted—maybe even flogged. All I was in danger of now was looking silly, and after almost two years as Michael's squire I was accustomed to that.

As I said, the day dragged on, until suddenly it was time to paint our faces and depart and the minutes started hurtling forward.

We rode into town in the Barkers' fancifully painted wagon, perched on their belongings with the little dogs crouched between us—when they weren't on our laps. They too seemed . . . not nervous, but quiveringly eager. Their ruffled collars got in our way more than they seemed to bother them.

At least Trouble was tied securely to a tree, "guarding" the picketed horses. He had wanted to accompany us so badly that I triple-checked the knots that held his tether before we left.

The cart lurched onto the cobbles long before I was ready for it, and my stomach lurched, too. Michael was smiling his cursed this-will-be-an-adventure smile, and I swore at him under my breath.

With Rudy gone, he was the one who helped Rosamund down from the cart. Barker stopped several blocks short of the square, so we could sneak in and "mysteriously" appear when the curtains opened. At least, that was Makejoye's plan. I hoped the exercise would settle Rosamund's nerves, for she looked absolutely terrified.

I think the brisk walk did us all good. I couldn't see Rosa's color under the gaudy paint, but some of the stiffness drained from her posture, and her breathing steadied. As for me, moving cloaked and unobtrusive through a crowd brought back memories older than my con-man days. If not all of them were pleasant, at least the familiarity was soothing. This time I risked nothing.

The crowd gathered in the square was larger than I'd expected, almost filling it. Pie sellers were hawking their wares, their rough voices giving texture to the chatter of the crowd. The lighters were just starting to kindle the torches when the Barkers' wagon rattled into the square.

Edgar and Edith stood on the driver's seat and bowed, as one of the two lads we'd hired that afternoon came forward to take the reins. They jumped down, Barker turning a few cartwheels in the process, and began, with comic clumsiness, to unload the small platforms and bright-striped hoops.

I suddenly wondered if Makejoye hadn't outsmarted himself. The square was packed with people, and how the Barkers would clear a path . . .

I needn't have worried. At Barker's shrill whistle the dogs burst from the wagon, and *they* cleared the space before them, herding the crowd aside like so many sheep, yapping at the recalcitrant. When one cocky youth refused to stand aside, instead of nipping, the dog lifted a leg, in a way that made the threat only too plain. The boy leapt back and the crowd roared with delight.

Skirting the mob's fringes, we might as well have been invisible.

Sunset's orange glow made the well-worn costumes and props look fresh and bright. The dogs leapt and clowned their way toward the stage. A grubby lad, perhaps eight or nine, sidestepped in search of a better view and ran into my legs. His mouth fell open at the sight of my painted face, and I lifted a finger to my lips and winked.

The wide grin of a child with a secret stretched his cheeks. I pointed to the steps of one of the guild houses—farther off, but high enough to give a good view—and mimed climbing.

He grinned again and took off like an arrow. As I strolled up the stairs to the wings of the stage, only one pair of eyes in all the oblivious crowd was on me. Master Makejoye knew his business, it seemed, and my qualms for the performance began to diminish. Until the Barkers drew the curtains aside and revealed the bright-lit stage, Rosamund, and Gloria.

"My dearest friend," said Rosamund, in a quivering voice so soft that I could barely hear her, "I . . . I hope . . ."

"Ah, Carolee," said Gloria in a voice they could hear on the other side of the river. "You shouldn't fret about your lack of speech. Some men prefer women who are silent and mouselike."

Falon, who stood behind me, choked, for that line was emphatically not in the script. But if Rosamund didn't pull herself together, a mute heroine might—

"My speech is fine," said Rosamund—and if you couldn't have heard her across the river, at least the back of the crowd stood a fighting chance. Real indignation made her tone almost natural. "As you well know, Elaine. Just because I don't chatter all the time like . . . like a bold woman, it doesn't mean I have no speech."

Makejoye, on the other side of the stage, hissed

softly; Gloria and Rosamund got the hint and the play went forward as written. By the midpoint break my nerves had vanished into a sweaty, panicked exaltation. My only costume change for the second half consisted of putting on a different doublet, so I was able to watch Makejoye work the crowd.

He'd taken his viol up onstage and commanded their attention with a melody that set feet tapping throughout the audience—children and young couples danced wherever they could find the space. When he finished, there was a moment of absolute silence, then kind of a roaring whisper as the whole audience took a breath at once, followed by exclamations of awe and shouted demands for another tune.

"In good time, my friends, in good time. For it strikes me that while you've seen something of all of us, we barely know any of you, and that doesn't seem fair." The viol mourned, and almost broke my heart.

"You, sir, yes, you in the front, come up here and talk to me." He had to take the man's hand to lead him up to the stage—a laborer of some sort by his clothes, come in from the countryside for the performance. His tanned, lined face was wary as he gazed at the gaudy actor.

"So, sir, are you enjoying the play? More interesting than the milk pails, I trust?"

"Here!" The man looked as if he'd swallowed an

egg whole. "What do you know about milk pails?"

"You're a dairyman, are you not?"

"How'd you know that!" His astonishment was so sincere even I knew he wasn't a shill, and the audience murmured their appreciation.

"Why, because of the way your girl was clinging to you," Makejoye answered smoothly. "No one"—his voice dropped to a whisper that carried farther than most men's shouts—"handles women like a dairyman, as all the girls know." The viol mooed.

The flattered, red-faced farmer shook the actor's hand and returned to his embarrassed wife.

Then Makejoye challenged the crowd to send him people whose professions he might not guess, "No, not you, sir, there's far to many potters in this town for that to be a puzzle. Someone harder, if you please."

All herb-mixers carry the faint scent of their wares, though the crowd apparently didn't know it, for they were astonished. The clerk he no doubt told by the faded ink stains on his cuffs, though even Makejoye guessed wrong as to who he clerked for, to the audience's delight.

They'd have forgiven him for murder at that point. The jokes were flying thick and fast, each topping the next—they laughed till they were clutching their ribs with tears on their faces.

"A jester," Michael whispered, a note of awe in his voice. I felt the same, for jesters are almost as outdated and mythical as knights errant.

"And a good one," I whispered back. A man of many talents, Master Makejoye. What in the world was he doing scrounging for contracts in obscure towns?

I got an inkling of the answer later on, as I listened to young Lord Gaspar lament how he was forced to a path not of his choice by the foolish conventions of another time. It hadn't sounded quite so . . . radical when I read it in the script. In a time when barons all through the realm were struggling to keep their people from running to the towns, some of the young lord's romantic problems seemed to have political overtones. Of course this was a town, but still . . .

"Isn't this a bit . . . unwise?" I asked Gloria, who happened to be on my side of the stage at the moment.

She grimaced. She really was pretty, though not as spectacularly lovely as Rosamund. "If you think that's bad, you should . . . ah, think again, Master Fisk. It's nothing but a young man whining about wanting to marry against his family's will."

"Of course," I replied. But I frowned as I said it. Players often have different versions of the same script—the story the local baron might see would be subtly different from the version that played when all the audience was villagers and common folk. Even if someone objected, the worst it was likely to bring them was a pointed request to leave, and perhaps a few bruises. A flogging was rare. But if Makejoye had political leanings, maybe it was good he wasn't playing in Crown City.

It was almost time for Gloria to go on and give Gaspar his lover's desperate plea for rescue.

"Shouldn't you cut Rosa a little slack for the rest of the night?" I asked softly. "If you step on any more of her lines, Makejoye will demote you from best friend to scullery maid."

She grinned, unrepentant. "But as Callista pointed out, she probably won't be with us very long. Besides, I've almost dragged a real performance out of the wench."

That was true; sheer self-defense had forced Rosamund to fight for the chance to say her lines, to command the audience's attention. So far, she'd muffed only half of them.

Gloria's cue came, and she rushed out onto the stage, her sweaty costume looking rich and real in the clear lamplight.

Soon it was over. We straightened from our final bow, and I realized I'd never been so exhausted in my life.

Makejoye stepped forward one last time. "You've been a splendid audience," he told them. "And I hope you've enjoyed our performance as much as we've enjoyed pleasing you. If you wish to leave a small token of your gratitude, the lads holding the horses at either wagon will be happy to accept it on our troupe's behalf. Now we bid you good night."

Michael looked startled. "I thought Lord Fabian was paying them."

I grinned at him. "What's the difference between a traveling player and a bandit?"

Michael sighed. "I don't know. What?"

"The player expects you to clap when he's finished."

Mistress Barker, who stood between us, snorted. "That's the truth, isn't it?"

"Nonsense," said Makejoye, joining us. "A few fracts won't hurt them and might do us a deal of good."

"Can I ask you something?" I'd been wondering all night. "How did you guess the dairyman? I figured out the others, but he looked like he'd bathed."

"He had." Makejoye grinned. "When most folk ask, I tell 'em it's a trade secret, but since you're one of us . . . It was the softness of his hands. Dairymen rub grease on their cows' udders to keep them from chapping, and their hands are as soft as a fine lady's. But I believe I see opportunity approaching. Master Potter, what did you think of our performance?"

"Councilman for the Potters' and Brickers' Guild," Falon murmured, as Makejoye went to greet a thin, plainly dressed man. "Lord Fabian's rival for control of the town. With any luck he'll feel obliged to hire us for a different performance, and pay even more to score off his lordship."

If the guilds managed to organize sufficiently to get the town charter transferred from Lord Fabian to them, Lord Fabian would lose his cut of the town's taxes, and the guilds, whose taxes would then go straight to the High Liege, would pay far less. Hiring players to put on a few shows was a cheap price for both parties to pay in that kind of struggle. If Makejoye was clever, he could make a lot of money here. If he wasn't careful, he might get caught up in a fight too big for any player to deal with—but all that was tomorrow's problem.

The audience was leaving. With them gone, the cool breeze could reach the stage, and I was grateful for it. Edgar Barker was taking the tired dogs back to camp. Edith watered and closed up the phosphor mosslamps, preparing to go with him. The rest of us still had work to do.

We changed out of our costumes, men on one side of the stage, women on the other. Then the ladies packed up costumes and props, while Rudy brought out hammers and crowbars for the rest of us to take the scenery off the scaffolding. He was showing Michael and me how to pull the nails without leaving dents in the panels when we discovered that one member of the audience hadn't left.

"You!" Rosamund's voice was full of loathing—I wished she'd project that much emotion on the stage. "What are you doing here, you horrid little man?"

"Now, Mistress Rosamund." Quidge was a lump of darkness in the shadow of the steps. "You know perfectly well what I'm doing, and no wrong to you intended. Couldn't we discuss this?"

"No," said Rosamund, though it sounded like a reasonable request to me. "Of course I know what you want; I meant, how did you find me? Not that it will do you any good this time, either!"

Quidge looked mournful, but there was a glint in his eyes I didn't care for. I joined the others, who were converging at that side of the stage.

Rudy threw a manly arm around Rosamund's shoulders, and Michael, preempted from that, hovered protectively beside her. Even Makejoye paused in his negotiations with Master Potter.

"You think you're safe here, don't you, girl, with your new friends. You trust 'em?"

"Of course I do." Rosamund put her arm around Rudy's waist. "Oh, Rudy, this is Master Quidge, the bounty hunter my uncle sent after me. Master Quidge, this is Rudy Foster, my betrothed."

I heard a choking sound beside me and glanced at Callista. She'd played the heroine's spiteful stepsister and somehow managed to suppress her remarkable allure. If she hadn't, the audience would never have believed she had reason to be jealous of any woman. She was rumpled, sweat stained, and tired, as we all were, but the lamps tinted her smooth skin to honey. Amusement glinted in her eyes as they met mine.

"Breeding will tell," she murmured, and I laughed.

"Pleased to meet you, Master Foster," Quidge replied, irony smoothing his rough voice.

"I'm sorry I can't say the same," Rudy replied. His accent was a good match for Lord Gaspar's, but it would take more than a noble accent to intimidate Quidge.

"And I'm sorry to bring bad news," the bounty hunter went on, not sounding sorry at all. "But the truth is, lass, you can't trust 'em. You asked how I found you so quick?" I was wondering that myself. "I just wrote to your uncle and asked where young Rudy was. Master Makejoye's been keeping your uncle informed of all his movements these past five months.

I'd have intercepted you on the road if it hadn't taken a bit of time for your uncle's letter to reach me. I wish you'd read it, for he's deeply worried about you. And he'd not betray you for pay, like this lot here."

Rosamund stiffened. It was Rudy who spun to Master Makejoye. "Hector, you didn't!" It was a protest, not a question.

"Lad, what would you?" Makejoye shrugged. "I hadn't the least notion the girl would turn up, and he offered ten gold roundels just to tell him where you were. Since I knew you didn't intend to abscond with her, where was the harm? Though candidly, even if you had planned to steal her away, I'd have done the same. How many times must I tell you all, I cannot challenge a man like Baron Sevenson."

"A wise choice, sir," said Quidge. "You see, girl, they won't protect you, but your uncle will. I can't guess how much he's already spent trying to see you safe. Just let me take you home, and—"

"No," said Rosamund.

Rudy released her and started down the steps, his handsome chin thrust out. "Maybe Hector won't protect her," he said. "But I will!"

He leapt from the steps as he spoke, but Quidge was ready for him—and a better fighter than Rudy would ever be. He caught one of the boy's out-flung arms and ducked beneath it, slamming Rudy's body to the cobbles as he did.

The matter should have ended then, but acrobats know how to fall. Rudy hit the ground rolling and sprang to his feet, coming back at Quidge with fists clenched.

"Michael, do something!" Rosamund shrieked.

"We'd better stop it," said Michael, "before someone gets hurt. You take Rudy, Fisk, and I'll reason with Master Quidge." It was probably a fair division; though Rudy was less skilled, Master Quidge was more likely to answer to reason.

Having no desire to see anyone hurt, I laid down my hammer and followed Michael down the steps. We closed in behind our respective targets—no small feat, for they were prancing around each other, fists flying. At least, Rudy's fists were flying. Quidge was mostly blocking, aiming a blow only when he thought it might get through. Rudy had a reddened streak along one side of his jaw, but acrobats are good at ducking, too, and it looked like the fight might last longer than I'd expected. Except that we were going to stop it, of course.

I stepped up behind Rudy and wrapped my arms around him, spinning him away at the same time in case Michael failed and Quidge took an ignoble

advantage—highly probable, from what I'd seen of
him.

Rudy swore and tried to throw me off, so I barely
glimpsed Michael stepping in front of Quidge. I don't
know where communication broke down, but Quidge's
fist whipped past Michael's ear. Then they were dancing and trading blows, as Rudy twisted like a serpent
in my grasp and tried to stamp on my feet.

"Try reason!" I gasped to Michael. He was a better
fighter than Rudy, and after working all spring as a
bouncer was in better practice as well. He and Quidge
might actually do some damage.

Rudy shoved me backward trying to ram me against
the building behind us, and I dug my heels into the
cobbles and pivoted so we both hit the stone wall
sideways. It hurt.

"Stop fighting, you jackass. We're trying to *help*
you!"

A breathless curse was my only answer. Men fight-
ing for their lady's favor seldom want help, a point
I should have remembered when Michael assigned
Rudy to me.

I was too busy to watch, but I could hear the slap of
boots on stone and the occasional thud of blows. All
in all, I have seldom been more grateful to hear the
whistles that heralded the arrival of the watch.

Rudy heard them too and stopped struggling, so I released him. We had our shirts tucked in and our hair tidy by the time the deputies arrived.

Michael, also fighting for his lady, curse him, was still trying to land a punch when two of them grabbed him from behind. At least he had the sense not to fight them, but so did Quidge.

"They attacked me," he panted to the deputy who seemed to be in charge. "The players! They're a public menace. They should be locked up. The men at least!"

A quick-witted fellow, but the deputies weren't idiots either. "So they attacked you, did they?" The one in charge looked at Makejoye, Falon, Rudy, and me. I struggled to keep my breathing even. "All of them?"

"No, just that one," Quidge admitted, gesturing to Rudy. "The man I was fighting is unredeemed—you can't charge me for it."

"Ah." The lead deputy turned to study Michael, and the two who gripped him tightened their hold. "We've heard about him. But as for you, Master . . ."

"Quidge. Oliver Quidge. I was hired by Baron Sevenson to return his niece to her home. I have letters from him," Quidge reached into his doublet and pulled out a tight-stitched leather case, "explaining the situation and requesting the aid of any baron whose fief the girl should enter. They give me full authority to act as his agent and take her back to him."

"Only if you drag me, screaming, every step," Rosamund put in. "These nice men would never allow that, would you?" She turned a melting gaze on the deputy in charge.

"Well, Mistress, that's for the sheriff to say, but—"

"I have authorization from her uncle," Quidge insisted. "And I was assaulted. You have to take them in."

Thereby getting at least two of Rosamund's protectors out of the way. At the moment, I could think of worse ideas.

"I must say, Roy, I think he's right." Master Potter sounded amused, in a plain, quiet way. "You should pass this one on to higher authority. And though I know nothing about eloping nieces, I have to say it was the young player"—he nodded to Rudy—"who jumped Master Quidge. The other two were trying to break it up."

"The other *two*?" Deputy Roy asked, and all eyes turned to me. Why do I let Michael talk me into these things?

The upshot was that they took all four of us to the sheriff, adding Rosamund and Makejoye for good measure. At least we didn't have to go far—nothing like committing a crime on the steps of the town hall to produce prompt service.

The inside of the building showed signs of the great hall it had been. The foyer's ceiling was two stories high, with a great stone stair leading up to a gallery that gave access to the second floor. Even at this late hour light showed under many of the doors, and a few weary clerks and tabarded armsmen waited on the benches that lined walls whose stone was softened by tapestries and decorative molding.

We went down a short flight of stairs, down a long hall, and down more stairs—to the dungeons, no doubt. I was feeling fairly cheerful. If the deputies threw Michael and me out, we could leave Rosamund in Makejoye's capable clutches. And even if she was thrown out with us, we'd be leaving the wreckers behind. Of all our problems, they worried me the most.

We clattered to the bottom of the steps and were met with the news that Sheriff Todd was speaking with Lord Fabian. Upstairs.

By the time we reached the second floor, Rosamund was breathing hard. The deputy, sneaking surreptitious peeks at her heaving breasts, was trying to pretend that he wasn't.

Lord Fabian's office had carved double doors in

front of it, and instead of barging in, the deputy knocked so gently that he had to try again to gain the attention of those inside. He explained his mission to Lord Fabian's clerk, and eventually we were ushered into his lordship's office.

The floor was of parqueted stone, with some very good rugs. I wondered if they were locally woven—if so, the town had another export, for such things cost high. The candlesticks were silver; if solid they could be fenced for eight gold roundels each—three if they were hollow.

Lord Fabian sat behind a massive desk strewn with papers. Sheriff Todd had just risen from the plain, straight chair before it.

Deputy Roy explained the situation. Again.

"Humph." Lord Fabian snorted comfortably. "You say you've letters from Baron Sevenson, rogue? Let's see them."

He was short but solid, like a scaled-down bull, with a dark beard shadow though he'd obviously shaved this morning. There were enough candles lit to heat the room on this mild summer evening, and his maroon doublet—velvet, not wool—hung over the back of another chair. His fine linen shirt dripped with lace, and the ruby in his ring was worth more than any haul I'd ever fenced.

Quidge handed over his papers, and Lord Fabian read them. Only when he finished the last page did he pass them on to Todd.

"So." His eyes rested on Rosamund appreciatively. "You're Sevenson's niece?"

"I am," Rosamund admitted. "But not his chattel, sir, whatever he may think."

"I'm sure"—Michael's soft voice startled me—"that you recognize the writing, my lord. I believe you've done business with my father."

Lord Fabian's gaze turned to him.

"*You're* Sevenson's son?" Lord Fabian sounded dubious, and well he might—in his ordinary clothes, Michael looks more like a down-at-heels armsman than a noble's son. "But Todd says you're . . ."

"Unredeemed," said Michael. "'Tis a long story. My father was very disappointed in me."

"I can imagine." And the image seemed to please Lord Fabian, for his frown smoothed away and the corners of his mouth turned up. "I expect he's disappointed in this chit, too, eh girl?"

Even Rosamund had caught on. "I don't know about disappointed, but I know he'll be furious. And frustrated. Really, really upset, as long as he can't get me back."

"I'm sure he will be. So, Lester, what do you think?"

Todd wasn't blind to the undercurrents either. "I don't know, sir." He tugged his lower lip unhappily. "Master Quidge's papers are in order, but all Baron Sevenson can do, within the law, is ask you to let him take the girl."

Fabian's hand slapped down on the desk and we all jumped. "Cursed straight, that's all he can do. This is my fief and my town, whatever Simon Potter thinks."

"But if the players are disturbing the peace . . ." Todd protested.

"Perhaps I could send for my papers," said Master Makejoye hastily. "I'm Hector Makejoye, and my troupe's honesty is certified by the guild. I have letters of recommendation from every town and baron on my regular route. They'll all—"

"I've no need to see your papers, man. I checked you out with the guild before I hired you. In fact, I'd like to make arrangements for a concert later—just music. I could hear that viol in here. But as for the rest of this . . ."

Todd saw which way the wind was blowing. "I asked Master Sevenson and Master Fisk to stay," he said, "in case I should need to question them further about the other night. They reported the fire, you know."

"Well, that settles it," said Lord Fabian. "I'm not going to let Sevenson's domestic . . . embarrassments

interfere with solving serious crimes. Master Makejoye,
I'm placing Mistress Rosamund under my protection
and I order you not to remove her from my fief. If
Sevenson wants her back, he can petition the High
Liege to have me return her."

"But that could take months!" Makejoye looked
aghast. "My lord, I've contracts in other towns. If you
wish to protect Mistress Rosamund, perhaps you could
take her into your household."

"No!" Now Rosamund and Rudy looked aghast, but
it was Rosamund who spoke. "I won't—"

"No." Lord Fabian lifted a hand. "I have no desire
to interfere with true love. None at all." Wicked delight
gleamed in his eyes. "Don't look so glum, sir player.
I think knowing where she is will motivate Baron
Sevenson to take action quickly, and I'll compensate
you for any contract you miss. Good night."

Makejoye, too, knew when he was beaten. This man
would care nothing for the fact that his reputation for
keeping his bargain was worth more than any single
contract he might lose. He simply bowed and followed
the rest of us out.

"What did your father do to that man?" I asked
Michael on our way down the stairs.

"Beat him out in a timber deal," Michael replied. "I
don't remember the details, just Father smirking over

it. I wasn't even sure I'd remembered the name aright, till I saw how he reacted to the mention of Father's."

"Curse the man," sighed Quidge. "He warned me some of the barons I'd present those letters to might not cooperate. He also said that if he was forced to go to the High Liege over this, he'd cut my fee in half. I'm suitably grateful for that, Master Sevenson, let me tell you."

"And I," said Michael, "am suitably sorry, of course."

I laughed, and Quidge turned his scowl on me. Then he shrugged. "Oh well, at least I came across an old friend here. Lass, if you should change your mind, I'm staying at the Slippery Wheel, and I'd be pleased to escort you home whenever you say."

"Never," said Rosamund from the shelter of Rudy's arm. "You nasty, horrid, wretched . . ."

Quidge bowed and slipped down the stairs in front of us.

"He loses with good grace," Michael murmured, watching the little man cross the foyer. There were fewer people on the benches now, the day finally winding down.

I snorted. "Assuming he has lost. I wouldn't believe that man had given up till I saw him buried—and maybe not then."

Quidge stopped in his tracks, his back stiff, staring at an armsman who was going out the door. Then he hurried after him. Michael's brows lifted questioningly, and I shrugged.

"Another friend, maybe? Cheer up, Master Makejoye. The way your luck is running, by the time you're free of Huckerston, you'll be ready to retire and play the Crown City stage—then you won't have to worry about broken contracts."

Makejoye groaned.

"Mayhap 'tis you who should cheer up, Fisk," said Michael. "You've been wanting to be more settled, and now we've the chance. Why, we might bide here till the wreckers are caught."

His face brightened at the prospect. I didn't moan, but it was a near thing. At least it looked like I'd have a permanent address long enough to get a letter or two from Kathy.

## CHAPTER 4

# Michael

Fisk must have taken my teasing seriously; he scribbled up a letter to Kathy, including the information that we might be here for a time, and sent it off on a northbound cargo ship. He said he thought it only fair to let her know that Rosamund had reached her Rudy safely.

I wished he'd be as scrupulous about informing his own family, for none of his sisters were forbidden to write to him. Indeed, long, acerbic letters from his sister Judith came to us whenever I sent her an address. Fisk had parted from his family on difficult terms, and he got angry all over again whenever one of Mistress Judith's letters arrived—though he read them anyway. This traumatic family fight was now a year and a half past, and part of me thought that Fisk should be further along the path to forgiving them by now. But I was on worse terms with my father than he was with his brother-in-law, and if I meddled in his affairs, Fisk would certainly point this out. I did consider sending Judith word of our whereabouts, but I wasn't as confident that we'd remain here as Fisk seemed to be.

The life we led was pleasant enough. I did a bit of hunting and a few odd chores. Master Potter, not to let his rival for the townsfolk's favor outdo him, came to camp the morning after our meeting with Lord Fabian and hired us to play in the market square four days hence. He'd wanted a concert for the guild masters afterward, but Makejoye, sensible of Lord Fabian's tender pride, convinced him that a session of jesting with a few songs thrown in would please his colleagues better. Both he and Master Makejoye would have preferred to have this take place sooner, but Potter said a storm would start at midafternoon on the third day and last till early night—not as violent as the first, but steady. When we asked how he knew that, we were told of a mad Savant called Nutter, who predicted storms with uncanny accuracy.

To most folk all Savants seem a little mad. But I had never heard of any, Savant or no, who could truly foretell weather, and I looked forward to seeing if the prediction came true.

The delay gave Master Makejoye a chance to set up

a new production, offering Fisk and Rose more challenging roles, while I played a smuggler, a groom, and part of three crowds.

I also assisted the Barkers with working Tipple into their dog act—a thing I enjoyed as much as Tipple seemed to. She likes attention and apples, and dogs, too. The little dogs—Mitzi, Holly, Bo, Tuck, and Rabbit—were amazingly quick to learn. The chaos that occurred the one time True got loose and tried to join the act was horrendous, but I laugh when I think back on it.

The Barkers weren't the only ones adding to their act. Master Potter would get a different, more comical play, and some other acts as well. Gloria would dance, and Callista would fill the mid-play break with a puppet show. They also planned to set up Rudy's tightrope. Watching him practice on one of the wagon tongues, just a few feet off the ground, I perceived something I hadn't noticed before.

I believe I mentioned that Gifts are not magic, but watching Rudy tumble and roll, I sensed something within him. 'Twas not magic, exactly. Now that I can see it, I know that magic fills the things that possess it. Rudy didn't glow with eerie luminescence, but when he worked at his tumbling, something arose to lend his muscles extra strength, his reflexes an extra edge of speed. Mayhap 'twas magic, only blocked somehow, so that only a bit of it worked on him. Or mayhap 'twas not magic at all, but something akin. Since the time Lady Ceciel's potions had changed me, I had begun to see that magic was not as simple as I had assumed. I shuddered at her temerity in meddling with it, and was glad I had resolved never to use it.

But watching Rudy showed me something else, alas, for Rose watched him too. He seemed to be a decent fellow, though not extraordinary aside from his looks. But whatever he did, Rose found it wonderful. I saw that the ropes in Master Makejoye's winter bed, where Rose now slept, had gone slack, and I spent most of the morning drawing them tight. She thanked me prettily; but when Rudy left a single flower on her pillow, she went into raptures and wore it in her hair all day.

So when I saw someone sneaking out of camp in the midst of the night, 'twas of Rudy I thought, and a shameful hope that he might be up to no good leapt in my heart.

It was the night before our performance in the market square, and I had risen late to answer nature's summons. Ordinarily, in a camp of mixed gender, I would have been better dressed. But the rain had come on as predicted, so Fisk's and my bedrolls were spread over the scenery panels in the prop wagon, and

I'd worn naught but my shirt to bed.

I rose silently and poked my head out the door. The rain had stopped some time ago, but the woods still dripped. The Creature Moon had set, and the rising Green Moon hid behind the clouds. Listening carefully, I heard no one else stirring, so I pulled on my boots and climbed out of the wagon in my shirt, turning away from camp into the grove beside us.

I was coming back toward camp when I saw a cloaked figure hurrying through the trees off to my left. I dove for cover behind a clump of bushes—not because I was suspicious, but because the shirt I slept in was too short for decency.

Whoever 'twas had plainly not seen me, but neither could I identify him. Or her, mayhap, for the long cloak covered the person head to toe. It appeared his business abroad was more complex than mine, for he strode out briskly toward the main road. And for all his haste, he moved silently.

My suspicions leapt, and as I've confessed, the thought that it might be Rudy was the first to occur to me. But eyeing the person narrowly, all I could say for certain was that he was too tall to be either of the Barkers, Gwen Makejoye, or Gloria.

The only way to know was to follow.

I had to keep back, for 'twas too dark to see the

ground and small twigs snapped beneath my feet. The rain-wet undergrowth chilled my legs, and droplets ran down into my boots, but my attention was fixed on Rud— the person I followed. Mayhap there were innocent reasons for someone to set off like this, in the midst of the night, but none came to mind. It couldn't be connected to the wreckers, because that had been going on for years before the players arrived here. Still . . .

Once out of sight of the camp, the person turned onto the rutted track that admitted the wagons to the clearing. He moved faster after that, and I too was forced to hurry—harder for me, dodging between the small trees, but I dared not follow him into the open lest I be seen.

In only minutes he reached the road and turned east, away from town, striding off with the confidence of one who knows where he goes. I took to the track myself then, and ran, reaching the road just in time to see the cloaked figure step into a coach, which waited some hundred yards from where I stood.

The Green Moon emerged from the scuttling clouds to show one white hand reaching out to pull up the step; then the door snapped closed. The reins slapped the horses' rumps and they set off at a trot. I couldn't see the driver's face.

Wild thoughts of racing after the carriage, leaping up, and clinging to its back went through my mind. But even assuming I could catch the trotting horses on this mud-slick road, the carriage's back appeared to be completely smooth, with nothing to grip or stand upon. No, what I needed was a horse.

I ran back down the track, heedless of puddles. The horses were tethered on this side of the camp and I'd nothing to fear from the dogs. The Barkers' well-loved beasts were tucked safe in their wagon, and True was sleeping curled against Fisk's side.

I did think of going back for my britches, but knowing that the carriage might even now be turning onto one of the lanes that branched off Wide Road deterred me from wasting any time. If it left the road before I caught sight of it, 'twould most surely be lost.

I plunged into the tree where we'd hung the bridles, and snatched up Chant's. I considered riding Tipple, for Chant's weakened leg might fail if he slipped, but I'd no more time to waste saddling up than I had to dress properly, and I was unsure how Tipple would take to being ridden bareback.

Chant and I, however, are old friends. He snorted warm breath over my hands as I slid the bit between his teeth, prancing with interest at being taken out in the middle of the night. Some horses don't care for night riding, but Father trains the destriers for use in all circumstances. I grabbed a handful of his mane and wiggled onto his smooth back, and Chant stepped out willingly.

The other horses pricked their ears, but they didn't stamp or neigh, for they knew me well.

We had to take it slow until we reached the road—in the shadowy scrub any faster pace would invite disaster. As we drew near the main road, I saw a figure turning off it toward our camp. I pulled Chant into the shelter of the trees. My first thought was that 'twas the person I'd followed, though how he had returned so soon . . . Then I saw that this person wore a long coat rather than a cloak, and a plain, rather lumpy hat. It seemed night in the players' camp was busier then I'd thought. The traveler was quite close when the capricious moon peeked out and caught his face—Rudy! But if this was Rudy, then who . . .

I wrestled with this question as he passed, oblivious to our presence. There was no doubt of his identity. Unless he'd changed his clothing for no reason I could fathom, and left the coach only moments after he entered it, he couldn't be the person I had followed. So who under two moons was it?

I did think, then, about whether I should continue on, but whoever 'twas had looked so furtive . . .

I had to wait till Rudy was past before taking Chant onto the road, and then I urged him to a trot, since I knew the coach would be far down the road by now. But a carriage is always slower than a man on horse-back, so there was no need to risk Chant's weak leg galloping through the dark on this mad errand.

Even a trot was rough, and the lack of stirrups forced me to grip Chant's body hard with my legs. The better part of an hour passed, and the insides of my knees chafed against his smooth hide. I was deeply grateful that I hadn't saddled him, for exposed as I was, the edges of the saddle leather would have scraped my bare thighs raw. The discomfort brought weak thoughts of giving up and returning to my bed. Surely the coach had long since vanished down some dark lane.

It was sheer stubbornness that kept me moving forward, but I was beginning to question my sanity—and not the first time someone has done that—when I rounded a bend and came across the very coach I followed.

'Twas pulled off to the roadside, with another coach beyond it, and the black-cloaked person I pursued stood by the window of the second coach speaking earnestly to its passenger. Or passengers, for all I knew.

Passengers who'd brought half a dozen men-at-arms riding along beside them, several of whom were staring at me.

One of them leaned forward, interrupting his master's meeting, and the cloaked figure spun. They were too far off for me to hear what was said, but the upshot was plain enough. They all drew their swords and galloped toward me.

Fisk has taught me many useful things in the years he's been my squire; one of those things is that there is a time for running, and this was obviously it.

I spun Chant and sent him galloping down the road, so fast the cold wind combed my hair. Much as I hated to, I would risk him spraining a tendon to keep myself from being slain—and against six, even if I'd had a sword, that was exactly what would happen.

But the rogues' horses were running, too, and it soon became apparent that they hadn't spent the last hour at a brisk trot. They were fresh, Chant was tired, and they were gaining on us.

Something hissed over my head. Glancing back, I saw one of them had stopped, and the jagged dark shape in his hand was a crossbow.

I turned Chant into the woods and set him zigzagging between the bushy trees. I hoped the rogues wouldn't risk galloping though the shadowy woods, but 'twas a slim hope, and it died when I heard them crashing through the underbrush.

Chant's gait dropped to a canter, perforce, and so did the others'. I knew he would run till his noble heart burst, but Chant would fail before their horses did. And even if he didn't, 'twas a sacrifice I couldn't accept.

Jigging around trees and rocks, barely able to keep my seat without a saddle, I considered jumping off, on the chance that they might follow Chant and give me time to flee. 'Twas the counsel of despair; in a proper forest it might have worked, but among these low, scrubby things they would soon catch a glimpse of Chant's bare back and then they would return to find me. Afoot and unarmed, I had no chance. I was desperate, and in that moment of desperation the serpent of power in my belly began to uncoil.

'Twas the last thing I needed and I thrust it back, ducking as branches lashed my face. Even if I wished to use it, I didn't know how, there was nothing to use it on, and . . .

Then I saw the rocks. They weren't extraordinary in themselves, just an outcrop of the earth's bones, which by some chance formed two uneven spires that had put me in mind of broken teeth when I saw them while hunting some few days past. A chasm lay beyond them.

'Twas not much of a chasm as such things go, mayhap thirty feet deep, cut by one of the streams that ran down to the sea. But 'twas too wide for a horse to jump, even in daylight with four sound legs.

'Twas not, however, too far for a magica horse.

There was no time to think about it. Chant's lungs heaved between my legs, and we would reach the chasm soon. I dropped the reins to his neck—no sacrifice, since I'd been letting him choose his own course since we turned off the road—and laid both hands on his rippling withers.

I willed the serpent of power to rise and felt it shift, sluggishly, like a wary fish nibbling at the bait. I was beginning to panic when I remembered that it hadn't worked that way before; instead of will I let my need command it. My dread of the swords behind me. My fear for Chant, with his weakened leg and his mighty courage. My passionate desire to escape, to live, to laugh in the bastards' faces and prove to my father that I could do it, I could.

The serpent came to life, uncoiling into a mass of unfocused energy. It flowed like luminous water through my arms and hands, and Chant began to glow.

I felt him start, snorting in astonishment as fatigue left him, and his weary legs found a speed and power they'd never had before. He picked up his pace, whipping though the trees, his canter suddenly faster than most horses' gallop. I heard a cry of astonishment behind us as we started gaining ground, but then the trees fell away and the chasm lay before us.

'Twas easily fourteen feet across, and I felt Chant hesitate; he knew nothing of magic, and 'twas a jump he couldn't possibly make. But I leaned forward and signaled him on, and the years of trust between us worked a magic more powerful, to my mind, than any that flowed through my hands. He committed himself to try, timing his strides so he'd be positioned to leap when he reached the edge.

Only when he sank on his haunches, gathering himself to spring, did I remember that he hadn't jumped since he'd injured his leg six years ago. Not to mention the fact that I had been allowed to ride Father's magica horses only on the flat, under his close supervision, that I had never jumped any horse bareback, and that this was not, mayhap, the smartest thing I'd ever done.

I wrapped both hands in Chant's mane, bracing myself as best I could, and 'twas well I did, because he almost leapt out from under me. I had seen magica horses jump, but I'd never imagined how much speed, how much power, they expended.

A shout of terror and delight broke from me as we sailed through the sky, for Chant shone like a new-made moon, and 'twas as close as I may ever come to flying.

We landed on the other side with a good eight feet to spare. But while magic made the leap possible, it did nothing to spare me the jolt of landing. I pitched forward on Chant's neck and would have tumbled to the ground but for my death grip on his mane. As it was, I slipped half off, and only a furious twist that wrenched every joint in my spine let me haul myself onto his back again.

Chant bolted into the trees, now running from himself as much as any pursuit. I let him go as he would, speaking soothingly. The brightness faded slowly from his dappled hide, as if the magic I'd poured into him evaporated with use.

I knew when the last of it was gone; that was the moment his leg gave out and he came to a limping stop, panting and shivering.

I swore and slid down, stroking his sweaty neck before reaching down to examine his weak leg, unsurprised to find it swelling. I felt it carefully and found no sign that anything had broken, to my considerable relief. 'Twas only then that I looked up and met his eyes. "Sorry, my friend. I didn't mean to startle you like that, but I didn't have much choice."

Was that sufficient excuse for breaking my oath never to use my freakish power? An oath I'd sworn for good reason?

Chant blew against my chest and nuzzled me, evidently feeling he'd earned a treat. I'd have agreed had I anything to give him. Forgiveness is simple, for horses.

We set off in the direction of camp, both walking, since I'd no wish to tax Chant's sprain any further and by the time our pursuers made their way around the chasm we'd be long gone. Who had they been? And who had gone to meet them, and why?

I found no answer to any of my questions. Fisk, no doubt, would ask whom my use of magic had harmed. The answer was no one, except mayhap myself. Was my honor wounded? If so, I didn't feel it, or much of anything except a singing joy at being alive.

Not even relief, however, could make the scrape of boot leather on bare heels less painful. By sunrise we were still several miles from camp, I was limping as badly as Chant, and I had no britches. Explaining this to the players would be hard enough. Explaining it to Rosamund . . .

"We survived," I told my weary destrier. "We should be grateful for that, right?"

'Twas not as consoling as it had been, and I found my steps slowing for reasons that had nothing to do with blisters. Which was foolish, for I of all men know that there are many things worse than embarrassment. Public embarrassment. Embarrassment in front of—

Chant drew a breath and released an earsplitting neigh, and I heard the patter of paws behind me. I spun to face the sound, just in time to receive two muddy paws on the front of my shirt and a wet tongue across my face—across my mouth in fact, which made me glad 'twas not open at the time.

"True! Good boy. Down. What are you doing here?"

True, frisking under my petting, declined to answer. But I wasn't surprised when Fisk's cynical, humorous voice replied, "I motivated him. In fact, I told him if he didn't prove useful for something I'd skin his worthless hide and throw him into the cook pot. He took off on your trail like a deerhound. Do you think the same technique would keep him out of my bed?"

Tipple came toward us through the brush, whickering as she saw her stablemate. Her rider looked more amused than anything else, especially when he observed my state of undress. But I would have forgiven him any wisecrack just then, for he carried my britches over his arm. Fisk is a very good squire.

"It was obvious," he replied to my question, as I gratefully accepted my clothing. "You were gone, your boots were gone, but your britches were still there. So were your stockings. Do you have—" I pulled off my boots, wincing, and he sighed. "Yes, I see you do. Don't put your stockings on yet; I've got salve and bandages."

So he did, in the pack on Tipple's rump, along with water, and biscuits and honey, sticky and crumbled in their oiled paper but delicious all the same. There was even an apple for Chant.

A *very* good squire.

The one thing he hadn't brought was the ointment I use on Chant's leg, but I wasn't unduly concerned. The swelling wasn't severe, and most of the salves and ointments in our medical chest were magica. This was something we couldn't ordinarily afford, but the one advantage of my changed senses that I was willing to use was the ability to easily locate magica plants and herbs. So I'd made the acquaintance of Litton's herb-mixer, telling her, truthfully, that my mother was a skilled herb-talker. I knew how to harvest most magica plants with the proper sacrifice, so the Green God takes no vengeance. Those plants I couldn't harvest safely I brought to her attention. In exchange she gave me a share of the medicines she produced, a bargain that pleased me well, though Fisk said I should have held out for coin.

But even magic doesn't heal in an instant, so I rode Tipple back to spare my blisters and Fisk led Chant, silent as I told of the night's adventure.

In the end all he said was "I suppose I shouldn't be surprised."

"You're not surprised that half the camp is sneaking out in the middle of the night, meeting carriages, with *armed* escorts, and—"

"Oh, that. That is surprising, though there might be a number of reasons for it. We'll figure out who it was when we get back to camp and ask them. I meant, I shouldn't be surprised by the mad things you do."

"I suppose you'd have gone back to sleep?" I asked tartly.

"No," said Fisk. "I'd have waited till whoever it was came back, and watched which wagon they went into."

This was so sensible, it silenced me for several minutes. The choice of wagon would have revealed the person's identity clearly—of the two Makejoyes only Hector was tall enough. Callista slept in the wagon that held costumes and the smaller, more valuable, props. And if the person went to the men's wagon, it had to be Falon, since it couldn't be Rudy. Though what *he* was doing out in the middle of the night was yet another puzzle.

Eventually my embarrassment faded and curiosity grew in its place. "How?"

"How what?" Fisk asked.

"You said when we get back, we'll figure out who it was and ask them. How can we determine their identity now?"

"By the time-honored method," said Fisk smugly, and refused to elaborate, curse him.

The players paid little heed to the tale Fisk told, before I could stop him, of an early hunting trip and an unfortunate stumble that had lamed Chant and delayed my return. The only ones who expressed interest were the Barkers, and their concern was for Chant rather than me.

I rubbed a deal of magica ointment into his leg and wrapped it tight. Then I brushed him down, gave him an extra helping of oats, and returned to camp to find Fisk sprawled on the driver's seat of the Makejoyes' wagon, watching Callista's puppets perform. All the players were putting a final polish on their acts, except for Gwen Makejoye who was, to my sorrow, putting away the breakfast dishes.

"I thought we were going to find out who I followed,"

I told my squire pointedly, but softly withal.

"That won't take long," said Fisk, smiling as he watched the puppet wife beat her husband around the small stage. Callista did both voices herself, but so cleverly I could swear I heard two folk shrieking at the same time—and I could see her.

"Here, this'll keep you busy for a while." Fisk handed me four biscuits and a largish chunk of still-warm sausage.

"Thank you." My speech was somewhat muffled by the first bite. "But I still want to know how we're going to find him."

Fisk sighed. "I suppose this is a good time for it. Meet me around back." He turned and crawled into the Makejoyes' wagon as if he had every right to do so.

I wandered around the wagon, out of sight of the clearing where the actors worked, and found him sitting on the folding step examining Master Makejoye's spare boots.

"It wasn't him" was the first thing he said.

"I suppose his boots told you that? You know, when boots and doublets start talking to you, it's a really bad sign."

He rolled his eyes in exasperation. "Look at yours."

I propped one up on the step and did so. 'Twas coated with orange-gold mud.

"Oh. But how do you know he's not wearing—"

"I looked," said Fisk, "as soon as we got back to camp. His boots are neither muddy nor clean enough to have just been washed. Nor are any the others are wearing, except for Rudy's."

"Yes, and what was he doing, sneaking in, in the middle of the night?"

Fisk shrugged. "No way to know. But to find out about the others—"

"We have to search the other wagons." I resolved to let Fisk do the searching. He's better at that kind of thing, and better yet at coming up with excuses if he's caught. As it turned out, excuses were unnecessary. The next wagon we searched was Callista's, and kicked beneath her cot was a pair of sturdy boots, the rusty mud plain upon them.

"Well," said Fisk, "this isn't what I expected. It looks like half the camp really was abroad last night. I wonder what Edith Barker was up to."

"Surely 'twas not Callista I followed," I said. "I mean . . . I suppose it could be. She's tall enough."

"It was *you* following me?"

Both Fisk and I spun at the sound of her voice, but I was the one who blushed. The puppets hung like dead rabbits over her arm, strings and sticks dangling.

"Oh dear. I'm glad you're all right. They said they

didn't catch you, but . . ." She was trying to look sympathetic, but the amusement showed through.

"Michael," said Fisk, "meet the mysterious, cloaked figure. Callista, meet the evil stalker. What were you about, if you don't mind my asking?"

His tone reduced it all to foolishness, and I confess it stung. But he'd also asked the important question without sounding offensive, which was more than I could have managed.

"I probably shouldn't say." A demure expression transformed her face, making her look both innocent and sly. Then she set the mask aside and laughed. "But since next time you might break your neck, or get yourself skewered . . . I was meeting a lover."

"I thought this was the first time you'd been to this town," I protested, before I realized how tactless the comment was.

"These things can happen quickly, Sir Michael. He saw our performance the other night. While the rest of you were talking to the sheriff, he bought me some wine and told me all about how his rich wife doesn't understand him."

"I see," I said stiffly. My face was hot. Fisk was grinning.

Callista snorted. "I hope so. If you don't, your keeper should take better care of you." She cast Fisk a slanting glance and he laughed.

"Guilty as charged. It's a challenge, you know. He runs off so—"

"Forgive me, Mistress," I interrupted. "It won't happen again."

She sobered. "In all truth, Michael, you should be more careful. He thought you were someone hired by his wife, and ordered his men to bring you back to be dealt with. I assume that means bribed, but even so . . ." She shook her head.

"It won't happen again," I assured her once more. Sincerely, for the way I felt now, I never intended to poke my nose a single inch beyond my own business.

"Just to ensure it, I'll spare you the rest of the search," she went on, with a bit of friendly malice. "Falon was out last night, too, for I met him on my way in. He often goes into town at night. He gambles. Badly, I'm sorry to say."

"You don't have to tell us this." I was beginning to fear what she might reveal next. "Come on, Fisk, we have to, um . . . leave."

He strolled after me without haste, laughing under his breath. Curse him. "I'm sorry, but you should have seen your face. If it was anyone but Callista, I'd say that was quick work. As it is . . ."

" 'Tis a perfectly innocent, credible excuse," I sighed.

"Well, mayhap not innocent, but . . ."

"But not our business, Noble Sir. I trust the point's been made."

"Amply," I told him gloomily. "I feel as great a fool as you might wish. But did you notice what she didn't say?"

My clever squire frowned and eventually shook his head, which restored my battered self-esteem.

"She didn't mention Rudy, Fisk. She didn't even know he'd gone out, much less what he was up to. So we still have one mystery on our hands."

## CHAPTER 5

# Fisk

For once Michael agreed not to pursue it, but I knew that would last only as long as his embarrassment—which wouldn't be long. Immunity to embarrassment is essential to knight errantry, along with immunity to common sense, and any sense of self-preservation, as near as I can tell.

Soon it was time to go into town and set up for our performance. This time the two houses of the main stage set had a jumble of other buildings between them, different-colored shutters, and a fountain in the center of the stage. The "water" consisted of mica-covered willow wands that glittered like frost in the summer sun. Setting up the tightrope and nets for Rudy's act took longer than constructing the stage.

Falon and I stayed behind to watch the set today, and I managed to confirm that he'd been out gambling last night. And had lost, though like most gamblers he didn't realize that losing is a chronic condition.

*Ever meet a rich gambler, boy?* Jack's cynical voice echoed in my memory.

Tonight's crowd, packed between the market stalls, was even larger than the first, and it was Rudy's acrobatics on the tightrope that captured their attention as the others crept in to join us. Safety nets notwithstanding, the sight of a man balanced so delicately over a great height was riveting. Then he started doing cartwheels.

This play was simpler, more comical, and bawdier, but the exhilaration of performance was the same. It was also shorter, and afterward we left the breakdown of our set to some of the Potters' and Brickers' guildsmen, under Falon's supervision, and crossed the river to the Potters' and Brickers' guildhall. Inside was a great square room, each side lined with long tables. The banners of various guilds rippled in the warm air that rose to the high ceiling.

They'd cleared one end of the room to give Makejoye a stage of sorts, but for the first part of this private performance he left the stage and strolled among the tables, trading quips, topping puns, and making the dignified guild masters laugh till their sides ached.

Michael and I were able to enjoy most of the

show, for those of us no longer performing had been recruited to serve wine and the light pastries to which Potter was treating his fellow guild masters.

Michael's teasing aside, I've no deep prejudice against most work, though table server doesn't pay enough to tempt me. But it's an easy task—or it would have been, had the side of the room Michael and I were assigned to serve not held the Bankers' Guild master. The first annoyance was that he'd brought a pack of hounds with him. They were well behaved, but there wasn't enough room for them, so Michael and I had to step over or around them whenever we passed behind the table.

I saw Michael eyeing them and was unsurprised when his quiet comment that they were fine animals produced the information that they were all magica.

"The best possible guards," the guild master bragged. He was very plump, flesh puffing out on either side of his rings. His doublet's hem and collar were trimmed in fur, and that thick velvet must have been unbearably hot on this high summer night. But he declined to shed it, preferring instead to keep Michael and me hopping with calls for cooled drinks, and once a fan, though how he expected us to produce that out of thin air . . . If the master-of-house hadn't managed to locate one, there might have been trouble. At least he hadn't quite the gall to ask us to fan him with it.

"They protect my person and my vault," he went on grandly, "better than any human, for their senses are sharper and nothing gets by them. They can't be bribed or blackmailed, and even someone with a Gift for animal handling can't seduce them. Even aquilas doesn't affect magica dogs."

I blinked at that. Michael and I had once used aquilas to escape from a particularly disastrous predicament, but I'd never heard of it being used on a guard dog. It made sense, though, because aquilas subverts the will; a man who drinks it will agree to anything. If it worked the same on dogs, they'd probably lead you to the silver, and help you pack it, too.

"They cost high," the banker went on. "But I'm a generous man. I lend them to my neighbors when they've a need, don't I, Dawkins?"

For a fat fee, I'd bet. His clerk, a slight, bespectacled man, nodded agreement in the automatic manner of the thoroughly cowed. Then another call for service took us away.

"You shouldn't encourage him," I hissed to Michael, stepping over the last of the sleek, gray forms. The beast looked up, but its tail didn't thump the ground as Trouble's would have. I found that oddly chilling.

"I know," Michael murmured. "But I've never seen

so many magica hounds in one place—he must have gathered them from all over the south."

"And it cost a fortune." I nodded impatiently. "But he's got that—no surprise, given all the shipping that leaves this port. You can buy anything with enough money, Noble Sir."

Even knowing that was true, I was disgusted to see the poor clerk fanning his master as the room grew warmer.

During the interim in Makejoye's performance, Gloria danced. The soft clash of her finger cymbals was no lighter than her feet, the torches' flame no brighter or more fluid than her body.

The banker's gaze was avid, and I had a dreadful premonition that we would be called on to perform for him sometime in the next few days.

At least it gave his clerk a moment's respite; I saw him over by the wine barrels talking to, of all people, Ebb the tapster. I searched the banners on the other side of the room till I found the loaf and key of the Tavern and Innkeepers' Guild—Joe Potter sat beneath it. I wondered if Quidge was still staying with them and what he was doing these days. We'd seen no trace of him, but he hadn't struck me as a man to be idle for long.

In the last act of the performance Makejoye played his magica viol and his wife sang, and even the banker fell silent.

I heard this music around our campfire nearly every night, but I found my steps slowing, my thoughts drifting on the run of the melody.

When it was over, the wealthy, powerful guild masters left their tables and pressed forward to congratulate the fiddler, shaking his hand—and more to the point, leaving tangible signs of their appreciation. I saw the banker approach and contrived to be near, though I'd a fair-enough notion what would pass.

"Well played, sir, well played."

"Why thank you, Master . . ."

"Burke. Lionel Burke, master of the Bankers' Guild. You must perform at my home. Just a few of your best acts, for my family and friends."

"'Tis not his habit to ask, it seems," Michael murmured.

"But none of this girlish warbling," the fat man went on. "I want your dancer, that luscious puppeteer, and the ropewalker too. Must have something to please the ladies."

Even Makejoye looked wary at this. "We are a troupe, sir. You may request any acts you like, but we come together and go together."

It was a more polite warning than I could have managed.

"Fine, fine." The plump hands waved. "My clerk will

arrange the details. Dawkins!" The unfortunate man jumped. "Arrange the details with Master Merryjoye here." He turned and waddled off, his hounds silent as shadows at his heels.

"You needn't look so worried," Lester Todd had sneaked up on us without my noticing. "He's a . . . sensual man, but he's too indolent to chase someone around the room, and too rich to need to. If your girls say no, he'll just summon others."

"And take his anger out on the troupe later?" I knew this would be Makejoye's most pressing fear.

"Ah, that probably depends on how tactful the 'no' is."

"That's contemptible," said Michael. "And as for the way he treats his clerk . . ."

Todd sighed. "Willy inherited the job from his father. He's bright and skilled. He could go to another employer, if . . ."

If all his independence hadn't been bullied away.

We watched as Dawkins completed his business with the anxious-looking Makejoye, then scurried after his master.

"What's the difference between a merchant and a bandit?" I asked.

Todd shot me a startled glance. "I don't know, what?"

"The merchant tells you you're getting a good bargain."

Todd laughed and took his leave, and eventually we were free to make our way back to camp. Burke had hired us to perform eight days hence, at a price so high that I knew Makejoye had hoped he would refuse it. I could have told him it wouldn't work; a man with a whole pack of magica dogs could afford anything he wanted.

On the other hand, even if Burke proved a nuisance, it wasn't likely to be lethal. Things could be worse. I was feeling almost optimistic . . . until the next morning, when Todd and his deputies rode into camp to tell us Oliver Quidge had been murdered.

For once it wasn't Michael or me the sheriff suspected.

"Half a dozen witnesses saw you meet him at the Slippery Wheel," he told Rudy. "And you left together, even though it was still raining. What were you talking about, Master Foster?"

So that was where Rudy went on the night of the storm. Michael and I exchanged wary glances. The others simply looked worried, except for Makejoye, who looked exasperated as well.

Rudy was trying to look calm and composed, but

he couldn't quite pull it off. "We were talking about Rose. He sent for me. He wanted me to make her leave. To convince her I didn't love her anymore." His eyes strayed to Rosamund. "I told him to go to . . . I told him no. Then I tried to convince him to leave. To stop wasting his time, because if she's strong enough to come all this way, to brave such danger just to be with me, then nothing can separate us."

Except, possibly, Baron Sevenson. But it was clear Rudy believed what he said, and Rosamund blushed and clasped her hands. As to the rest of his story . . . He wasn't as bad a liar as Michael—few are—but it sounded awfully thin to me.

Todd's intent gaze told me he thought the same. "Where did you go after leaving the inn? Did he take you to his camp?"

"Yes," said Rudy. "But he was alive when I left him."

The four men Todd had brought with him exchanged glances, though that sounded like the truth to me. One of them led a saddled, riderless horse.

"His camp?" Michael asked. "I thought he was staying at the Slippery Wheel."

"He did for a time." Todd's sharp gaze turned to Michael, and I swore under my breath. So much for minding his own business.

"He hadn't much money," the sheriff went on. "He chose to camp outside the town to spare his purse."

"Oh," said Rosamund. "I didn't know that."

And if she had, she'd have what? Given him money to stay at an inn while we camped? Bribed him to leave? . . . Why hadn't I thought of that? It might not be the best use of Rosamund's jewels from her point of view, but it would have been cursed useful for Michael and me.

Todd turned back to Rudy. "So you knew where his camp was?"

"Yes," Rudy admitted. "I told you he took me there. But he was fine when I left. He was sitting by his campfire, with a pot of herb tea brewing."

"Did you tell anyone where his camp was?"

"No, I didn't tell anyone about it." Rudy looked surprised at the thrust of these questions, but I began to understand.

"Sheriff, when was Quidge killed? Do you know?"

Todd's lips tightened in annoyance, but he replied, "As a matter of fact, we do. A charcoal burner had a camp near his, and he heard him screaming—then the sound of his fall. He fell into a ravine last night, about an hour after sunset."

Jaws dropped around the circle.

"But I was on stage then!" Rudy exclaimed. "I couldn't possibly have killed him."

"No one said you did," said Todd patiently. "I was merely trying to determine who could have known where his camp was."

And he wasn't above trying to rattle us while he did it, but I was too grateful to care. For once, both Michael and I had cast-iron alibis.

But Michael was frowning. "Why do you say he was murdered if the charcoal burner heard him scream and fall? Did you find signs of struggle, or—"

"We'll be looking for that," said Todd, sounding even more annoyed. "But you misunderstood me. The charcoal burner heard him screaming for help before he fell. We're going now to search his camp and bring the body back to town."

That would be what the spare horse was for. His words were simple, but they brought the picture vividly to mind. A grimy man, lying in his bedroll. The cries coming in on the night wind, as he sits up and wonders. Then the sound of falling, cracking stone. A broken body on the rocks.

I'd seen enough death lately for any given year, so I was exasperated to hear Michael say, "Do you mind if Fisk and I go with you to look at the camp? We're two of the few people you know couldn't have done it."

Todd opened his mouth to refuse, then realized that a chance to observe such suspicious folk as us at the scene of the crime might be worth something. "All right. Master Foster, too, if he wishes to come."

Rudy had the sense to decline, but Michael borrowed one of the wagon horses, a big dun brute, and we both joined the deputies, and another man in a neat gray doublet who turned out to be the town's foremost herb healer. The deputies, so friendly the other night, ignored us. But Michael did a good job of pretending he didn't notice.

Quidge's camp was on the other side of Wide Road, which put it closer to the coast than I'd have cared to camp with a murderous gang of wreckers in the vicinity.

"Maybe it was the wreckers who killed him. Maybe he saw something he shouldn't have." I was speaking to Michael, but Todd overheard. "I've thought of that, Master Fisk. They don't usually throw their victims over cliffs. In fact it would be a nuisance for them, because they'd have to go down to be sure he was dead."

A nuisance. But I had to admit he had a point.

We started with the body. The charcoal burner had needed to return to his fires, but he'd given the sheriff good directions. We found a path down the bluff that the horses could manage, then picked our way up a small, stony canyon.

I took one look at the twisted form on the rocks and decided I didn't need to examine another corpse, thank you very much. Michael went forward with the others and watched the doctor. Their voices carried between the stone walls, so even with my back turned I couldn't escape it entirely.

"He hit his head when he fell," said the doctor. "Landed on it, by the way the skull's crushed. His spine's broken, too—either injury would kill him. No surprise, from that height."

The ravine's sides were over sixty feet high.

"Is there any sign he fought with someone?" Todd asked. "Any injuries not caused by the fall?"

"If he died immediately after, there might not be much a bruising from a minor blow. There're no marks on his face." I heard the whisper of cloth on cloth. "Hmm. There are some peculiar punctures on his forearms, but nothing like the bruise a rope might leave. No bruising on the hand that didn't hit the rock. No bruising on his chest or sto— Wait, there's something here! This man has magic in him!"

Many healers have the sensing Gift.

"In him?" Todd sounded baffled. "What do you mean, in him?"

"I mean in him," said the doctor tartly. "As if he took some magica medicine, or ate a magica plant. It's fading, but it's definitely there."

"Could he have done that?" the sheriff asked. "Eaten some magica plant by accident?"

I still wasn't looking, but I heard a shrug in the doctor's voice. "Anyone can, though most folk aren't that careless. And the Green God seldom imposes death as a penalty. Do you know if he was taking any medicine? Was he ill?"

"I've no way of knowing," said Michael. "He looked healthy enough."

There was more along those lines, none of it surprising, except for more of those odd punctures on the man's ankles and calves, which the doctor said might be rodent bites. Eventually the deputies wrapped the body in a blanket and carried it off.

Michael looked as squeamish and somber as I felt. Random death is bad enough, but when it's someone you know, even slightly . . . I was glad to leave the echoing walls and feel the sea breeze on my face.

We were all quiet riding up the bluff, and I wasn't sorry to see the doctor and a deputy depart for town with the shrouded corpse.

Finding Quidge's camp was harder, for he'd tucked his tent into a small grove, and it was all but invisible unless you were looking from the right direction. The canvas had probably been bright blue once, but years of sun and rain had faded it to a dusty slate that blended with the foliage. As we approached, I saw that the canvas was patched in places, and the seams looked threadbare. Before I started feeling too sorry for the man, I reminded myself that Michael and I didn't even have a tent. A tent costs high, and so does a packhorse to carry it. Speaking of which . . .

"Where are his horses?" Michael exclaimed, and went to look for them.

Todd's brows lifted, and he nodded to one of the deputies to accompany him. For my part, I was hoping to get a look at Quidge's possessions. No one stopped me as I entered, though the way three men crowded the tent might have justified it. The bottoms of the canvas sides had been secured by a ring of stones and then pulled into the tent to make a partial floor. A worn, round rug covered the center—snug enough, especially compared with a bedroll under open sky. The bluish light that came though the canvas showed us Quidge's bedroll beside the tent's center pole. The rest of the space was taken up with a large pack saddle, with pack; a pile of pans and dishes; and a stack of kindling in one corner where it would stay dry, along with the tent's occupants. You've fallen far, financially, when a battered tent can make you jealous.

"Davey, go through the pack." Todd stood in the

center—the only place he could stand upright. "If you insist on being here, Master Fisk, you can go through his bedroll and the firewood."

We were all curious about the pack, but I shook out blankets and felt through pillows under Todd's watchful eyes, while the deputy pulled a stack of clothing from the pack and did the same. He'd made it all the way to the pack's bottom and I was dismantling the woodpile when he made the first discovery.

"Look at this. He kept a journal, sir."

Todd and I both turned to the deputy.

"What does the last entry say?" Todd demanded.

"It's dated second Scaleday, Cornon," the deputy began, and I frowned—that was the day after his altercation with us. " 'I think I'm on to something. Swear I recognized J.T. yesterday.' "

"J.T.?" Todd interrupted.

"Just the initials." The deputy leafed through the earlier pages. "It looks like he always used initials to refer to the criminals in the cases he worked on, sometimes with a note to remind him of the crime. Murd. Rob. Assl."

"Never mind," said Todd, rather unfairly. "Go on."

" '. . . recognized J.T. yesterday. Surprised me no end—over two years since he was reported dead. Threw out his warrant so no descript. but I'm pretty sure. I wonder—faked own death, or forged papers and some sheriff's seal? Or bribed? Better go carefully. Told T. about it just in case—J.T. the kind who's all too likely take up with gang of wreck. Reward for them would set me up good.'"

I started to ask what the reward was and quelled myself. Look where greed had gotten Quidge. Though it would certainly buy a tent and a packhorse with change to spare. I must have moved, for Todd's gaze fell on me.

"That's enough, Davey. I'll go through it carefully back at the hall."

"There's not much more." Davey sounded disappointed. He could probably use the reward, too. "No description. He doesn't even say where he saw the man. It looks like he wrote things down only when he wanted to make a record for a case he was working on. The stuff before that is all about Mstrs. R."

I smiled to hear Rosamund set down like a criminal and wondered what her crime was. Elop-Plyr?

Todd glared at Davey and we went back to work. Davey also found a packet of old warrants—people Quidge evidently watched for wherever he went, as a bounty hunter must, I suppose.

All I found was Quidge's purse, hidden beneath the firewood. I dumped it out on a blanket at Todd's command. It made a small pile, mostly sharp-edged fracts, few of them gold. All the roundels were silver or base.

"He really was broke, poor bastard," Davey murmured. I winced, for the contents of Michael's and my purse were even leaner. But if Quidge's purse was here, then where was—

"Sheriff, we've found something you should see," Michael called. Todd set Davey, whom he trusted, to gather up the pitifully small pile, and I followed him outside.

A brown horse and a mule were tied to a tree a short way off, but Michael and the queasy-looking deputy led us away from them to a small pile of garbage, buzzing with flies.

I wondered what this was about; any camp accumulates such stuff, especially if you're there for more than one night—along with a privy pit. I was hoping that wouldn't be next on the tour when Michael knelt and waved the flies away, pointing to a small heap of gray-brown fur and bone.

"This was magica," he said. "'Tis fading now, like the magic in Quidge's stomach, but if you bring the doctor back he'll confirm it. And we found this not far off." He held out a shining wire loop, with pegs dangling from its end. A simple snare, just like half a dozen Michael and I carry with us.

"You think he caught a magica rabbit in a snare and ate it?" Todd sounded incredulous, as well he might. "Magica hardly ever gets into snares, and when a rabbit does, it goes invisible, so you can't mistake it."

"So I've always heard," Michael agreed. "But there was magic in Quidge's stomach, the remains of a magica rabbit in this midden, and . . . come look at this."

He led us toward the cliff now, but I already had a notion of what had happened and some of the other deputy's queasiness stirred in my gut. I'd have preferred touring the privy.

Michael stopped before a small patch of mud—one of many puddles left by the storm—but this held the impression of a man's skidding boot, and another track that might be . . .

"Rats," said Michael. "There are rat tracks all through this area, in the mud, under the bushes. Anywhere the earth will take a print."

"You're saying it was an accident?" Todd demanded. "That he somehow caught a magica rabbit, ate it without realizing, and . . . and . . ."

Michael shrugged. "We found the snare. He had bite marks on his legs and arms. Your deputy can show you more tracks."

"But he was on to one of the wreckers!" Todd

protested. "Or so he thought. This can't be a coincidence. At least . . . The Furred God does take life sometimes, but I still can't believe . . ."

No matter how we rehashed it, that was our conclusion. Todd chose to leave Quidge's tent where it was, taking only the journal, purse, warrants, and horses back to town. He would send some grooms with a cart to pack up the rest of it for Quidge's kin, if they could learn who that might be.

The sheriff accompanied us all the way to the track that led to the players' camp and saw us start down it, curse his nasty, accurate suspicions. The moment he was out of sight, I pulled Tipple to a halt and turned to Michael, only to find he'd done the same.

"You first," I told him.

"I don't believe it," he said passionately. "Any hapless hunter might shoot or snare a magica creature, and pay the Furred God's price for it if there's no Savant to hand, but never a rabbit, Fisk. Never. 'Tis their Gift to become invisible when they wish to avoid notice. Truly invisible, and 'twould be cursed hard not to notice that you'd an invisible creature caught in your trap."

"But you found the skin. There was magic in his stomach. The evidence—"

"Oh, he ate the beast," Michael agreed. "That much

is clear. But something happened, something that . . . that changed the rabbit's nature long enough to let it happen—and cursed if I know what, or how, or who could manage that. Only a Savant would have that knowledge, and they'd be the last to do such a thing."

"Um," I said, liking the trend of this conversation less and less. Murderous wreckers were bad enough; a murderous Savant was the last thing I wanted to deal with.

"Your turn," said Michael. "What troubles you?"

I didn't want to tell him, but sooner or later the same thought would occur to him—probably in the middle of the night, which would be even worse.

"It was something that wasn't there," I told him. "Quidge's document case, the one where he kept your father's letters. The one that probably held warrants for all his current cases. I'm surprised Todd didn't remember it—Quidge took it out in Lord Fabian's office, in his presence. But we didn't find it."

Michael's face was a study in alert speculation. "So either the killer took it with him—"

"And why steal a highly recognizable case, when you could just remove the papers that concerned you?"

"—or it's still there." Michael finished.

It didn't take long to return to Quidge's camp. This

time I searched the pack, feeling for secret pockets, but it was Michael who found it, tucked into one of the canvas folds under the edge of the rug.

"The papers from Father." Michael laid them aside and I picked them up. *Three hundred* gold roundels, just for Rosamund? I'd turn her in myself for that! I wondered how I could manage it without Michael stopping me.

"Here's the warrant with information about the wreckers."

I let that lie. There are limits to greed.

"This is all that's left," Michael went on. "'Tis a warrant for a young apprentice, just fourteen, poor lad, who struck his master over the head and slew him— small blame to him. They say he can be identified by missing toes."

"Missing toes?"

Michael nodded, his mouth tightening as he read on. "His master would cut them off as punishment. And not only this lad, but others who worked for him. His guild would have stopped it had they known. But when he was killed, they felt the apprentice should at least be brought to trial, so they put up . . . a reward." His voice slowed. And stopped.

"What is it?"

He handed me the paper. There was a description

of the killer, but the guild had been sufficiently concerned to print up a sketch as well. The artist had
talent; the boy gazing out from the cheap paper had
clearly grown into the handsomest, gentlest, noblest
Rudy Foster. We wouldn't even have to check his
toes.

Michael took back the warrant, folded it, and put it
in his pocket. We put the rest back for the sheriff to
find, when his grooms struck the tent or he remembered that something was missing, whichever came
first. Rudy was Michael's problem. And Rosamund's.
And probably, curse all lovers, mine.

## CHAPTER 6

# Michael

"But Fisk, if a Savant helped the wreckers arrange Quidge's death, then finding that Savant might lead us to them." We'd been having this argument since yesterday. I was tired of it—and I was winning.

"The last thing I want is to find any of these people." Fisk hunched his shoulders against the early-morning chill. I'd roused him from his blankets before dawn, that we might make some progress in our investigation before half the day passed. The sun was rising now, flooding the eastern hills with a radiant display that should have cheered the gloomiest of men. Unfortunately, Fisk is immune to beauty before midday. I'd even yielded to his request to leave True behind, though I know he'd have enjoyed the romp.

"Besides," I pointed out reasonably, "we owe it to

Master Quidge. If not for us, he'd never have come here, and he'd still be alive." I felt badly about that. He wasn't the most pleasant person, but he certainly hadn't deserved to die.

Fisk moaned. "That's so crazy, I'm not even going to dignify it with an answer. Quidge came because he wanted the three hundred gold roundels your father promised, and why you think we owe him anything . . ."

Trust Fisk to have noted the amount. But that gave rise to an argument that might stand a chance with my squire. "Think of the reward for bringing the wreckers in. 'Tis—"

"Be quiet," Fisk interrupted. "I don't care about the reward. I don't want to know how much it is."

I stared at him in astonishment. "You don't care about the *reward*? *You* don't—"

His expression lightened. "Maybe I do care, but I still don't want to know. You can't spend rewards if you're dead. These people are killers, Michael, and if you're right, then so is this Savant you're so eager to find. We're probably endangering the others with this hunt of yours, and we're certainly not helping anyone. And Rosamund . . ." His voice softened, which should have warned me. "Rosamund loves you as a brother, and nothing more. Surely you know that."

I did, but hearing the words felt like a cold blade sliding into my heart. "I'm not her brother! And feelings can change." I would find some way to change Rosa's. I had to. I had loved her so long, it was as much a part of my world as the wheeling stars, or the green rebirth of spring. I didn't even need to be in her presence to feel it, only to know that she was waiting at home for me to return someday and win her heart. Only now she wasn't waiting at home, and if I was going to win her heart, I'd better do it soon or she'd wed that cursed player . . . and a light would go out of the universe.

"The wreckers threaten everyone till they're caught," I told Fisk firmly. "'Tis a knight errant's job to capture them." It would also be a triumph to make any woman's heart swell with admiration and affection—but I wasn't about to say that to Fisk.

"But why would the wreckers even bother with such a clumsy, complicated murder? If they wanted Quidge dead, they'd just smash his skull in like they've done with dozens of sailors. They'll probably do it to us if we persist in this."

'Twas a good question. "I don't know," I admitted. "But Quidge thought he might have a way to find the wreckers, and now he's dead. That can't be a coincidence."

"And now you think you have a way to find them. How delightful! Are you listening to yourself?"

In fact, I wasn't. "Look, there's a farm cart ahead. Mayhap the driver can tell us how folk in these parts summon their Savant."

I kicked the hard-mouthed wagon horse, which I'd borrowed to spare Chant's lame leg, to a trot. Fisk swore, but he followed.

The carter, a bluff countryman, had a wagonload of bread fresh made for the market and still hot. My breakfast was not so distant, but I think the scent of new-baked bread could tempt the dead to rise.

"Good sir," I said, "we wish to speak with your local Savant. Can you tell us how to summon him?"

"Why, surely," said the carter. But he looked uneasy and took up the reins to urge his horse to a faster pace. I knew what troubled him.

"You've no need to fear. We've caused no trouble to anyone or anything. We only wish to speak to him."

Fisk snorted as if to disagree with some part of that statement, but he held his tongue.

"Oh." The carter let the reins fall. "Well, first off, our Savant's a she. But she's easy to summon. We take good care of her and she of us, just as it should be. There's a willow tree, about half an hour's ride north of town . . ."

He gave us directions and instructions, and when the subject of payment for her services arose, he kindly offered to sell us a few of his loaves.

"It'd be more if you wanted help—likely be more when you tell her what you need. But just for a chat, a couple of loaves will do. And you might buy a third for yourselves. She'll come to a summoning, but if you're not in trouble, she may take her time. I'll let you have 'em for a silver ha' apiece, and you'll find no sweeter anywhere."

I was reaching for my purse when Fisk said, "You sell them in the market for two copper roundels."

I've no idea how Fisk always knows such things, but I've learned not to question him in matters of money.

"Do you know the difference between a bandit and a baker?" he went on. "A baker—"

"—works warm in the winter," the carter finished, sounding resigned. "I sell 'em for four, stranger; grain's expensive around here. Besides, we're not in the market, are we?"

We weren't, and I'd have paid a few extra fracts to save the time and trouble, but Fisk got three loaves for ten copper roundels, which is why I leave all bargaining to him.

The carter's directions were as good as his bread, and there were enough Savant summoners in this town to have beaten a path up the narrow, dusty ravine where the willow grew. It perched beside a small spring, barely more than a seep, which vanished into the damp earth only a dozen yards from its source. But the willow itself was big and gnarled and old, and it held so much magic, it glowed like a torch, even in the sunlight. Its energy brushed my skin like cat fur as we drew near. Had my sensing Gift been this responsive before?

Fisk tethered the horses while I emptied my water bottle into the spring, as instructed. Then I drew my knife and, steeling my nerves, nicked my finger and then the willow's bark and pressed the cuts together. The magic was so intense, it felt as if my skin was scorching, but when I pulled my hand back, there was only the small cut I'd made and a bit of sap.

I stripped five glowing leaves, and Fisk made the fire in a ring of blackened rock that many others must have used. The magica light vanished as they burned, and I saw no trace of it traveling skyward with the smoke.

When the leaves had been reduced to ash, we moved away from the tree—by common consent, for Fisk said he found it "creepy." He didn't know the half of it. Our retreat slowed when we passed the stream's end and stopped shortly thereafter, though the willow was still in sight.

I had no wish to talk as we waited, but I was with Fisk. We were arguing when a woman stepped from behind the willow tree—how had she reached it unseen in this barren chasm? Unlike Fisk, I'd been watching for her.

In other circumstances I might have taken her for a countrywoman who'd dressed in her husband's britches to perform some chore. Her dark hair was braided down her back and she moved like a girl, though her sun-browned face was lined.

As she came toward us, I saw the confidence in her—a sense of total belonging, though whether the tree belonged to her or she to it, I'd not hazard a guess.

"You're not in trouble," she said. "So it must be something you want to do. I warn you, the price for interfering with magic is higher than most folk are willing to pay."

'Twas not a soothing sentiment, under the circumstances.

"Who says we're not in trouble," Fisk muttered, and I shook off the chill that had overtaken me.

"We're not in trouble, Mistress, and have no desire to make it. But there was trouble here some few nights past, and we wish to set it right. As much as death can ever be set right."

I told her the whole tale, for her gaze was clear and

honest, and even Fisk could not have suspected . . . Well, maybe Fisk could, by the way he stepped on my foot as I started to speak. But no reasonable man could imagine she'd had a hand in Quidge's death.

Her first reaction was like all the others'. "A *magica* rabbit? That's impossible. They go invisible when they're threatened."

"Yet it happened," I said. "Which is why we sought you. Is there a way, Mistress, that someone could suppress the rabbit's Gift? Long enough for Quidge to see and kill it, unknowing?"

She frowned. "I don't know. There are things I might try, if I wished to do such a thing. But no Savant would. We've nothing to do with the affairs of men, except to make peace between them and . . . what they've disturbed."

No Savant has ever said who or what they serve, though many folk have speculated, and some have even asked them. Indeed, she was more forthcoming than most, so I ventured my next question.

"You wouldn't, but I've heard there's another Savant in the area and that he's . . . ah . . ."

"Mad?" Her lips twitched. "Hmm. He'd have sensed the trouble. I did myself, but I was dealing with other business, and by the time I got free of that, it was over."

"What other business?" Fisk asked. He'd obviously

forgotten his avowed dislike of the affair, and was as intent on the conversation as I.

"I'm surprised Nutter didn't attend to it," she went on as if Fisk hadn't spoken. "But he's become a bit . . . He follows his own way these days, even more than most of us."

'Twas as good a description of madness as any I've heard.

"Do you know what causes his trouble?" I had no expectation that she would answer me any more than she had Fisk, but she sighed.

"He dreams, poor soul."

"Dreams?" I asked softly.

"Yes. Some time ago there was a great slaughter among the whale migration that passes this coast."

I'd not known that whales migrated, but I kept my peace and she went on.

"Some lordling had a bright idea, and he gathered folk from all the fishing villages and sent them out to hunt in their little boats. The whales, especially the magica, fought fiercely, and the slaughter was terrible. On both sides." She fell silent, lost in memory.

"When did this happen?" Fisk asked.

"About three centuries ago. Oh, I know it seems a long time, but it marked this place. It echoes even now, and Nutter hears the echoes in his dreams. He's come to believe that what he dreams is not the past but the time to come. Though given the death toll, I don't think anyone would try that again."

She rose, brushed off the seat of her britches, and picked up two of the loaves.

"Please wait, I have . . ."

"But we need . . ."

She turned and walked out of the ravine, as if we no longer existed.

"That was cryptic," said Fisk.

In fact, we'd learned more than I'd expected. We discussed it on our way back to camp, and as we unsaddled and brushed down the horses. Fisk wouldn't concede that this trail was worth pursuing, though he admitted that she might know ways to work the trick, and that if she knew such things, so might another Savant.

"That's *why* I don't want to pursue it," he protested as we walked into the circle of bright-painted wagons. "There's a very, very slim chance that you're right about this, and if— Do I smell burning stew?"

Alas, he did. We had made haste to return in time for the mid-meal; Mistress Barker was teaching Rose to cook, and I liked having the chance to praise her.

Even as I detected the familiar scorched scent— familiar, because I'd tried to teach Fisk to cook a time or two before giving up on the matter—Rose jumped from the costume wagon and hurried toward the hearth, reaching out her small, bare hands—

Fisk shouted a warning, but I saw he'd not break through her preoccupation in time and leapt forward. I feared for a moment I'd not make it, but somehow I reached her before her hands touched the hot iron handle and whirled her away. She gave a small shriek as I whisked her off her feet.

"You'll burn yourself! Use the hot pads, Rose."

"Oh." She blinked up at me, still clasped so tight I felt the stir of her body against mine as she took a breath. "How foolish of me. Thank you, Michael. But the stew . . ."

"Fisk will take care of it," I murmured. I could hear Fisk emptying his water flask into the pot and stirring; having burned the stew so often, he knows how to save it. But my gaze was fixed on Rosamund's tender mouth. In all the years I'd known her, why had I never kissed her? Some foolish notion of honor, I remembered. At least, it seemed foolish now. I—

"Rose!"

She jumped and pulled out of my arms. One of the hardest things I've ever done was let her go.

"Rudy, I'm a disaster of a cook. You should disown me."

"Never, dearest," said the murderous bastard. A

revolting smile replaced the glare he'd aimed at me. "Here, let me help you."

I didn't see that he helped her much by wrapping both arms around her and laying his hands atop hers as she lifted the kettle, now safely protected by the thick cloth pads.

"I think we were in time," said Fisk. "A bit scorched, but not inedible." His words were casual; the note of warning in his voice was directed at me.

Had he been anyone but Rosamund's betrothed, I'd have had no blame for the poor apprentice who'd struck too hard when he fled his vicious master. An unredeemed man might be so unjust; as a knight errant, I should do better.

I took a step back and looked away from them, struggling to make my voice sound natural. "That's good. I'm hungry enough to eat that stubborn brute I've been riding. Could you use another loaf of bread?"

My tension eased as the players came in for the meal. They praised Rose politely, although the stew did taste a bit charred.

Rose, in her sweet, honest way, gave the credit for saving it to Fisk, who laughed and gave her credit for burning it so that he could play the hero.

If I found the wreckers, played the hero in truth, would that make Rose see me as a man, instead of the cousin she'd grown up with? Was that, in fact, why I was so bent upon it? I prayed that notion never occurred to Fisk.

All in all 'twas a merry meal, and eventually even Rudy Foster and I were coaxed from our sulks. So 'twas even more alarming when Barker rode right into the camp, not leaving his horse at the picket line. "Hector, we've got a problem."

"What now?" Makejoye sounded more harassed then fearful.

"There's another troupe in town," said Barker grimly. "The Skydancers. They're working the market right now, drumming up business. If we don't do something—"

"They'll steal all our contracts!" Makejoye leapt to his feet and began spouting orders. Within moments all the men, including Fisk and me, were ahorse and riding for town to protect our territory from invasion. I didn't look at Fisk. I was having trouble enough controlling my laughter.

"It's serious, for them," said Fisk, watching a brightly clad dwarf somersault between his partner's legs. "If Makejoye has to stay here, with no contracts and the day-to-day expenses eating up his profits, it could cost him high."

We'd been sent to the market square to scout the competition, and it didn't look good. The Skydancers had no magica viol, at least none we'd seen, and they were no more skilled than Makejoye's troupe. But there were more of them, their costumes and props were newer and brighter, and with the lure of acts the crowd hadn't seen . . .

We wandered over to a woman clad in many shawls and scarves. Her face would have been ordinary if not for the fanciful butterfly wings painted round her eyes.

"Madam Mara has the Gift," she chanted. "Madam Mara can See. Guess your age; guess your weight within half a stone, by your own town's grain scale, right over there; or guess the month of your birth. If you fool Madam Mara, you pick the prize." Here she gestured to a chest full of bright crockery, jumping jacks, and other trumpery. "Only one silver roundel, and you pick the question! But I warn you, Madam Mara has the Gift to See. Guess your age; guess your weight within just half a stone . . ."

A plumpish matron took her up on it, giggling, and asked for weight. "You're right!" she exclaimed, her eyes widening in amazement. "A teeny bit low but within half a stone, for I sat in the grain scale just last week!"

I thought that Mistress Mara's estimate was as low as it could be to keep within the half-stone limit. Fisk was smiling.

"All right," I said. "I know there's a trick to it. Weight I understand; I might do it myself with a bit of practice. Age too leaves its mark, though 'tis harder to judge. But how can she guess the month of birth? That leaves no sign, and 'tis a one-in-twelve chance."

"Wait and see," said Fisk.

We lingered, and soon two boys, brothers by the way they quarreled, approached the woman.

"He wants to give you his money," said the older, pushing the younger—about age nine—forward. "I think he's a simp."

"Am not!"

"Are too!"

"My friends, my friends," Madam intervened. "I charge a silver roundel for a guess, young sir, and only if I guess wrong do you get a prize. I warn you, Madam Mara can See."

"Sure you can," said the urchin cheekily. "I want you to guess the month I was born."

He handed her a silver roundel and sneered at his brother.

"Hmm, let me see." She walked around him, and he stiffened with pleased self-consciousness. "That hair . . . the shape of the jaw . . . the length of the middle finger . . . I believe you were born in . . . Hollyon!"

"No!" The child hopped in excitement. "You're wrong, I was born in Wheaten! I win! I get a prize!"

"You were?" said Madam with artful astonishment. "Then you have defeated Madam Mara, and there aren't many who can say that! Choose your prize, young sir."

He chose a bright-painted whistle and tooted it happily. His brother dragged him off, muttering, "You nit, you can buy one just like it for fracts! It costs only half what you paid for it."

My startled gaze shot to the chest; all the prizes in it cost less than a silver roundel in the open market. The trick was that simple. I closed my sagging jaw and turned to face Fisk's laughter.


That night around the campfire the players held a council of war. Or mayhap 'twas a council of defeat.

"They have a contract," said Makejoye, "so we can't go to the guild. Though that's the strange part. It's written in Simon Potter's hand and bears his signature, but he swears he didn't write it. And when Lord Fabian accused him of trying to beat him out for the townsfolk's favor, Potter replied that the townsfolk were too smart to be bought by 'a handful of sparkling glass and a dancing bear.' Then they went at it tooth and claw and forgot about us."

He fell silent, his brooding gaze lost in the campfire.

"Well, don't nod off," said Gwen Makejoye tartly. "If Potter denies hiring them, how will they get paid?"

"Easily." Makejoye snorted. "Lord Fabian's booked a performance already, and Potter can't be far behind even if he is telling the truth about that letter being forged. Then everyone else will follow suit and hire the *new* players. If we hadn't a written contract with Burke, we'd not see another fract from anyone in this town. 'Since you've other players here,' I said to his lordship, 'perhaps we could go on to our next contract?' But no, we're important witnesses in a criminal case. By which he means, the poxy toad, that he won't give up his chance to tweak Baron Sevenson, and be hanged to what it may cost us."

"You could go on," said Rose. She was sitting on one of the fallen logs the players had dragged in to make benches around the fire. Rudy's arm tightened around her shoulders in protest, but she went on, "Michael and Fisk are his witnesses, and if I stayed with them, 'twould forestall all his objections."

"If you stay, I stay," said Rudy.

Makejoye smiled at her. "That's a generous offer, lass. But I already put that suggestion to his lordship and he said no. Handed me some drivel about proper chaperones. Ha! I'm about that far"—he held up two fingers, not far apart at all—"from packing up and sneaking out. Our contract with Burke's not for six days, and he'd just hire the Skydancers to take our place. We could be into the next fief by midday tomorrow, and that"—his fingers snapped sharply—"for Lord Fabian."

"Which is fine," said Gwen Makejoye, "till Burke shows the guild a broken contract and they renounce us. Then we get no contracts at all."

Makejoye's sigh should have put the fire out.

"Maybe that's what someone wanted," said Fisk thoughtfully. "To drive you out of Lord Fabian's fief so that Master Quidge, say, could have another chance at Rosa. That letter would have been sent before his death, whoever is behind it."

I eyed my squire with respect. Whatever his ethical lapses, Fisk's wits are exceeding sharp.

"How could he have known where the Skydancers were?" Rose asked. "I mean, he sent the letter to them."

"He could have asked at any guild office," said Makejoye. "Or gotten the news from a peddler, or another player—we traveling folk keep track of each other. That's how I knew the Red Mask had changed their route to miss this part of the coast. In fact, I know the Skydancers' regular route—the only reason Dancer was available was that two of his smaller towns canceled on him, right in the midst of his circuit. That's why he's so determined to stay—this fills a gap in his schedule. Master Quidge might have heard about that and seen a chance."

But he didn't sound convinced and neither was I. Quidge was a clever man, but that kind of twisted scheming didn't seem to fit what I'd seen of him. He was beyond our questioning now, but tomorrow I would take the next step in my search for his killer.

## CHAPTER 7

Fisk

In the morning Michael took the next step in his plan—reaching a new level of lunacy, even for him.

"But she said he usually comes when there's trouble with magica," he said. "And he doesn't come when summoned. So the only way to get him to come is to disturb some magica thing."

"Suppose he doesn't come anyway," I said, standing well back as Michael reached for the small lacy plant he could so easily identify as magica. "Or doesn't come in time."

Michael reached down and picked the plant with a single quick tug. "Then I'll take the consequences." He shredded the roots and leaves with the nervous determination of a man pulling splinters from his own flesh. "The Green God doesn't exact life for destruction of a plant—not even serious injury for a quick-growing thing like mouse-foot."

"If you say so." I waited till Michael had seated himself before I chose a place to wait; eight feet wasn't too far off for conversation, though Michael was amused by my precautions.

He was less amused when the first warrior ant sank its teeth, or pincers, or whatever ants use to bite with. He stripped off his clothes, dancing and swearing, and I brushed the bugs out of them while he slapped them off his skin. Then he ruefully examined the hard red bumps.

By the time we reached camp, he was limping, and he kept grabbing folds of his shirt when the fabric tickled him, crushing them between his fingers. I made the supreme sacrifice and didn't say I'd told him so. And if he mistook my intention when I said he'd made a better deal than I realized choosing magica itching salve over money, well, that was hardly my fault.

Actually, the salve worked all too well; by mid-afternoon he was ready to try again.

"Don't worry," I assured him as he eyed a small, harmless-looking plant the way most men look at a tooth-drawer's tongs. "I've got the medicine chest right here." Along with bandages, a pail of water, a blanket, some sandwiches for dinner, and Michael's sword, just in case. My knife is always in my boot, but I was more aware of its presence than usual.

My noble employer cast me a wry glance. "You're prepared for a siege." He pulled the plant and shredded it.

"Never hurts to be prepared," I told him.

Conversation at twelve feet was harder than at eight, but we managed fairly well as the afternoon passed into dusk. I was beginning to wonder if the plant he'd chosen wasn't magica, or if the Green God was asleep when he destroyed it. Also whether I should return to camp and fetch our bedrolls.

As it happened, I didn't have to—the black-and-white skunk that trundled out of the dusk and lifted its tail answered all my questions. Twelve feet was barely far enough, but nothing could save me from helping Michael deal with the consequences.

The stuff was too oily for water alone, so I went back to camp for soap and clean clothes. Then I went to fetch a melon from a nearby farm field, for Michael said his father's master of hounds used it when his dogs encountered this particular misfortune.

At least Trouble wasn't with us—if Michael's problem had been magnified by two, we wouldn't have been allowed back into camp for days. The way the

Barkers spoiled the mutt, I wondered if they couldn't be persuaded to take him off our hands, but my luck never seems to run that way.

I helped Michael work the crushed melon into his hair, though it made my hands stink. I must admit I was grateful to leave him, rubbing his skin with melon rind and swearing, while I buried his clothes. Clothing that I lifted with the shovel's handle and carried as far from me as I could get it.

Both moons were high when we finally returned to camp, and the players had gone to bed. The scent, though unpleasant, was no longer intolerable. And, as I helpfully pointed out, the nights were mild—there was no way either Trouble or I would share an enclosed wagon with him.

At this point I hoped he'd give up, but I should have known better. Michael endured the players' jests with his usual good humor, and midmorning found us once again sitting beside a pile of shredded magica plant. At least, Michael sat beside it. I was standing twenty feet off, prepared to run at a moment's notice. It made conversation difficult, but there was a subject I'd been wanting to bring up for some time.

"What are you going to do about Rudy?"

It isn't in Michael to prevaricate, even with himself, which was why watching him ignore the matter was beginning to alarm me. If I could have gotten Lucy back by turning the butcher's boy over to the law, I'd have done it in a heartbeat. Or . . . maybe not. Despite my furious anguish, even at the time I'd known that the choice had to be hers. And I wasn't her choice. Whether Jack had paid her off or not.

"I don't know." If there'd been any wind, the distance between us would have eaten Michael's words, but the day was still and hot, with only the whir of an insect to break the silence.

"He's wanted for murder," Michael went on. "'Tis my duty to report him to the sheriff of the fief where he's accused, so he can try for a Liege's warrant. Or hire some bounty hunter to haul him back. Or appeal to Lord Fabian for assistance."

"That's your duty," I agreed pleasantly.

"But he was only a boy, fleeing a savage master. He probably didn't mean to strike hard enough to slay."

"Probably not," I agreed. Though if that bastard had been my master, I'd have struck to kill the first moment I thought I could get away with it.

"Even if he was brought to trial, the judicars would almost certainly let him off lightly, considering the circumstances."

"Almost certainly." He'd get to the point that mattered eventually.

"He's in love with Rosamund."

Almost there. "Yes, he is."

"Fisk?"

"Yes?"

"If you don't stop humoring me, I'm going to go over there and do something about that smirk you're wearing."

A stranger's scratchy voice said, "Now why'd you want to do that? Sounds to me like you're winning."

We both jumped and spun. All male Savants are bearded—well, the only other one I've seen was—but this man's hair stuck out in patchy clumps, with a wildness I'd never seen equaled. His elderly coat and britches were neatly patched at the elbows and knees, but none of the patches matched his garments or each other. He was scrupulously clean, from his springing hair to his worn boots.

"I'm not winning," Michael told him. "It only looks that way."

"Huh!" He snorted, stepping into the small clearing between us. "She said you were a foolish lot and I see that plain enough. But she also said you'd not give up till you'd seen me, and I should go and get it over with before you tore up all the magica in the wood. Now you're seeing me. Satisfied?" He turned to go.

"Wait, sir, please. We've some questions for you if you'll spare us the time."

Only Michael could call a lunatic "sir" and mean it. Though so far the fiery old man seemed no more mad than any Savant. I hoped Michael remembered our agreement that it wasn't smart to blurt out your suspicions to the people you suspect. He should remember—we'd spent half an hour arguing about it.

"Oh, she told me you thought I'd killed some poor fool, putting magica rabbits in his snare." So much for precautions. But Nutter snorted again and went on, "What's one fool's death to me? Compared to the slaughter to come, one death is nothing—a puff of wind before a hurricane. The earth and sea will weep blood when the slaughter comes. But no one cares about that."

"We do care," said Michael. "But no man can undo the past. 'Tis the present—"

"No, it's the future." He turned his angry eyes to us, for we'd left our places to draw near him and now stood side by side. In a Savant's presence we were safe from the Green God—even a Savant as strange as this one. "All the voices of the earth," he went on, "they call it out. Earth isn't like that lying water—it speaks true. It speaks in the voices of the dying, their fear, their pain. And it will come!"

He shook his fist. It should have looked absurdly theatrical, but it didn't.

"It will come, and all folk do is laugh at my warnings."

"Maybe the earth doesn't understand about time," I said. "Maybe it changes so slowly, sees so much, that the past and the future are one to it."

The light, mad eyes fixed on me curiously. "He said you wouldn't care. Huh! Makes you wonder what else he was wrong about. But you sail in ships, don't you?"

"Who's 'he'?" I asked.

"Aye, you travel in ships, the both of you. As unnatural as a frog sprouting wings and taking to air. You know what happens to a flying frog? Snap!" He clapped his fingertips together. "The hawks get 'em. But they still take to the sea in ships, they do."

"Mayhap," said Michael gently. "But neither Fisk nor I can keep men from the sea. And Quidge's death is a matter we might do something about, if you'd help us."

"Aye, they pay no heed to my warnings, either," said the Savant, sounding suddenly weary. "I tell them it's going to storm, and they say, 'Thankee, sir'. But then I say that man and magica are going to die, and they laugh. Laugh!" But the fire was going out of him. He turned to leave.

"They laugh at me, too," Michael said urgently. "Come back, please. We can speak together as men who've been laughed at."

The old man stalked into the trees and away.

Michael and I gazed at each other. The sudden absence of so much passion was as shocking as its appearance.

"Do you think he did it?" I asked.

A frown creased Michael's brow. "He didn't deny it."

"He didn't confirm it, either."

We stared at each other again—then Michael sighed and bent to gather up my supplies. "If he did do it, 'twas not for gain or fear, for I see he is beyond such things. But think how useful 'twould be for the wreckers to know when a great storm approached."

"True." I picked up the basket that held our medicines and bandages. "But they don't have to work with Nutter for that—he evidently tells the whole town his weather visions. Remember Simon Potter telling us about the last storm?"

"Yet he must have helped them with the rabbit," Michael persisted as we started back toward camp. "And what was he talking about, 'He said you wouldn't care'? Who's 'he'?"

I snorted. "A voice from the earth, probably. Or no, it was that lying water."

"I care too," said Michael. "'Tis piteous to see a man so troubled. He might even have helped the wreckers and then forgotten it."

He'd forgotten something else as well, and neither Michael nor I remembered it until Michael—with a most uncharacteristic clumsiness—tripped, and fell on a rotten log where a tribe of hornets nested.

I was standing right beside him. I really should know better.


"I take it all back—magica medicine is a great investment. We should buy it before we buy food. As long as you persist in doing this kind of thing."

It had taken several applications of salve—even magica salve—to ease the burning stings. But it was finally working, and I thought soon I might sleep. It was a bit warm and smelly in the wagon, but tonight Michael and I were . . . tired of the out of doors.

"I've no more need to summon up Savants," said Michael wearily. "I've spoken to both of them, for all the good it did."

He sounded depressed anyway, so I might as well make it worse. We still hadn't finished our discussion.

"Michael, you remember what we were talking about? About Rudy? You never—"

The rap on the door was soft but clear, and we both

sat up and looked at each other—not that we could see much in the small amount of moonlight leaking through the windows.

"Come in," said Michael, and the door opened.

"I won't come in." Moonlight flowed over Callista's skin, washing out the gold so she glowed lily-white. Her dress exposed a lot of lily-white. "I was on my way out and I thought I'd stop and let you know. You've had a bad-enough day without having to follow me."

Several comments flashed through my mind, but I couldn't find one that wasn't risqué. Even the simple "good night" was fraught with peril. She waited a moment to see if we'd be foolish enough to try, then shrugged and closed the door.

There was a long moment of silence. Michael broke it. "Well, I'm embarrassed. How about you?"

"She's good, isn't she?"

"I wouldn't know."

I choked on a laugh. It seemed Michael too was thinking in double entendres. The wagon rocked as he lay down.

"But you see what I mean?" I persisted. "She's made it impossible for us to ask questions—much less get in her way."

"There's no reason we should wish to do either."

"I suppose not. And it does explain her dress."

"If you thought that dress needed an explanation, squire, you're more naive than I'd imagined."

I laughed again. "I'm corrupting you, Noble Sir. I meant the fabric. It's expensive."

"You noticed the *fabric*? And you priced it? You amaze me, Fisk."

"Yes, but Michael . . ."

"Um?"

"Never mind."

The time for that conversation had passed, but I'd have to bring it up again. He still hadn't decided what to do about Rudy Foster, and he wouldn't, he couldn't, until he faced the real problem. The real problem wasn't that Rudy was accused of murder, and was probably innocent. Or even that he loved Rosamund.

The real problem was that she loved him.


We both rose late for once—hornet stings are tiring. Climbing out of the wagon behind Michael, I perched on the step for a moment to enjoy the sunlit fresh-ness. Gwen Makejoye was tending the porridge pot, while her husband sat on their wagon seat, frowning over what appeared to be a new script. The inkpot was open beside him, and his fingers were marred with black stains. The Barkers were playing with the dogs, and they'd included Trouble in the game. Falon had put up a backstop against one of the wagons and was flipping knives at Gloria. She was yawning, which she didn't do when they performed. But sleepy as she looked, she took care not to move. Callista was nowhere to be seen. I guessed she hadn't risen yet and fought back a grin.

As for the rest of the company . . . Rudy and Rosamund had obviously been gathering firewood; they were just coming out of the forest, and he carried a load of dry branches under one arm and a bundle of neatly cut logs, bound with string, on his shoulder. Rosamund carried an armful of flowers and looked, no surprise, beautiful.

If I'd been her intended husband, I'd have handed her an armload of sticks, but Rudy didn't seem to mind working for two. In fact, I'd bet he was the one who tucked the flower into her hair.

He was gazing at her now, affection and amusement making him even more handsome. Michael's face still bore red blotches from several stings, and his dark scowl didn't help.

I hoped, without much conviction, that he was too wise to stalk over to them and make a fool of himself. I sometimes thought that Michael was as much in love with love as he was with Rosamund. Unfortunately, being in love with love feels just like being in love for real, and wisdom had never been Michael's strong suit.

"Good news, Hector," Rudy called as they approached. "We passed the sheriff on the road, going up with his men to get Master Quidge's things. He said he didn't think Lord Fabian would insist on your keeping Rose here much—"

"I thought you two weren't supposed to be un-chaperoned." Michael may have thought his voice was soft, but the rhythmic thump of Falon's knives ceased, and the Barkers hushed the yapping dogs.

The brightness of Rudy's expression vanished in a glare as fierce as Michael's, but Makejoye spoke before he could.

"That was just for Lord Fabian's benefit, and it seems he's losing interest. I hope he's losing interest. Rudy'd do the lass no harm, Sir Michael, were they cast up on a deserted isle. He means to marry her."

And if he and Rosamund wanted to do what Michael so clearly didn't want them to do, it would take a jailer, not a chaperone, to stop them. My guess was that they hadn't; Rudy seemed almost as honorable a fool as Michael, and somehow . . . Well, I didn't think they had. But I wasn't a thwarted lover.

Michael stalked across the clearing, clearly bent on making an idiot of himself. I sighed and climbed down from my perch, wondering if I should try to stop them if it came to blows.

Rudy evidently had similar expectations. He dropped the wood, the bound logs breaking free from their string, and stepped back a pace. Not from fear—he didn't seem to have any sense of self-preservation either—but to give himself room to swing.

Rosamund stepped in front of him. "I don't know what you're making such a fuss about," she told Michael firmly. "But if it's because you promised to watch out for me, or some such silly thing, then you're just . . . Michael, what is it?"

Michael had stopped and was staring at her feet— the anger leached out of his face, leaving something that looked like fear.

"Rosamund, step back."

She did, very quickly.

Michael knelt, fished among the shattered bundle, and plucked out a rough-cut quarter of a log, which to me looked like every other piece of wood in the pile. "This one is magica."

"Well, get it out of camp!" Makejoye exclaimed. "Not you, Sir Michael—you've had enough of that sort of trouble. Rudy, you're the one who's handled it so far—you take it."

"What do I do with it?" Rudy looked more alarmed by the log than he had at the prospect of being pounded by Michael, but he picked it up anyway. "No, Rose, you stay back. Go over there with Gwen."

"You need a Savant," I said. "I guess Michael and I haven't wasted the last few days after all, because we know how to find one. There's a small ravine half an hour's ride north of town, with a big, old willow in it. . . ."

We gave him the directions and assured him that he probably had time to get there before the Green God took action. Handling magica for which no sacrifice has been made will get you into trouble eventually, but not as quickly as destroying magica will. Especially if the appropriate moon is down. Usually.

Rudy departed, accompanied at a suitable distance by Falon and Edgar Barker, but I wasn't too worried. Magica wood is more potent than plants, but he'd had little contact with it and no hand at all in its destruction. If Gwen Makejoye had pitched it into the fire, on the other hand, things might have gotten nasty—and not only for Rudy.

"How could something like that end up in a bundle of firewood?" Gloria wrapped her arms around herself, despite the growing warmth of the sun.

"I don't know," said Makejoye grimly. "A better question is how Rudy came by it."

"It was lying beside the road." Rosamund bit her lip.

It had taken Makejoye's command, as well as Rudy's, to keep her from going with him. "Right by where the track to this clearing joins it. We thought it had fallen off a cart." Her voice quivered.

"Don't blame yourself, girl," Makejoye told her. "It's small harm done, when all's said. I wonder if there's more of that stuff in their load. Maybe we should ride into town and warn them."

"Or mayhap," said Michael, "'twas left there for one of us to find. Master Makejoye, could anyone besides Quidge want to drive you off? The Skydancers?"

"Why should they?" Makejoye flung out his inky hands in frustration. "We've not been offered a contract since they got here—the only one left is Burke's—and if they've a lick of sense, they won't want that one. *I'm* the one who wants to leave. I know how it looks, on top of the Skydancers, but what connection could there be? It has to be a coincidence."

As much as Michael and I discussed it, we could reach no other conclusion. Both Lord Fabian and Simon Potter were hiring the Skydancers now, and in the struggle for control of a town, a troupe of players was the smallest part of the morass of political maneuvering. Quidge was dead. We didn't threaten the wreckers—and even if we had, they dealt more directly with people who threatened them. A fact that didn't stop Michael from wanting to take another look at Quidge's camp once the sheriff had gone.

I made no protest. I knew he suggested it only because he couldn't think of anything else to try.

We went, looked, and found nothing—to my sincere joy. Then we went to a pond we'd found yesterday, while searching for magica plants to damage ourselves with. We did some duck hunting, which was the excuse for our absence we'd given the players, and Michael brought down several.

We'd taken Trouble with us, to give him a romp and because Michael insists he's a good retriever. In fact, Trouble won't go into a pond unless someone else goes with him—that someone being me, for in the absence of a useful dog, retrieving ducks is a squire's duty. Once he has company, Trouble charges in with a great deal of splashing, and then gets me even wetter by shaking all over me when I come out. On the other hand, I like roast duck.

All in all, it was a good day. Nothing stung or bit or skunked us. Michael was out of clues. Even the sheriff was losing interest in us. So the thing that occupied my mind as we returned to camp in the late afternoon was the prospect of duck for dinner.

Until we learned that on his way back from Quidge's camp, Sheriff Todd had arrested Master Makejoye.

## CHAPTER 8

# Michael

"What was he charged with?" I asked.

The players who'd gone with Rudy hadn't yet returned, but Mistress Makejoye, who'd followed her husband into town to present the guild's testimonials of their honesty and good reputation, had come back just before we did. Her hands were clenched on the useless papers, and she looked older than she had this morning.

Edith Barker sat beside her, an arm around her shoulders. The bright sunlight and gaily painted wagons made a strange backdrop for so many grim faces. My tenderhearted Rose was near tears, but she sat silent, waiting for something she could do to help.

"For his plays." It was Gloria who answered, her expression hard and anxious. "How they found them . . . *I* didn't know where that cupboard was, but that bastard found it in minutes."

"What plays?" The Makejoyes were players—of course they had plays. There was nothing illegal about it.

"The other plays, Michael," said Fisk, looking almost as concerned as the rest of the troupe. "The ones they put on when there aren't any lords in the audience. But you didn't put any of those on here, did you?"

Gwen Makejoye shook her head. "It was some fellow who'd seen us in another town." Her voice was hoarse. "Trundle, I think his name was. Prissy bastard. Said he found them 'offensive.'"

"But if you didn't perform them in Lord Fabian's fief, surely the worst he can do is ask you to leave," I said. "And that's just what you want."

"That probably depends on how offensive Fabian and his judicars find them," said Fisk.

"But that's unjust," I protested.

"We're players, Sir Michael," said Callista. "Here today, over the fief's borders next week. A stranger is always easier to mistrust than someone you know. Easier to punish, too, if it comes to that."

I'd learned that lesson myself in the last two years.

"How bad are these plays?" Fisk asked.

"That's the problem," Callista replied. "They're not bad, they're good. They leave the audience weeping and holding their sides, they laugh so hard. How much tolerance do you think Lord Fabian and the judicars will have for being laughed at?"

There was a long pause. I couldn't speak for the judicars, but remembering Lord Fabian's fierce, prickly pride . . .

Mistress Makejoye turned her head into Edith's shoulder and began to cry—the harsh, clumsy sobs of someone who doesn't do it often.

"He'll probably be flogged," said Fisk. "He'll survive it, at least, and be free to go. But when the Players' Guild hears about this . . . How long will it take them to read these scripts?"

Callista and Gloria exchanged glances. "Hours," said Callista. "Maybe a day. There are lots of them."

"Tomorrow." Gwen Makejoye scrubbed her face with her hands. "They were too busy today—Fabian is meeting with the captains of a convoy that just came in. Everything they take on here has to be searched for some cargo that was taken from the latest wreck. Some of 'em are making a fuss about it, so they set the scripts aside to read tomorrow. You sound like you have something in mind, Master Fisk."

"So no one's actually read the things?"

My heart beat faster; I recognized Fisk's expression.

"No, but Lord Fabian's got 'em locked in a strongbox, in his own office."

"What kind of lock? Padlock or inset?"

"A padlock, but he dabbed it up with wax and put his seal on it." Her mouth quivered. "From the ring he wears. It's no good, Master Fisk. Even if you could take 'em, or burn 'em, they'd know it was one of us. It might save my Hector the whip, but you'd earn it in his place, and the guild will cast us off anyway."

"Oh, if we're obvious about it," said Fisk. "But if all we do is replace those scripts with others . . ." He gestured to the Makejoyes' wagon, where the ordinary, innocuous scripts resided.

My heart began to dance. A flogging is no light thing, as I of all folk knew, but to fight injustice is the proper purpose of a knight errant and his squire.

"What about the seal?" Callista asked.

"There are ways to deal with wax," said Fisk. "Though on a surface that's not flat . . . hmm. I'll just have to see."

"You mean *we'll* have to see," I said.

Fisk eyed me askance. "Have you thought about what might happen if you're caught? All Makejoye or I will face is flogging. You're unredeemed. Anything could happen to you."

"At the sheriff's whim," I agreed. "But he can condemn me at his whim whether I do anything or not. If I never risk anything, for fear of what *might* happen, I might as well be dead. I can't let it stop me."

Fisk sighed. "You could, but I don't suppose you will. I need a scout. And besides, you got me into this. Oh, you're definitely coming, Noble Sir."

Fisk is a most excellent squire.

Fisk wished to start as soon as possible, but it took some time to prepare. First he assembled a tool kit, mostly from Callista's tools for the making and repair of the troupe's jewelry. His brows lifted when he saw how complete her small workshop was, and she told him she'd refurbished it recently, for she'd picked up a new store of cut glass from the local glassmakers and planned to enrich their costumes.

The others arrived while Fisk was packing up a pile of "safe" scripts, and we had to explain everything to them. Then 'twas time to don our disguises. In light of the arrival of a convoy of ships, Fisk decided we should go in as a ship's captain and his clerk.

Callista found us suitable clothes in the players' stores, and with my hair pulled back and tied at my neck—a style sailors oft affect—I looked quite nautical.

Fisk looked like himself, wearing a clerk's somber doublet and plain cuffs, but I knew he could look very different as soon as he had to. He produced "old" stains on his cuffs by thinning a drop or two of Makejoye's ink and smearing it on. Dried, it looked exactly like an ink stain someone has tried to wash away several times, and Falon's eyes narrowed thoughtfully as he gazed upon my squire.

But the players were busy too, since Fisk had called upon them to create a diversion. To go in full paint and costume would be suspicious, but they chose bright, flamboyant clothes, of the kind plain folk might imagine players would wear offstage. Alone, each of them would have caught the eye. Together . . . I will merely remark that as we trailed them into the town hall, no one was looking at Fisk and me. Especially since the Barkers had brought their dogs.

"Wait! You can't bring those beasts inside." The door clerk, a dignified man with snowy lace at his cuffs, leapt from his desk as the troupe swarmed into the echoing foyer. They were even busier today than the first time we'd been here. The stone benches along the walls were filled with sea captains and their clerks, and some of them sat upon the steps, or on the satchels that held their manifests.

Fisk's satchel, which held scripts and burglary tools, was larger than most, but in the midst of such a hubbub no one would notice that.

"We want to see my husband," Gwen Makejoye demanded in a voice that carried to all ears in the room. "Your bullies took him this morning on the mere suspicion that he *might* have written a play that someone *might* not care for, and we want to see him."

"Yes, madam, certainly, but you can't bring those dogs—"

"Well!" Edith Barker put her hands on her hips. "Have your ever heard of such a thing, Mitzi? This nasty man doesn't want you in his nice jail. I'll bet it's dirtier than your kennel, and full of lovely rats you could chase, but—"

The Barkers' signals were too subtle for me to see, but they must have given one; all the dogs scattered to explore the room, sniffing the seamen's boots and satchels. Rabbit jumped into the lap of a grizzled captain, who petted him with bemused delight. Indeed, grins were dawning all over the room, and Rudy performed a few cartwheels.

"Look, if you lot don't settle down, I'll call the guards—"

"Excuse me," Fisk murmured. His face was suddenly thinner, with a most lugubrious expression. "My captain and I have an—"

"—evict you. And take those dogs outside!"

"—appointment to see the master of the exchequer. I believe—"

"Yes, yes, take a seat, sir. Stop that! You can't do flips in here!"

At the word "flips," half a dozen dogs started doing them, so it hardly mattered that Rudy obediently stopped.

Fisk and I took our places against the wall and proceeded to enjoy the show. The harassed clerk was forced to summon half a dozen guardsmen to help the Barkers take the dogs out.

Then the clerk mopped his brow with a clean handkerchief and explained to Gwen Makejoye that, yes, she and her friends could visit the prisoner, but only in groups of two, and only if they permitted the guards to search them for concealed weapons.

"That's no problem," said Falon. "I'll give them to you now." He stripped off his coat, revealing an arsenal of throwing knives, and began unloading them onto the desk, despite the clerk's startled squeak. They made a tidy pile even before he started pulling out the concealed ones.

Edgar Barker opened the door, poked his head through, and asked if everything was going all right. The clerk's voice rose half an octave telling him to stay out.

Fisk asked the armsman who stood at the foot of the central stair, staring with widening eyes at the still growing pile of cutlery, where he might find a privy. He then followed the guard's directions to the corner of the room and down a shallow staircase.

Falon was persuaded to keep his weapons until the guards asked him to surrender them, and the fascination of watching so much steel vanish into one man's clothing entranced both the armsmen stationed in the hall. And myself as well, in truth.

Edith Barker poked her head in to ask what was taking so long, and a small dog peered around the door.

The clerk's face turned scarlet, and he said something quite unbecoming to a man of his dignity.

My ribs were beginning to ache, and judging by the guffaws around me I wasn't the only one.

Callista told one of the guards that she didn't carry concealed weapons, but she supposed he'd have to search her too. The guard suddenly forgot to breathe, and his comrades looked on jealously.

Fisk came back up the unobtrusive stair and told me he'd encountered the exchequer clerk in the corridor, and his master could see us now. He could have said that Lord Fabian was ready to have us dance naked for him, for all the attention anyone paid us. And that was before Edith Barker looked in again and caught Fisk's slight nod. The dog at her feet shot into the hall, dodged the startled guard's grasp, and dashed up the stairs.

Edith ran in pursuit yelling commands, which the

dog, trained to signals, ignored. The rest of the pack followed at her heels.

I staggered through the melee, wheezing and clutching my sides, as helpful bystanders tried to capture the dogs for the shrieking clerk. They were amazingly quick. The dogs, that is. Rudy was walking on his hands.

I followed Fisk down the steps—six of them; then he took me around behind them and opened a small door that led to a dark closet beneath the stairs. I crouched and crawled in.

The ceiling at its highest wasn't much more than four feet, and it lowered quickly. The largest part of the closet held several wooden chests, stacked upon each other, which I assumed held documents. In the shallower end were brooms, pails, and a feather mop on a long handle. That was all I had time to see before Fisk entered and closed the door behind us, and it promptly became very dark.

"That's that." He sounded incredibly smug, small blame to him. "The best way to get behind a locked door is to be on the right side when they lock it."

His voice was low, but not a whisper. Judging by the way the uproar above us had been muted, we probably could speak freely.

"What if they need a broom or a pail?" I asked.

"What if one of the dogs piddles?"

"That's why we're going to move the chests," said Fisk. "And we'd better do it before they get the riot under control."

We worked by touch, but 'twas not difficult to drag the stacked chests forward a few feet and wiggle though the gap to sit behind them. 'Twas not uncomfortable with my back against the wall and my legs stretched out before me, Fisk's booted feet nestled beside my hip.

"What if someone notices the chests have been moved?" The muted sounds of chaos and mayhem were fading, so I lowered my voice to a whisper. "What if someone wants one of the documents, or whatever's in them?"

"Judging by the dust, it would be the first time in a decade; but if they do, they do, and we'll probably accompany Makejoye to the flogging stake. Why do we always end up burgling places? And don't say it's my destiny—I hadn't done this for years till I hooked up with you. Now I'm always breaking into something."

"That's ridiculous. It would never occur to me to do this, and we haven't burgled anything since Worthington's house, a year and a half ago."

"What about the mayor of Fennic's house?"

"That didn't count—'tis not burglary if you're putting

things back. Especially if you didn't steal them in the first place."

Fisk can brangle endlessly when he's in this mood, but now he had something else on his mind. "Have you thought about what this means? Aside from the immediate consequences."

As it happened, I hadn't; but I thought about it now and saw what he meant. "'Tis the third shaft aimed at Master Makejoye and his troupe," I said slowly. "And like the Skydancers, and that magica wood that turned up so conveniently, 'tis designed to force him to leave. But Quidge couldn't have done this, so it seems . . ."

"Makejoye has an enemy," Fisk finished. "One who's prepared to do him real harm."

"But this is the first time he's been in this town—how could anyone hate him? Besides . . ." The implications of that thought stopped my voice.

"Besides?" Fisk prompted impatiently.

"No one from the town could know about those scripts. No one knew about the secret cupboard in his wagon except his own troupe—and us."

"Well, it wasn't us," said Fisk. "Even I'm not paranoid enough to suspect you or Rosa. But I'm not so sure no one else could know. Most players are rumored to have such things, and Makejoye's plays . . . It would be easy to guess he had them somewhere. As for the cupboards, any of his troupe who hates him is free to pack up and leave. And I can't see him evoking such hatred in anyone without Gwen being aware of it. She's no kind of fool."

"Mayhap hatred has naught to do with it," I said. "Mayhap someone simply wants to drive him off, as we thought Quidge did."

Hard as we tried, we could think of no motive for anyone to want such a thing, much less go to such lengths to obtain it, but our speculation passed the time. Which was just as well, because we'd a great deal of time to pass.

A dim glow crept under the door. Eventually I could make out the outline of the chest I crouched behind, but that was all. The stone floor and wall grew harder as the hours passed; in a space two feet wide and four feet high the number of positions you can sit or kneel in is very limited. I went through all of them twice, and the more comfortable several times, before the steps of the solitary night guard, whose rounds Fisk had insisted on timing for a ridiculously long period, passed over our heads once more. Fisk waited for a small eternity and then signaled that 'twas safe to for me to crawl out and stretch my cramped limbs. He dragged the satchel full of plays and burglary tools out of our prison and shut the door behind us. I must confess to an ignoble satisfaction that he rose as stiffly as I did.

"I wish we could hear the clock chimes from here," he fretted in a whisper. "My guess is that the guard's making his rounds on the hour. That's going to go awfully fast, now that we're moving."

"Then let us move," I said softly. Lord Fabian's office was on the upper floor. All we had to do was climb the stairs—avoiding the guard—break into the locked and sealed strongbox, replace the plays, and depart, without leaving a trace of our presence. Compared to sitting one more minute in that cramped hole, it sounded ludicrously easy.

The corridor was lighted by a single oil lamp, no doubt to aid the guard's peregrinations. As Fisk stretched, groaning quietly, I crept forward to the base of the stairs and started up them. I took care to keep low; we knew how often the guard passed, but we'd no idea where he went when he left our corridor.

The entry hall, lit by two lamps in brackets on the walls, was as empty as the hallway behind us. I heard no footsteps near or far, so 'twas safe to assume that he wasn't on the gallery above our heads.

Fisk came up behind me and stood, listening as intently as I. Since he was the expert, I waited till he nodded before stepping out onto the polished stone of the floor and hurrying toward the central staircase.

I'd not taken three steps when a gray shadow oozed from behind the stair, a growl building like distant thunder in its throat. And why I say shadow I know not, for the beast glowed like a swamp wraith. Ordinarily, I would have no doubts as to my ability to handle a guard dog. As it was . . .

"Fisk, back up."

"I have." Indeed, my squire's voice sounded some feet distant, but I dared not take my gaze from the dog to look. Its intelligent golden eyes were fixed on me, and it started forward, claws clicking on the stone. The warning growl grew louder.

"I'm leaving, there's a good lad," I said soothingly, easing back as I spoke. "You're a good dog and I won't challenge you."

My Gift for animal handling rose, as familiar to my wielding as Chant's reins, reaching out to the beast to convince it I was its friend, accepted and trusted. Any other dog would have lifted its ears and tail, and its growl would have faded, but Burke's magica hound came on. At least it had been trained to warn before it bit. I retreated, steadily, but did not run. Nothing tempts a predator more than fleeing before it.

The first of the steps caught me by surprise. I stumbled, and might have fallen if Fisk hadn't caught me. I recovered my balance on the third step, my eyes flashing to the dog. But far from charging, it—he, I now saw—tucked his hindquarters and sat. The growl stopped, and if his tail didn't wag, at least his ears lifted a bit.

"He's been told to keep people out of the entry," I told Fisk softly. "As long as we stay here, we should be safe."

"So persuade him to let us up," said Fisk.

I stared at him in astonishment before I remembered that he was blind to what I saw so clearly. "He's magica, Fisk. This is one of Master Burke's hounds. He said he lent them out, if you recall."

Fisk also remembered what else Burke had said. "Your Gift won't work on him?"

"No. I tried it."

Fisk's frown deepened. "This isn't good. I poked around quite a bit on my way to the privy, and as far as I can tell, that stair is the only way to get to the upper floor."

"They often made the old keeps so," I told him. "So if anyone broke in, the inhabitants needed only defend one stair. And they could shoot from the gallery, as well."

Fisk had no interest in historic architecture. "How does the guard get past the beast?"

"The dog's handler would have introduced him. But he didn't introduce us."

"If we could get a guard's tabard—"

"Dogs go by scent, Fisk. You'd have to smell like him, not look like him."

"And you can't get us past?"

"Let me try again." I spoke soothingly to the dog, remarking what a good fellow he was, pouring my Gift into the words. He let me climb the stairs without fuss, but the moment I set foot on the foyer's parqueted floor, his ears dropped and his growl rumbled.

"No," I told Fisk, falling back to the bottom of the steps. "I can't get us past him."

I expected his face to mirror the near despair I felt, but his expression was intent. "He only started to growl when you stepped onto the floor."

"I told you, he was ordered to keep people out of this room."

"But for him, the room is the floor?"

"I don't follow you," I admitted.

"I'm going to try something." Fisk stripped off his boots and doublet as he spoke. "If this doesn't work and he sounds an alarm, get back under the stairs—if you don't get caught, you'll be free to act later."

I was also the one who'd get into the most trouble if we were caught, but I couldn't allow Fisk to take extra risks because of it.

"What are you going to do?" I asked.

He was already at the top of the stair and waved me to silence. "Nice doggy," he announced unconvincingly.

The dog watched with unwavering yellow eyes.

"Here goes," said Fisk nervously. He stepped onto the baseboard. 'Twas near a foot high but only an inch wide, and he had to grasp one of the lamp brackets to keep his balance. I moved forward to catch him, but he eased his feet along the narrow stone ridge and into the entry.

The dog cocked his head—he whined softly, uncertain. But he made no move to attack as Fisk transferred his grip to the crevasses of a decorative bas-relief of the Waterweis crest, then made his way forward till he could step onto one of the stone benches.

He turned slowly and looked at the dog, who looked back with an intensity that promised a charge at the first wrong move Fisk made. But not yet.

"You're right," I told my white-faced, sweating squire. "The room is the floor. But neither the benches nor the baseboards run between this stair and the central one, so unless you can climb to the gallery over sheer wall, I don't know what we've accomplished."

"It's not sheer," said Fisk. "There's carved bits all over it, and a nice three-inch ledge all around the room, right at gallery level, if you could just get up there."

"But you can't," I exclaimed in some alarm—he

looked far too serious about it.

"No," said Fisk. "But I know someone who can. Wait till I get back to you, and we'll go fetch Rudy."

'Twas not so preposterous as it sounded, for the players had chosen to await us at an inn not far from the town hall. And as Fisk pointed out, as long as one of us stayed behind to let the other in, we wouldn't have to break in again. But it felt strange to slide the bolt on the rear door and watch Fisk slip off into the darkness.

I shot the bolt behind him and went into the nearest office to await his knock, preparing to hide behind the desk if the guard wandered by.

In truth, 'twas not the oddity of interrupting a burglary to go and fetch someone else that troubled me, but the fact that I didn't want to work in so close and precarious a matter with Rudy Foster. Yet he cared more for Makejoye, had more right to come to his aid, than Fisk or I. Would I have questioned Falon's right to help? Or Gloria's? I feared not.

The guard did pass as I waited, though he didn't trouble to open the door to the room where I crouched, not even breathing, in the darkness.

I had time to imagine a number of things that might happen if Fisk should knock when the guard was passing, but the knock came some time after the guard had gone by.

"How long ago did the guard go by?" was the first thing Fisk said when I opened the door. He and Rudy surged in on a wave of cool, fresh air. Rudy's eyes were wide with excitement, but his expression was one of steady determination.

"How should I know? There's no clock in here."

Fisk took Rudy's arm and drew him down the hallway. "You must have some idea—five minutes ago? Almost an hour?"

"Somewhere between that," I replied, earning myself a glare. "All right, I'd guess 'twas about twenty minutes. What difference does it make?"

"It makes a difference because I don't want him strolling by while Rudy's spread over the wall like a tapestry," said Fisk. "The sure way is to hide under the stairs till he passes again—then we'd know we have a full hour."

That idea held no appeal. "I think it was about twenty minutes," I assured him.

"If the wall's like you described, I can get up it pretty quickly," said Rudy.

Fisk hesitated at the foot of the steps; then he nodded. "All right—let's do this fast."

I introduced Rudy to the dog as best I could, while he examined the wall and removed his boots. The urgency of the moment made the coiled power in my gut stir sluggishly, awakening to the possibility of adding itself to my useless Gift. Even as I crushed it down, I wondered if that might work—if I let my magic enhance my Gift for animal handling, would it overcome this beast's magic resistance? And if it would, did I have the right to reject it at the risk of Hector Makejoye's pain? Or would its power burn my weaker Gift away, that I might never use it again? Or make it so strong I couldn't close the door upon it, so that every animal I met fell madly in love with me, and followed me down the streets and byways. The possibilities were endless and almost all bad. No, I had a choice this time, and I refused to use it.

Rudy was a far better climber than Fisk. He slid along the baseboard and onto the bench, then paused to examine the challenge before him, his hands twitching as he mapped future hand- and footholds. Then he grasped a lamp bracket, hooked his toes over the top of the Waterweis crest, and started up.

I held my breath as I watched. He made use of the smallest cracks and protuberances, and I hadn't even imagined a man could climb so. His toes were as strong and flexible as his fingers, and I noticed, with a sudden lurch of my stomach, that he was missing one of them on his left foot. The scarring at the stump was white with age. I looked at Fisk to find his steady gaze upon me, and looked away.

I couldn't blame Rudy for what he'd done, but he was my rival for Rose's hand, Rose's love; and the crumpled paper in my pocket was a weapon that could bring him down. Not kill him, of course. Not even do him much damage. But if I wrote to the sheriff of that far-off fief, sooner or later someone would come, deputies, bounty hunters, and they would call him a killer and take him away. Rose would weep and ask to go home, and I would escort her, console her, and show her that another, better love awaited her.

Then Rudy, clinging to very little that I could see, stretched up one foot and stepped onto the ledge that ran the length of the room at the same level as the gallery floor. To a ropewalker three inches of solid stone must seem like a high road, and he slipped along it swiftly and vanished onto the gallery above us. His hand came down, reaching for something. Fisk promised the watching dog that he wouldn't do anything, stepped forward, and swung a coil of rope up to slap his palm. Rope and hand vanished.

"He knows where Fabian's office is," Fisk murmured. "And Gwen gave him good directions for finding the strongbox. They're all waiting for us, back at the inn."

Including Rosamund, who would see Rudy as the hero of this perilous night despite all the risks that

Fisk and I had taken. If Rudy was accused of murder, even if he was acquitted, would the Players' Guild continue to accept him? Or would their members' need to be perceived as good and lawful citizens force them to cast him off? To forbid his employment by any troupe that sought their endorsement? I shivered.

"How will he get the box down? He can't climb with it."

"That's what the rope's for," said Fisk. "He can lower the box and set it swinging till we can catch it."

"Oh. But tell me, what would you have done if the guard had answered the door instead of me."

"Demanded to see Lord Fabian," said Fisk promptly. "In my best drunken manner. Don't be silly."

It sounded chancy to me, but no more so than the rest of the enterprise, and risk is the business of a knight errant. And turning in your comrades, just to get a rival out of your way? What kind of thing was that for a decent man to contemplate—much less to do? Yet 'twould be so simple. Just a letter . . .

I was so lost in thought that the soft footsteps on the floor above made me start. The strongbox thumped against the gallery's rail loudly enough to make me wince. Then it descended rapidly to dangle in midair, several feet beyond our reach. 'Twas larger than I'd expected, about three feet by two by two.

The dog circled it, growling low in his throat, then stood on his hind legs to sniff it. But this strange intruder wasn't human, and he settled back to watch again.

Rudy's hand reached down to set the rope to swinging—then we heard the steps, distant, but drawing steadily nearer. My heart began to race.

I'd have hauled the box back up, but Rudy had other ideas. The box descended to the floor, in a silent rush that made the dog yelp. Then Rudy's face and arm appeared below the edge of the gallery—he must have been hanging outside the rail—and he pitched the rope to Fisk, who snatched it and dragged the box to us like a fisherman hauling in a net.

'Twas well swathed in rope, but the scrape of fiber on stone was so noisy, I'd have sworn the approaching guard could hear it. His steps were growing louder than my heartbeat, and I knew we'd have no time to run for one of the offices.

I jumped from the steps, down into the shadowy corner beside the stair cupboard. The moment Fisk had the box in his hands, he heaved it into mine; I staggered, biting back a grunt of effort. The thing was solid oak, bound in iron, and must have weighed two stone.

Then Fisk leapt down and pushed me into the step's shadow, and we crouched there, listening to the footsteps. They changed subtly when the guard walked onto the polished floor.

"Hey, boy. Slow night, huh?"

The steps changed again as he went onto the stairs and started up.

I looked at Fisk, who shrugged. If Rudy wasn't well hidden, there was little we could do about it. Fisk eased open the cupboard door; we pushed the strong-box in and followed it. My objections to my erstwhile hiding place weren't as strong as I'd thought—the safe, silent darkness was most welcome, and my heart rate slowed. A few minutes later the steps passed over our heads, and we waited several minutes more before crawling out.

"Help me get the box into the light," Fisk whispered. "I have to see for this."

"Isn't it too exposed?" Even as I spoke, we carried the heavy chest toward the corridor lamp.

"Less dangerous than shining a light where there isn't supposed to be one," said Fisk. "We can drag it into the room across the way if anyone comes."

We came to a stop in the midst of the lamplight, and Fisk knelt to examine the padlock that fastened the hasp. Or more precisely, the wax seal that covered the joining of the lock's body and its looped top.

"So much for the old hot knife," he muttered. "The

silly thing's in a right-angle bend."

"You mean you can't get through the seal." I fought to keep my growing panic out of my voice. The last narrow escape had overstrained my nerves—in fact, I was beginning to understand Fisk's aversion to burglary.

"Don't worry." Fisk turned the chest and eyed the hinges closely. "There's always a way if you look . . . hmm." He opened the satchel and pulled out a candle. "Light this, will you?"

I lifted the wall lamp's cover and did so. "Where's Rudy?"

"Waiting for us. He has to put this back when we're finished." Fisk took the candle and held the flame under one of the small knobs at the end of a hinge pin, and despite my nervousness I knelt to watch. It took several interminable minutes, but then a small silver bead appeared at the joint between knob and pin, and Fisk hissed—a soft, satisfied sound. "Soldered with lead. Find the pliers for me. The larger pair."

This took time, for Fisk's satchel held an amazing assortment of tools, all wrapped in felt so they'd not clank. Moments after I'd found the pliers, he twisted off the knob, and it took no longer to repeat the process on the other hinge. Tapping out the pins was the work of seconds, even though we took the time to muffle the hammer with felt. Then we lifted the lid from the back, leaving padlock and seal untouched.

"Always a way," Fisk murmured. "Just like Jack said. Here, help me with these scripts."

I've wondered about this Jack Bannister, whom Fisk so often quotes but will not speak of. The philosophy Fisk cites tells me the man was a cynic and a rogue. Fisk's refusal to discuss him, and the way he refuses, speaks of pain, mayhap betrayal. But as I've said, Fisk seldom talks about himself.

Once the safe scripts were within the strongbox and the hinge pins replaced, we hauled it down the corridor to where Rudy waited.

"What took you so long?" he whispered. "Never mind, just get the rope up here."

It took several tries to swing the end of the rope into his waiting hand, and the dog chased it, yapping softly, as we dragged it back after each failed attempt. Eventually we succeeded, and then 'twas our turn to wait as Rudy replaced the chest in Lord Fabian's office.

My heart rate only doubled as I watched him spider down the wall to join us; I'd been through so many alarms by now, my nerves were numb.

"I looked over some of the papers on Fabian's desk while I waited," Rudy told us as we hurried down the corridor.

I didn't know when the guard's next round would come, but 'twould be soon. We were almost at the door now. Almost free.

"One of them was a reward offer," Rudy went on, "for information leading to the wreckers' capture. Do you know how much they're—"

"No." Fisk pulled back the bolt and opened the door. "And I don't want to. Get out, and wait for us around the corner."

Rudy nodded and slipped out, but Fisk spent several more endless minutes, looping a thin string around the bolt's knob and testing how much power was needed to slide it forward. Then he looped the string around the knob one final time, stepped out with me, closed the door, and pulled—bolting the door behind us.

"You are a very good squire," I told him.

"And a better burglar," he said cheerfully. "No, don't run, that looks suspicious. Walk casually, like you're coming back from a tavern."

I managed to slow my steps, but for all the exhilaration rushing through my blood, my mouth was too dry to whistle. Sometimes Fisk is quite amazing.

## CHAPTER 9
# Fisk

Hector Makejoye was released late the next morning, amid the cheerful bedlam of happy people who frankly enjoyed letting the world know it. In fact, the scene that took place in front of the town hall was almost as distracting as the diversion they'd put on yesterday. Only Gwen Makejoye, thin arms wrapped tight around her husband, said nothing at all.

Eventually we retired to the sunny, noisy taproom of the inn where we'd spent the night and answered Makejoye's demand for an explanation. "Indeed." His voice, for once, was too soft for anyone beyond our table to hear it. "I thought I was about to pay the price for my misspent life. How under two moons did you switch those scripts?"

The players, who'd heard our story before, told him

more than Michael, Rudy, or I. When they finished, Makejoye looked at Michael and me and said, "You're one of us now, my friends. Never forget it, because I certainly won't. And as for you"—he turned to Rudy—"I believe I'll have to stop complaining about being tied here by the heels. If you want to wed the wench, I'll do what I can to help. Well, within reasonable limits."

But something else had been troubling me. "It may not be easy for any of us to stay. You have to admit it now—someone is trying to drive you off."

"Aye." Makejoye's breath gusted out on a sigh. "I gave that some thought in that—in that cramped little cell. But I'll be hanged if I can think who it might be, or why. I told Sheriff Todd the other things that happened. Gave him a bit of an explanation why someone would turn me in over my perfectly innocent scripts. I'm afraid he wasn't impressed. Said this John Trundle must have taken offense at something that touched him personally. And since the fellow has traveled on, we can't ask him."

I turned my ale mug on the table's smooth wood, leaving small wet rings. Something about the sequence of events made me uneasy. "Did you get a description of this Trundle?"

"No, why? He was passing through, or so he

claimed. I doubt he was local—too big a risk that someone might recognize him."

"Hmm." I half agreed. He probably wasn't local;
Makejoye was right about the risk, but it would have
been good to have a description of his enemy. Or just
someone hired by his enemy? No way to know, but
unless Rosamund came to her senses—and watching the way she clung to Rudy's arm, I decided that
seemed unlikely—we were tied to these folk. And this
last "prank" might have had serious consequences.

"At least I got something out of the deal," said
Makejoye more cheerfully. "When I complained to
Lord Fabian about what staying here was costing us,
he gave us another contract. Said he'd always intended
to hire me to play for his friends, though it was clear
he'd forgotten all about it. But he's having a big party
tomorrow night, at his home up the river. He wants
Gwen and me to make music for his guests, and I
talked him into hiring the rest of us as well. He's got
a big garden behind his house, going down to the
riverbank. One of those tangled affairs, with lots of
paths and clearings and shrubbery. We can set up the
tightrope in the central clearing, and other acts—Falon
and Gloria, Callista's puppets, the Barkers—in smaller
clearings, scattered about. We won't even have to hire
a boy to keep an eye on the wagons—that's Fisk and

Michael's job. Isn't that a splendid plan?" He beamed at us, and the others exchanged laughing looks.

"But what can I do?" Rosamund demanded.

"Ah, I haven't overlooked you, lass. You may have noticed that some of the farm carts coming into town carry flowers?"

Rosamund clearly hadn't, though I had.

"Well, you can be a wandering flower seller. We'll stop the carts as they pass our camp in the morning and buy some flowers off 'em. Keep them cool in a shady part of the stream during the day, while you pick wildflowers to stretch 'em out a bit, then tie them in small bundles and sell them to Lord Fabian's guests for four times what we paid."

Rose was delighted—she was clever at arranging flowers and might even make some money. Rudy smiled dotingly, and Michael scowled at his smile. The truce imposed by last night's emergency was clearly at an end. The players were too pleased by the prospect of being paid to worry much, but I wasn't sure which worried me more: our mysterious enemy or Michael's looming romantic crisis. At least he seemed to have given up on tracking down the wreckers.

The next morning Master Makejoye wanted us to work on a few scenes from the new script he'd been writing.

It wasn't finished, but he wanted to see how the scenes played out.

It was interesting to watch him move people about the stage, and change their lines as problems arose. It was even more interesting to watch everyone's reaction to the story, in which a poor (but honest) farmer and a dashing brigand (who'd been forced into banditry by the machinations of an evil sheriff) competed for the love of a wealthy merchant's daughter (who'd been forced to run away from home when her evil uncle inherited the family business).

Rosamund, who played the heroine, was the only one who didn't see it. "She'll marry the one she truly loves," she speculated, smiling. "Otherwise 'twill be a tragedy, and I'll be very upset with you, Master Makejoye."

"Oh, it won't come out badly," he said. "Though I think the farm lad's uncle is about to be thrown in jail on a trumped-up charge. But can I have yet another evil sheriff . . . I know! It's the same blighter who forced poor Oliver into brigancy! Then bringing him down can be the climax, and the two of them . . ." He wandered off to his inkpot, murmuring to himself.

"Which of the two do you think Melisande will fall in love with?" Michael asked Rosamund, not sounding nearly as casual as he'd have liked. The others exchanged amused glances, except for Rudy, who scowled.

"Whichever Master Makejoye chooses," said Rosamund. "He'll probably save her life in the end—that's how these things usually work out."

Rudy's scowl deepened, and Michael looked thoughtful.

"Though I hope 'tis young John, since Rudy's playing him," she added.

Rudy grinned and Michael's face fell. Michael had originally been cast as Oliver, but after his first attempt at sounding dashing, Makejoye had given the role to Falon.

I met Gwen Makejoye's eyes, and she started talking about the need for some new costumes. I hoped she'd speak to her husband later—there should be limits to artistic blindness—and that we'd see no more rehearsals of this particular piece till Michael and I were gone.

Michael and Rudy both helped Rosamund tuck her damp flowers into the coolest part of the prop wagon, and the heat of the animosity between them should have wilted the silly things.

I separated the two of them, insisting Michael ride with me, while Rudy drove a wagon. I even let him talk me into bringing Trouble along, for between fretting whether Chant was starting to limp again—he wasn't—and rescuing Trouble from chasing squirrels over the sea cliffs, Michael wouldn't have time to be upset about how the small driver's bench pushed Rosamund up against Rudy's side.

Even so, it was a good thing Lord Fabian's house wasn't far up the river. I'd formed a mental picture of an old stone keep like the town hall, and that was foolish. The wealthy had moved out of such drafty, inconvenient places shortly after the first High Liege imposed peace and moved into more comfortable houses. Lord Fabian's house was built of the local brick, three stories high, with local glass sparkling in its many windows. It seemed I'd been right about the amount this town brought into the family's coffers. No wonder he and the guilds were at daggers drawn.

It was Fabian's steward who came out to greet us as we pulled up in front; he promptly directed us around to the back, where we might set ourselves up in the garden and call on the grooms for any assistance we needed. The gardens were as described. Makejoye, who was also aware of the tension between Michael and Rudy, told the women to help Rosamund move the flowers down to the riverbank, while the rest of us set up Rudy's tightrope.

They chose a couple of big trees at the edge of the clearing and pulled out the round collars that would attach to them—they had an amazing assortment of hardware for fastening the tightrope to everything from windowsills to grain towers. The net was an easier proposition: Supported by a series of tripods, it could be set up anywhere and, properly staked down, would easily handle a falling man's weight. Rudy and Edgar Barker climbed up the trees to attach things and winch the rope tight; the rest of us had the net up before they finished.

The ladies emerged from one of the many twisting paths in time to watch Rudy give the rope its final test. I wasn't sure if Rudy, forty feet above, could see the glow on Rosamund's uplifted face, but Michael certainly did. Rudy stepped out of the trees' leafy shelter and onto the rope with the casual cockiness of a man about to show off for all he was worth.

He never got the chance. We heard the rope's strands snapping, and the way it jerked could have unseated a squirrel. A man, even an acrobat as talented as Rudy, never had a chance.

I'd helped set up the net myself, but panic shrilled through my nerves as I watched him fall. I couldn't blame Rosamund for screaming. He tucked, spun in midair, and extended his arms and legs to hit the net spread-eagled on his back. As I believe I've said, acrobats know how to fall. Had he expected to do so, I doubt he'd have minded, but the suddenness of it startled us all. Rudy's face was almost as white as Rosamund's as he climbed over the springy ropes and rolled off.

"It just broke," he said, sounding almost simple in his astonishment. "It was perfectly solid; then I felt it start to twist and then it snapped."

Rosamund burrowed into his side, and he clasped her tight. Barker was already starting up one of the trees.

Makejoye took a deep, sustaining breath. "We'll know soon enough," he said, though even from the ground you could see that most of the rope's strands had parted, a bare few holding it suspended. For so many strands to break with no previous sign of wear . . .

Makejoye and Falon exchanged grim looks, and I could see from their faces that Gwen and Callista had reached the same conclusion. Michael was watching Rosamund and Rudy, and something about his bleak, closed expression sent me to his side—though whether I thought he needed comfort or restraint I couldn't have told you.

The rope slithered down and we converged. Falon

reached it first. "A good job." His voice was coolly critical, though his face showed the strain we all felt. "They went in with a very small, sharp knife and cut the insides of the strands, so the damage wouldn't show unless you looked really close. I'm surprised it held when we winched it up, but with the net in place there was no danger. Our prankster is being careful."

"This is no prank." Gwen Makejoye's voice shook. "This is . . . it's torment, that's what. And the worst of it is that they must have sneaked into camp without us even seeing them. I want the dogs out at night, from now till we leave this accursed place."

That wouldn't help, if it was one of them. I couldn't imagine a stranger being able to creep into the prop wagon during the day, and at night, Michael and I—

"But why would anyone do such a thing?" Makejoye demanded. "I know that Burke and Lord Fabian are struggling for control of the town, but would Burke go this far simply to ruin a rival's show? And how would one of Burke's men know which rope to cut?"

"Suppose it's not one of Burke's men." Rudy's voice was rough with the aftermath of fear. "Those two sleep in the prop wagon. They could have done it easy."

I might have been offended except that a) he was right, and b) he was looking straight at Michael.

"Now, lad," said Makejoye soothingly. "Let's not

go flinging words about because we've had a scare.
We were all in town last night—anyone could have
gone into camp and done the mischief. We'll just have
to check our gear carefully, and the costumes, too,
Callista. It wouldn't do for, ah, certain seams to be
ripping when we're onstage.

The thought of the havoc that might be caused by
tampering with "certain seams" brought scattered
chuckles, and the rest of the players started to relax.
But not Rudy.

"A stranger couldn't know where you kept your
scripts," he argued. "A stranger would have no reason
to do such things." He was breathing hard, his growing anger urging him on, and there was no way to
stop him. Even as Rosamund's hands tightened on his
arm, he continued. "But an *unredeemed* man might do
anything. Especially if he wanted one of us out of the
way. How scum like him would dare to court a girl
like Rose I'll never understand, but this time he's gone
too far!"

So had Rudy. The angry red patches on Michael's
cheekbones stood out against his pale skin. Even as
he took a breath, struggling for control, I saw him
losing it.

"Yes, I am unredeemed," he began hotly. "But my
intentions toward Rose are true, honorable, and for

her good and not just mine. She'd be no worse off
with me than with a—"

I grasped his arm and brought my boot heel down
on his toes just in time to stop him from saying "vagabond player," in the midst of a crowd of vagabond
players. Or something worse.

He stopped, his breathing harsher and more ragged
than Rudy's. Then he turned and walked away, not
looking at anyone.

"Go with him, Fisk," Rosamund commanded
urgently.

I did, though I took my time about it. It would
do Michael good to walk off his anger, and I had no
desire to chase him across half the fief.

As it happened, he didn't go far. I found him sitting
on a bench in one of the bushy nooks that faced the
river, gazing at the water's ripple and swirl.

I sat down beside him and waited for some time
before he spoke.

"She's in love with him."

"Yes. She is."

"I could stop him, Fisk. I could get him declared
unredeemed, too. I could destroy him."

I doubted the elderly warrant was powerful enough
to accomplish all those things, but I nodded anyway.
"You could."

"But even if I did, I'd still be nothing to her. Just the cousin she grew up with, who went and got himself unredeemed."

I didn't say anything.

Michael took the crumpled warrant from his pocket, tore it to bits, and cast them into the river. Assisted by the breeze, the pieces drifted into the water, hesitated a moment on the surface, then sank in the best melodramatic tradition. I was glad to see them go. Watching Michael hang on to that paper had begun to worry me.

He talked a long time then, going by natural stages from shock, to anger, to a bitter depression that I feared would last for some time. I went through the same thing when Lucy dumped me, and it enabled me to be patient with Michael. I even refrained from telling him he was well rid of the lovely nitwit, though the temptation was great.

I'd modified my original impression of Rosamund so far as to add good-hearted, and she'd probably suit Rudy well enough. Had she wed Michael, they'd have bored each other to tears inside a year. But I didn't say that either, as I like my teeth where they are.

When dusk fell and the guests began to arrive, we returned to the wagons to keep an eye on them as per "the plan." This was beginning to seem a more necessary precaution than I'd thought. Someone was tampering with the players' equipment. It wasn't Michael or I, and for all my conviction that Rudy was right, that it had to be an inside job, I couldn't for the life of me think of any reason for the players to sabotage themselves.

Once the guests, in their shimmering satins and rich velvets, were spreading through the gardens, I excused myself and patrolled the shrubbery till I found the man I wanted.

"Sheriff, may I speak to you a moment?"

Todd was dressed for the party, in mustard-colored velvet and snowy lace, but he came with me anyway. I showed him the rope and watched his lips tighten. "You can't call this an accident or a coincidence," I said. "No matter who's behind it, sooner or later someone is going to get hurt, even if it isn't intended. You have to see that."

"Yes," he admitted. "This kind of mischief almost always ends badly, whether anyone intends it to or not."

"Then let us go! If you declare that you no longer need us as witnesses, Lord Fabian has no excuse to keep us."

He fingered the cut ends of the rope. "I can't do that, Master Fisk. If nothing else, we may finally have a chance to catch—" He broke off suddenly, but I didn't need a translation.

"If you mean this mysterious cargo you're searching the outbound ships for, they'd have to be crazy not to have destroyed it by now. And has it occurred to you that this Trundle fellow might be the T in Quidge's journal?"

"He might, but so might any man in town whose name starts with T. There's more than one," said Sheriff Todd. "Though you seem to be bringing suspects out of the woodwork. I wonder why that is, Master Fisk."

"I don't care why it is," I said. "I care that we're in danger here, and so should you, *Sheriff*."

Todd shook his head. "I'm sorry, but I can't help you." He looked like he was sorry—but Lord Fabian paid his salary.

"On your head be it," I said nastily. "I just hope 'it' doesn't turn out to be blood."

I turned and stamped back to console Michael some more, though his broken heart was rapidly becoming the least of my worries. The thing that concerned me most was that I wasn't surprised. To first create fear, then provide a practical motive to act, was a tried-and-true method con men used to herd a mark into a snare. If our enemy continued to follow the pattern, the next step should be some assault on Makejoye's business or finances. It isn't often that I hope to be proved wrong.

The performances all went well, despite the players' slight hesitation whenever they picked up a piece of equipment. But even the backup tightrope performed as it should, and they made a tidy sum in tips, in addition to Rose's flower sales and Lord Fabian's fee.

This lightened everyone's mood, but I was still relieved when Rudy apologized to Michael the next morning. "I was frightened by falling, sudden like that," he finished. "And I was . . . well, I was frightened. But that was no excuse for saying what I did—I didn't mean it, and I'm sorry."

I saw Rosamund's fair hand in this noble declaration, and think Michael saw it too. He struggled to find an even more noble and great-spirited reply, but the effort was beyond him.

"'Tis naught," he muttered, and turned away. Rudy had the good sense not to pursue him.

I wished we could leave. Constant contact with the lovers would only exacerbate Michael's despair, but I also knew that he wouldn't leave while she was in danger. I couldn't even argue that if we left, the danger would cease, since I hadn't a clue who was harassing

the players. Or why. Or what the next attack would be.
No wonder I was nervous.

We were to perform at Lionel Burke's home that
night—the last of our contracts.

The house was smaller than Lord Fabian's, another
sprawling pile of mellow brick, glittering with windows, with two wings sweeping out behind. There
were benefits to being rich in a town that had its own
glassworks.

The place was in better taste than I'd expected from
Burke's choices in performance art. The statues were
mostly nude, but not entirely, and if the tapestries
were too violent for my taste, they weren't obscene—at
least in the public part of the house.

We hadn't seen our employer yet—it seemed he
was resting in preparation for the exhausting evening
ahead. It was his clerk, Willy Dawkins, who fussed
nervously over the placement of the long pole on
which Rudy would work, and the tables that lined the
great hall where the party would be. Even with every
window open, the big, paneled room was hot enough
to bring up sweat on the bodies of the men setting up
the tables.

Burke came down an hour before his guests were
due to arrive, clad in a burgundy silk dressing gown
that might have made some ship a respectable sail.

He proceeded to make several arbitrary and pointless alterations in Dawkins's room layout, and the clerk hurried to make the changes, spectacles flashing in the light from the setting sun. Then Burke turned to Makejoye.

"Where's the tightrope?"

"We couldn't set it up in this room, sir." Makejoye sounded respectful, but there was no groveling in this voice, and I deduced that watching poor Dawkins shrink from his master's bullying had disgusted him as much as it did me. "The ceiling is too low. But this pole will serve the same function. You'll see it's much the same size and shape as the rope, and though you can't see it, it has the same qualities of flexibility and tension. In some ways this low performance platform is more impressive, though it might not appear so to the unsophisticated eye. It's still six feet off the floor, and without a net the danger from a fall is actually greater. Also, at this range the audience can more clearly see the difficulty of what Rudy does; the degree of balance required, the straining muscles."

The man might not fawn, but he had flattery down to a high art, and he obviously knew what would appeal to Burke.

The banker pursed his lips. "Very well, I'll allow it." It was that or raise the ceiling. "But I want something in exchange for my concession. The young man will perform without a shirt."

"This is a display of skill and control, good sir." Makejoye's voice grated. "Not a—"

"I don't mind," said Rudy hastily, seeing that Hector Makejoye had been pushed too far. "I often work without a shirt when I'm practicing. It won't bother me."

"Fine then," said Burke, as Makejoye visibly tried to get a grip on his slipping temper. "Dawkins will take care of anything you need, as soon as he's checked to see if my bath's ready."

Dawkins scurried out and Burke followed, leaving the rest of us staring at each other.

"What's the difference between a banker and a bandit?" I asked softly.

Michael snorted. "What's the worst flaw in your character?"

"My addiction to those stupid jokes," I recited with him, and watched the others laugh, a bit louder than the mild jest warranted.

"I don't know why we're all so tense," said Callista. "It's not like we haven't dealt with 'handy' men before, and he can't do anything to us in a room full of respectable neighbors. All we have to do is not go off alone."

"I know," said Makejoye. "And still I wish I'd never accepted his offer."

Despite our misgivings the evening started off well. Those of us not performing were once again drafted to wait tables. In his own home Burke was served by his own servants, and had his dogs shut up somewhere, though the hard-faced men-at-arms who guarded the stairs provided sufficient discouragement to keep anyone from straying where they weren't supposed to go.

The first course was a clear broth that smelled of chicken and garlic, followed by some largish fish, breaded and browned. The people around the tables were becoming familiar; I saw the same faces I had seen at Potter's after-play performance and roving Lord Fabian's gardens last night. Joe Potter and Ebb Dorn were at the table I served, and Simon Potter sat in the place of honor beside Burke. In the few moments when his expression was unguarded, his mouth pinched with distaste. Judging by that, and by Lord Fabian's conspicuous absence, I deduced that this event was supporting a guild takeover of the town; I could think of nothing else that would place a man as powerful as Simon Potter in such close proximity to a man he clearly disliked.

Sheriff Todd was also present, though placed at the table farthest from his host. He'd retaliated by dressing far too plainly for the occasion, and I have to say he looked happier with his lot than Simon Potter did.

Most of the guests ate sparingly, evidently realizing the meal was far from over, so I was able to cadge a good dinner as I watched Rudy's performance.

I'd already seen most of his tricks in camp, but Makejoye was right about close quarters giving the audience a different perspective. And his shirtless state gave a very different perspective to the ladies, who cast him the covert glances women use when they want to stare but can't for fear their husbands will object.

Rosamund, I saw with some amusement, was not so bemused by Rudy's bared chest as to miss this, and I feared that several of the ladies at the table she served might suffer some small mishaps as the evening went on.

The next course was fowl, and much larger. There was duck in a sweet lemony sauce, turkey roasted with herbs, doves . . . well, you get the idea. After that came Callista's puppets. She wore a demure, high-cut gown and had somehow left her remarkable allure at the door, but the puppets made up for it. In deference to Burke's taste the skit was bawdier than any she'd performed so far; the puppets' wooden gestures lewd, their painted faces leering in the candles' flickering light. But the wit that made the thing sparkle came from Makejoye's fluent pen, and even

Simon Potter laughed aloud.

I was snickering along with everyone else when a lad pushed past me. He was about ten, with thick, straight hair, a bit grubby and far too roughly dressed for this room on this night. No one else seemed to notice him as he made his way behind the tables to Michael's side and handed him a folded piece of paper.

Michael gave the boy a few fracts—too many, by the skip in his step as he hurried off—but most of my attention was on Michael, whose laughter vanished as he read the note. He looked for the boy and took an impulsive step after him, but the urchin was already slipping through the nearest exit. Then he looked for me, half a room away from him, and when he caught my eye made an unmistakable gesture for me to stay where I was. He turned and followed the urchin out of the hall. After two years, you'd think he'd know me better.

I reached the exit too late to see him, but I could hear his steps in the deserted corridor that led to the rear of the house. That suited me well: If I couldn't see him, he couldn't see me, and if he didn't see me, I wouldn't have to argue with him.

My feet made little noise, even when the thick rugs gave way to bare wood as I passed into the servants' quarters. I had come within sight of my slippery employer when he reached the back door, and I had to dart into a darkened alcove to keep from being seen when he turned to look back before stepping outside.

Unlike Michael, I took the precaution of pushing the curtain aside to peek out before opening the door. The night was overcast, but enough moonlight leaked through for me to see Michael stop by the low stone circle of a fountain in the center of a three-sided courtyard. He looked around expectantly, clearly in search of the person that mysterious note had summoned him to meet. I'd bet gold to brass it was unsigned, and demanded that he come alone. Even Michael knew such notes are always a trap—unfortunately, that knowledge wasn't enough to stop my employer. If I opened the door, the sudden spill of light would alert everyone that he hadn't come alone, and possibly divert whatever catastrophe now threatened. On the other hand it would alert Michael, and he'd probably try to send me back to the hall, and then go find some other stupid way to do himself in.

It was the work of moments to extinguish the corridor lamps, so no one noticed the door easing open, and the soft splash of the fountain covered any sounds I made.

Even in the muted light the flower beds were lovely, and the shady arbors at the far corners would offer excellent concealment. But to reach them I'd have to cross the open garden, so it was fortunate that there was a balcony running the length of the main part of the house, which cast a deep shadow over the door. I slipped quietly along the wall into the even deeper shadow of one of the two sets of stairs that descended on either side of the courtyard. Unlike the last staircase I'd lurked beneath, these were high; I'd plenty of room to stand in comfort and curse my noble employer as he lingered obediently by the fountain, perfectly positioned for someone to shoot him, or whatever they had in mind.

We waited so long that my mental diatribe about people who did exactly what their enemies wanted them to had begun to repeat itself, when a startled cry broke the stillness.

I spun to the sound, which had come from the stairs at the opposite side of the courtyard. I was quick enough to see most of it—the man was falling. His shoulders and head hit the steps with a sickening crash, and his momentum was so great that his legs swung up, sending his limp form into another sloppy roll before he started skidding down the stairs.

Michael was already moving, so fast off the mark that he managed to arrest the man's fall before he reached the bottom.

I was standing on the lowest step when he turned, black blood staining the hands that had cushioned the man's head. A woman was screaming, very near.

"It's Ebb Dorn, the tapster." He sounded as stunned as I felt. "He's dead. I think his neck is broken."

Only then did the doors fly open, lamplight glaring as Burke's guards spilled out, charged up the steps, and seized Michael.

"A bit late, aren't you?" I asked.

The screaming subsided to choking sobs. Michael's expression closed as understanding descended on him.

"It wasn't me," he protested stiffly, no doubt sounding utterly guilty to a stranger's ears. "He fell. I was trying to stop him."

"That's for the sheriff to decide." But the armsmen's tight grip proclaimed that they'd already made up their minds.

Todd was fetched out of the party—discreetly. Master Burke wouldn't want his entertainment interrupted by so trivial a matter as a man's death. Dorn lay on the stair where Michael had halted his fall, so the sheriff might see the scene just as it was when they found it. The step beneath his head was dark with blood, his eyes open and blank. I shivered and looked away.

Then Todd arrived, his already grim expression

darkening to a scowl as he took in the scene. The guardsmen told their story, and it sounded cursed convincing with Michael standing there, his stained hands dangling.

"He didn't push him, Sheriff." I put all the assurance I could into my voice, squelching the despairing whisper in my heart, *no use.* "He was standing by the fountain when Dorn fell. I was under the steps over there, watching him."

"Sure you were," said Todd. He turned to one of Burke's guards. "I need you to ride to town. I want half a dozen deputies, the doctor, and a wagon to carry the body back. Tell them—"

"But it's true, Sheriff," a girl's voice said nervously.

We all spun. She was clearly a maid—pretty, as I'd guess all Burke's maids must be, with curly hair peeking from under a cap that looked as if it had been donned in haste. The lacing on her bodice was tight and tidy, as if she'd just knotted it. But it was the protective hovering of the young manservant behind her that really gave the game away.

"We both saw," she went on, gesturing to her companion, who looked profoundly uncomfortable. "We were . . . we were in the arbor there." She nodded at one of the leafy nooks that gave such good cover. "Then he came out and stood by the fountain. We hoped he'd leave, but he just stood there, like he was waiting for someone. He didn't budge till"—her gaze lit on Dorn and skittered away—"till that poor man fell."

Todd weighed this a moment and turned to the man. "Is that true?"

"Yes sir, it is. But, um, could we go now? I'm supposed to be on duty in the stables. If Master Perkin knew . . . Can we go, please?"

Todd got their names and dismissed them—if he didn't promise not to tell the master of house what they'd been up to, he didn't threaten them with it either. Myself, I was so grateful that I hoped they not only got away with it but married and had twins.

"What brought you out here, Master Sevenson?" Todd asked.

The story of the note sounded incredibly fishy, even when Michael produced it, and Todd's frown deepened. "Are you in the habit of answering an unsigned summons?"

"Yes, he is," I replied before Michael could. "It's a mental deficiency."

"It said someone had been making inquiries about Rosamund," Michael put in defensively. "I thought Father might have sent another bounty hunter."

Todd sighed. "And you, Master Fisk?"

"I saw him get the note and followed him," I said.

Michael looked indignant. "I told you not to."

Todd and I ignored him.

"So we were just in time to witness another accidental death," I went on. "The sheerest coincidence, no doubt."

Todd winced. "Did you see anyone at the top of the stairs before Dorn fell? Or aft—"

Light burst from the opening door and Joe Potter hurried into the courtyard. "What's going on, Lester? They say Ebb—"

His gaze found the corpse and his face went blank with shock. "What in the . . . Did he fall?"

"We're not certain," Todd admitted. "He came with you?"

"Of course," said Potter absently. "Guild's clerk. But how could this happen? He wasn't all that tippy. How could he have fallen so hard?" His face darkened, anger and grief replacing shock, and I took one man off my list of suspects—not even Hector Makejoye could have put on a performance like that.

"That's what I'm trying to find out," said Todd patiently. "He was with you; when did he leave the hall?"

"About . . . I don't know, fifteen minutes ago? Twenty? He just slipped out. I assumed he was going to the privy, or maybe out for some fresh air. It's hot in there. He left just after the start of the puppets."

About the same time as Michael and I. Potter's gaze found Michael, resting on his stained hands.

"No," said Todd quickly. "We've got reliable witnesses who saw Master Sevenson at the bottom of the steps when Ebb fell. He couldn't have done it."

"But he's . . ."

"Unredeemed." Michael sighed. "But this is none of my doing, Master Potter. And I'm afraid I'm a poor witness. I saw the man falling, and by the time I thought to look to the top of the stairs, anyone who might have been there was gone. Fisk?"

"I did the same," I admitted. "I heard him cry out, and looked up just in time to see him fall. I was watching Michael before that." So were the young servants, and the tumbling body had arrested their attention too. There could have been a dozen men up there, and none of us would have seen them.

"He fell hard," I said slowly. "Very fast. But I couldn't say whether he was pushed or not."

That was pretty much where the matter ended. Todd dismissed Michael and me and went on to question Potter about any enemies Ebb Dorn might have had.

Michael washed his hands in the fountain, and

we returned to the hall to watch Gloria dance, but I was barely aware of my surroundings. If not for the note that had summoned Michael to be blamed for the crime, I might have been able to dismiss it as an accident. As it was, it had to be murder—the second murder, if Michael was right about how Quidge had died. But except for that note, there was less to link us to Dorn than to the bounty hunter.

There had to be some connection—not only to the murders, but also to the harassment the players had suffered. Jack didn't believe in coincidence, and there were too many at work here. But I'd be hanged if I could make sense of the matter.

We told the players about it on the way home, and they were as shocked and baffled as we were, though more inclined to think it was an accident.

Michael agreed. In fact, Michael agreed so easily that my suspicions were roused, and I finally noticed the air of suppressed excitement about him, totally inappropriate in a man who had just escaped the gallows by sheer luck. If those lovers hadn't been there . . . I shivered again.

It wasn't till we were finally alone, in the familiar dark of the prop wagon, that I got a chance to ask, "All right, what are you up to? You know something."

"Not yet." The satisfaction in his voice sent a chill

washing over me, even before he went on, "But I should know more soon. We've a clue, Fisk! Our first real clue in this whole wretched affair."

"What clue?" I demanded, too alarmed for subtlety. Michael in pursuit of a clue is about as safe as a cocked crossbow in the hands of a jealous husband.

"Todd missed it, too." He sounded smug, curse him. "The lad who handed me the note, Fisk. He wasn't 'just passing through'—he was local. If we can find him, we can find out who hired him and trace the thread all the way back to the killer."

I got very little sleep that night.

## Chapter 10

# Michael

"How do you intend to locate one boy out of the hundreds, maybe thousands, in this town?" Fisk picked a stocking out of the tangle we'd left on the prop wagon's floor, squinting to determine if 'twas his or mine. He was unreasonably exasperated this morning, but he'd finally stopped asking if I realized where I'd be right now if not for the young lovers who'd witnessed Dorn's death.

I realized it so well that I'd slept rather badly, but as I told Fisk, the best way to be certain our enemies could do us no further harm was to reveal them to the law. And the first step was to find them.

"I've an idea about that," I told my squire. "I think you'll approve, for 'tis perfectly safe though it may cost a bit."

Fisk grimaced. "If it buys us some safety, I'd be

willing to pay. Although"—he rummaged in our bags and fished up my limp purse—"we'd better pawn another of Rosa's jewels if you're planning on spending more than a few fracts."

"We can't do that," I objected. "'Tis our quest, not Rosamund's. Oh, I should mention that I found her jewel bag—that false bottom is quite clever. If I hadn't known what the case should look like, I'd not have suspected it.

"I meant to tell you." Fisk looked even more exasperated, and I wondered why. "But so much was happening that I forgot."

"'Twas a good idea," I said. "So much so that I thought they'd be even safer in the Makejoyes' hidden cupboards, so I gave them to Mistress Gwen for safekeeping."

Fisk dropped the boot he'd just lifted and stared at me.

"I was going to tell you," I said. "But we were changing clothes to burgle the town hall when I found it, and after that I forgot." I had intended to tell him, for I'd a clear notion of his reaction should he suddenly find them gone. I saw no need to mention that I'd deliberately refrained from discussing it with him beforehand, fearing he'd not care to let the precious things out of his keeping. Fisk has reformed to my complete satisfaction, but some habits die hard.

"It figures," he muttered.

"What?"

"Nothing. But I hope your boy-finding scheme doesn't cost much, Noble Sir, because if you won't hit Rosa up for it, we don't have much to spare. I'm sure she'd be glad to loan . . ."

She might have, but I refused to ask her. I still had some lingering hope of overcoming her blindness where I was concerned. I had loved too hard, too long, to simply give up now. And in any case, my scheme was cheap enough.

We rode into town, since Chant's leg was fully healed, and my fear of being framed for further crimes helped me to forget that Rose had chosen Rudy over me for a long . . . well, minutes at a stretch.

There were few clouds, but the air had a sodden feel to it that I feared presaged a storm. The town seemed sleepy; people walked more leisurely in the heat, with their starched caps and collars wilting.

I accosted the first likely-looking urchin I saw. "Lad, would you like to earn a few fracts?"

He looked wary but approached me. I dismounted so as not to loom over him more than need be. I'd have knelt, but he was of the age to find that insulting. He had crooked front teeth and dark hair—though clean, it might have been several shades lighter.

"I'm looking for a boy who brought me a note last night," I said. "I mean him no harm nor trouble; I only wish to know who gave him the note."

"What's his name?" asked the urchin, sensibly enough.

"I don't know it," I admitted. "But I'd recognize him if I saw him. He's about your age, a bit taller, with thick, straight, light-brown hair and eyes a bit darker."

The boy snorted. "There's hunnerds of kids look like that. You're kidding yourself if you think you can find him."

"I probably couldn't," I admitted. "But mayhap you can. I want you to choose some helpers, and each of them, along with you, will get a brass roundel. For every youth they bring me who answers my description I'll pay two brass octs; one for them, one for the boy they bring."

"Huh," said the child. "One brass oct's not much."

"But as you said, there are hundreds of lads who might fit my description, so it should add up. And if I find him, the boy who brought him to me will get a silver roundel, and you get a silver roundel too."

A gleam lit the child's eye. "If I bring him, do I get both roundels?"

"That seems fair," I said. "But you'll want some helpers anyway. There's a lot of boys to go through, and I'd like to find him today."

"What happens if you don't?" the boy asked.

I thought fast. "The reward goes down. From a roundel to three quarts, then to a ha'."

"Got it." The lad nodded and darted away, and I turned to Fisk, torn between pride and apprehension. He really doesn't like to spend money.

Fisk's gaze was somber. "Noble Sir, I'm afraid we have a problem."

"What?" I confess I was stung; I had thought the scheme a good one.

"You've been traveling with me too long," said Fisk. "You're getting clever." A slow grin spread over his face. He turned Tipple and set off for a nearby shop.

"Where are you going?" I asked.

"To collect some brass octs. We're going to be paying out a lot of them."

Indeed we did. The boy I'd first approached—whose name turned out to be Jed Potter, though he claimed no relationship to our erstwhile landlord—deputized half a dozen cohorts, and they produced a parade of boys, of all ages, shapes, sizes, and walks of life. After I refused payment for a few who bore no resemblance to my description, the selection became less random.

There might not be hundreds of boys answering my specifications, but there were enough. I wondered if my enemies had deliberately chosen a child of common appearance and coloring to make a search more difficult. It seemed too much cleverness, but when I said as much to Fisk, he pointed out that our enemies had been clever enough to murder two men and almost get me hanged. He added that underestimating them would be a really bad idea.

Fisk appointed himself head of the exchequer, but the sack of sharp-pointed octs he wielded was growing thin when young Jed came panting up to us in the late afternoon.

"I think I've found him, Sir Mike, but he won't come. He says if you get him in trouble, his da'll wallop him; but I know where he's hid." He slowed a bit, eyeing me. "You meant it when you said he'd not get in trouble? His da drinks."

"I meant it," I answered. "His father need never know a thing about it, and we'll pay well for his assistance."

Jed thought that over, then nodded. "Follow me."

I took Jed up before me on the saddle, to his delight and Chant's snorted resignation. He directed us seaward, to the part of town where the docks and warehouses lay. 'Twas lower and flatter than the residential part of town, for here the river broadened, branched, and slowed, allowing the townsfolk to dig canals so the barges could bring in cargo.

Fisk was looking at the harbor, still some distance off. "I count eighteen sets of masts," he said. "Big convoy."

Jed snorted. "It's all right, but it's the only large shipment we've had this summer. My mam says if the wreckers scares off many more ships, this whole town'll dry up and blow away. Your horse is a destrier, isn't he? Like they ride in the tourneys? How fast can he go?"

"At a gallop in the countryside. In towns he only walks."

I saw what his mother meant—though the convoy was large, the harbor was less than half full, and only a few of the tall, creaking cranes were in motion. The cry of the gulls sounded louder than it should.

"That's still a lot of space to search," Fisk murmured. "I wonder how small the mysterious unidentified cargo is."

I wondered if Fisk realized that he wanted the wreckers to be caught as much as I did. The trail we followed must lead back to them—who else had cause to kill Quidge? But I confess I could think of no reason for the wreckers to harass Makejoye's troupe, or to kill Dorn. Two murders in the space of weeks—they had to be connected. But how?

"Nobody knows what the cargo is," said Jed. "Sheriff's men are keeping real quiet about it. They've tried to find cargoes the wreckers took before but they couldn't, and my mam says they won't find it this time neither. How much does a destrier eat?"

"A lot," I said.

Fisk looked startled. "You know the deputies are looking for the wreckers' loot?"

Jed grinned. "You think they can search every crate loaded onto all those ships and keep it secret? Everybody knows. The captains are sore about the delay, but I don't see why 'cause none of 'em would be leaving till after Hornday anyway. Old Nutter says we've got another big blow coming in that night."

Three nights hence.

"Ten-year-olds know they're looking," Fisk muttered. "No wonder they never find the cargoes. It's at the bottom of the bay now, whatever it was."

Jed nodded sagely. "That's what my mam says. There's another ship due in same time as the storm, the *Night Heron*, and Mam says likely the wreckers'll get it too. We're here, gents."

He guided us down a narrow alley between a warehouse and a cooper's yard, and into a small, weed-covered lot behind. It held naught but abandoned equipment, crates, and broken casks, and I saw at once why 'twould appeal to boys. If the lad we sought chose to avoid us, we'd never find him in this warren.

But Jed slid down Chant's shoulder, stepped up to the ramshackle remains of a water tank, and called confidently, "Come out and talk, you wart. I know you're there, and if you don't show your face, I'll climb up and make you."

For a moment I thought his confidence misplaced. Then a muffled thump sounded in the broken tank and half a face peered through a gap in the crumbling slats. A familiar half a face. My heart began to pound.

"You and who else," a young voice answered. "I'm not afraid of you, Jed Potter, and they're too big for the ladder."

"That's him, isn't it?" Jed demanded, and I heard Fisk fishing out our purse without waiting for my reply. Jed slipped away, and I tethered the horses and approached the old tank.

He was right about the ladder; I'd not have trusted the decrepit wood with a child's weight, much less my own.

"You've no need to climb down," I told the boy. "We only want to know who asked you to give me that note last night. And we'll pay well."

Fisk, always alert, pulled out a silver roundel and flipped it.

The eye widened, then narrowed warily. "No, you're

not getting me down. I didn't have nothing to do with it. I just brought the note."

"You've heard about Master Dorn's fall?"

"I didn't have nothing to do with it!" His voice grew shrill. "We used to tease him sometimes, but that was all. I didn't do *anything*." His breath caught.

"Of course you didn't." I said with all the assurance I could muster. "Master Dorn fell down a flight of stairs. How could your note be responsible for that?"

The single hazel eye searched mine, hope dawning. How long had this poor lad hidden, fearing he was somehow responsible for a man's death?

"You're sure? Honest, for real?"

"Yes. Think about it. Notes don't make people fall down the stairs."

"What if you did it?"

"Then Sheriff Todd would have arrested me," I said. "He was there last night, you know. You've done nothing wrong, and neither have I. But if you tell me about the man who gave you the note, mayhap between us we can make something right."

The boy's face vanished, and for a moment I thought I'd failed—then the hatch at the bottom of the tank squealed open and a pair of scuffed shoes emerged, followed by grubby legs, in grubby britches. He wasn't wearing stockings.

I sat on one of the crates to appear less threatening,

and Fisk followed my example. He spun the roundel between his fingers, making it flash. The implicit invitation drew the child several steps nearer, though he stayed well outside our reach. His face bore a spattering of freckles I'd not noticed in the candlelight; his expression was deeply suspicious.

"What do you want to know?"

"Who gave you the note?" I asked patiently.

The boy shrugged. "I don't know. Never seen him before."

Not a surprise, but disappointing. "Can you describe him?"

Another shrug. "He was old." For a boy his age that covered anything from twenty to ninety, but he went on without prompting. "His hair was almost all gray—just a bit of dark in it."

"Was he a sturdy old man," Fisk cut in, "or feeble?" He rose slowly, so as not to alarm the boy, and walked a few steps in an old man's tottering shuffle. The boy giggled.

"Not like that. He looked like a working man."

"And a stranger," I said thoughtfully. "I'd guess you know many of the working men in this town. Was he a sailor, mayhap?"

"No," said the boy. "They dress different. I thought . . ."

I waited.

"I thought he might be a farmer, in for the day. They sometimes look like that when they come into town."

"Were his hands hard or soft?" Fisk asked.

"Hard." The reply was confident. "That's part of why I thought he was a working man."

"Did you notice anything else about him?" I touched the place below my eye where I'd ridden into a jagged branch when I was only a little older than the boy before me. "A scar? The color of his eyes? Something about his clothes?"

If there was anything distinctive about the man, he hadn't noticed it, and I rather thought he would've. Those hazel eyes were as sharp as they were wary.

"A middle-aged countryman with no distinguishing features." Fisk summed it up. "That's even worse than a boy with straight brown hair."

He flipped the coin and tossed it to the child, who caught it but didn't run off. "You swear that note didn't have nothing to do with Ebb dying?" he asked again.

"I swear," I said. "It might have been sent to bring me to the scene, but he'd have died exactly the same no matter what you did with the note."

Color seeped into the child's face; now that we'd paid him, we had no reason to lie.

"Would you . . . What's your name, lad? Oh, don't look like that, I just want something to call you. I'm Michael Sevenson, by the way, a knight errant in search of adventure and good deeds, and this is my squire, Fisk."

The boy's eyes widened; then he shrugged, caring little for adult craziness. "Cappy."

"All right, Cappy. If you saw this old man again would you recognize him?"

"Yeah. The note didn't make him fall, but the people who sent it killed him, didn't they?"

He wasn't a fool, for all his youth.

"I think so," I said gently. "Though 'tis possible he simply fell. An accident."

Cappy didn't believe that any more than I did.

"Will you help us find the man? We'll pay you a sliver roundel a day."

"A ha'," said Fisk. "Unless this takes a lot less time than I think it will."

"What about it?" I held the boy's gaze with my own. "You say you used to tease Ebb Dorn. There aren't many ways you can apologize for that now. And you get to ride a horse."

His eyes flew to Chant and Tipple. "The destrier?"

"The destrier." I'd thought that might turn the trick.

"A silver roundel a day?"

"A ha'," Fisk repeated firmly. "Unless Sir Michael has another bright idea?"

"Sorry." I motioned for Cappy to follow me over to Chant. "This time we have to do it the hard way."

There wasn't enough daylight left, so we arranged to meet Cappy next morning. I worried that he'd not show, despite the lure of riding a destrier and being paid for it. But the next morning found him, tousled and yawning, beside the well where he'd told us to meet him.

He woke up swiftly when I swung him onto Chant's rump; he gripped the saddle's cantle with one hand and the back of my doublet with the other, and asked if we could go for a run, "Since the streets are empty, near enough."

'Twas not that early, and folk on their way to shop and work yard were streaming onto the cobbles. But the day's heat was not yet oppressive, so I promised him a gallop down the first empty, uncobbled road we came to.

We started our search among the farms at the city's western edge, simply because 'twas nearest.

At the first farmhouse the goodwife told us they had no men who matched Cappy's description working their farm, nor did the next house up the road.

But Merril's uncle Hap might be the man we sought. And so might Master Kellan, up Cowslipper Creek, or Master Ridgby who grew grapes over by Pirate's Lay, and had a brother who answered that description too, now that she thought on it. . . .

Sturdy old men with no distinguishing features were even commoner than brown-haired street urchins, and while the urchins had come to us, the farmers were all afield and we had to go to them. At least Cappy got his gallop before the heat set in.

What I remember most about that day is the dust and the stillness. Fat clouds scudded overhead, and I feared Nutter was right about a storm building. I saw no ships amid the waves' sparkling dance, and I hoped they were all making haste to shore.

Eventually we made our way inland. We spoke to old men amid fields of grapes, beets, squash, grapes, flax, more grapes . . . The early crops were ripening, and it had been a good year. Huckerston wouldn't starve, whatever the wreckers did to their trade.

As Cappy rejected man after man, we were able to add to our description and skip the old men shorter than Fisk, and the ones whose hair was all gray or white. But there were still too many of them, and we'd not visited an eighth of the farms that surrounded the city when we stopped for a luncheon of corn biscuits, cheese, and melon that a farm wife had provided. The melon brought back memories that seemed funny now, and we amused young Cappy with the tale of the skunk. He needed some amusement, poor lad.

"How long are you going on with this?" he demanded. "It could take *years* to visit all these farms. The guy could die of old age by the time we get there."

"Then you should be delighted," Fisk told him. "A silver ha' a day for *years* would set you up in a good apprenticeship."

"Huh," Cappy snorted. Unfortunately his mouth was full. He wiped melon juice off his chin with the back of his hand. "I've seen your purse, mate. You don't have that much."

"It won't take years," I said. "I should guess three or four days to cover all the countryside. Unless we get lucky."

I wasn't sure Cappy could withstand another day of squirming boredom; after a certain number of hours even a destrier is just a horse. By late afternoon I was wondering if I should give him the reins and start his first riding lesson now, or use that as a lure to bring him back on the morrow. Then our luck came in.

The old man in the dusty straw hat, propping braces under the sagging limbs of a laden apple tree, looked much like any of the dozens we'd already seen—but Cappy's slim body stiffened behind me, and the hand grasping my doublet tightened.

"Good sir," I called. "Would you spare us a moment?"

He looked up, startled at being interrupted in the midst of his own orchard. But he stepped forward willingly and removed his hat, revealing a sun-browned face and a pleasant smile.

"It's him," said Cappy. There was no doubt in his voice.

The old man didn't notice the boy until he spoke, and dismay vanquished his smile. "You're the lad I gave that note to—curse me, I feared it might be trouble." His eyes searched Fisk's face, and mine, resting on the small scar beneath my eye. "You'd be the one the note was for, wouldn't you, sir?"

"Michael Sevenson," I said. "I'm a knight errant, in search of adventure and good deeds, and this is my squire, Fisk. We've been looking for you for some time, Master . . . ?"

"Sanders." His brows had flown up when I introduced myself. Now his pale eyes crinkled, but he fought manfully and did not laugh. "I thought there was something strange about that note," he went on, the humor fading from his face. "I couldn't see why the fellow didn't deliver it himself if it was so urgent, or have the town crier carry it. But I couldn't see any harm in it, either. Was I wrong?"

His eyes were steady on mine and I couldn't lie. "The note itself did no harm, but we fear the man who gave it to you may have. A man fell down the stairs to his death that night, and 'twas your note summoned me to witness it—and mayhap be blamed, but for some luck and the goodwill of others."

"To his *death*? But how could . . . No, tell me everything."

"We'd prefer it," said Fisk, "if you told us everything. Who gave you that note?"

"I didn't know him." Sanders looked deeply concerned, as might any good man finding himself involved in such a scheme. "I don't go into town much these days, but I'd a broken plow blade for the smith, and I stopped at a tavern to talk to some friends. It was dark before I started back. A man stopped me on the street. He said he'd a note to deliver to a man at the big party Banker Burke was having, but he was late for another engagement and had no time to take it himself. Said he'd pay me a silver quart to hire a boy to take it in. I told him I'd deliver it if it was so important, but he said no, a lad would cause less commotion slipping through the crowd. He didn't want to anger Master Burke, disturbing his party." He turned worried eyes from me to Fisk, seeking understanding. "Burke's got a temper, and the money to back it up. So I looked about till I found a likely lad"—he nodded to Cappy, who nodded gravely in reply—"and sent him in. And now you say a man's dead?"

"'Twas not your fault, Master Sanders," I assured him. "It might even have been an accident. I believe the sheriff has called it so. Can you describe the man who gave you the note?"

My reference to the sheriff seemed to reassure him. "Aye, right enough. He was a youngish fellow, in his thirties I'd say, on the short side and very slender. Kind that gets bullied sometimes, as a kid." My heart was sinking—there must be thousands of such men in Huckerston, but he went on, "I thought it lucky he'd the brains to go for clerking."

"What made you think he was a clerk?" Fisk asked. At least that narrowed it down. There couldn't be more than three or four hundred clerks in a town this size.

"Well, he dressed like a clerk," said the farmer. "Kind of plain, with no lace or ruffles on his cuffs. But mostly it was because clerks' vision goes faster; all that reading and figuring, hard on the eyes. You don't see a lot of folk that age in spectacles."

\* \* \*

I stopped the first town-bound carter I saw—he was hauling a load of raw clay for the potteries—and paid him to take Cappy back with him. I told them both 'twas because Fisk and I had no need to return to town, but the truth was that if I couldn't share my tumbling speculations soon, I might burst. 'Twould be both unfair and dangerous to burden young Cappy with more knowledge of this affair.

Fisk paid him off, and the carter too, and we watched them roll away. The slanting sun of late afternoon cast humps of shade across the road—a welcome respite, since the day was hot enough to send sweat trickling down my spine. The moment they were out of earshot, I said, "Burke. It has to be Burke."

Fisk drew up Tipple's reins and set her walking in the direction of Makejoye's camp. "Not necessarily. Willy Dawkins can't be the only slim man in Huckerston who wears spectacles."

"But 'tis the perfect alibi!" I exclaimed. "Burke was at the party, but the note came from outside. And what better place to plan a murder than your own house."

"Almost anywhere, I'd think," said Fisk dryly. "It almost guarantees that you're one of the suspects."

"Not if you were in full view of every important person in town for the whole evening," I countered. "As I said, the perfect alibi. No one suspects him.”

“Except you, Noble Sir,” said Fisk. “How do you think he pushed Ebb Dorn down the stairs—not to mention why—while in full view of every—”

“He didn’t do it himself,” I interrupted. “’Twas probably one of those hard-looking men-at-arms. Just as ’tis they who go out and wreck the ships for him.”

“So you think Burke is the brains behind the wreckers?”

“Tell me you don’t think ’tis all connected,” I demanded.

Fisk’s scowl deepened, but he couldn’t deny it.

“Fisk, what’s the difference between a banker and a bandit?”

He gave me a suspicious look. “A banker makes you fill out contracts.”

“Exactly. As head of the Bankers’ Guild, Burke has access to all the insurance records—which means he has access to the ships’ manifests. He’d know better than anyone when to send his men to light the fires.”

Fisk was scowling again, as he does when he wants to disagree with me but can’t. “He’s pretty . . . trusting to send his men out without supervision. Most criminal gang leaders want to be there when the job goes down.”

“Well, I can’t see Burke scrambling up and down

the cliff paths. Besides, it lets him give himself an alibi. He probably has a subordinate among his men whom he trusts, who commands in his absence. A troupe of men-at-arms would be a perfect cover for a wrecking gang—he can hire them from out of town without anyone thinking it strange. People expect them to be tough, dangerous, and good with their swords. And they have no ties to the local community—'tis far safer than trying to find a local bully who'll commit murder after murder and not talk."

Remembering the cold-eyed men who'd handed me over to the sheriff, I had no difficulty thinking of them as the wreckers—now. At the time the thought had never crossed my mind. No more than it had crossed the sheriff's, or anyone else's.

"This man is clever, Fisk," I said slowly. "Underestimating him would be a bad idea."

"Well, I refuse to burgle his house," said Fisk. "One of those hounds was bad enough, and if his armsmen really are the wreck—"

"No one's asking you to burgle his house," I said. "I've never asked you to burgle anything—'tis always your idea. We have to figure out another way to find evidence against him."

"I don't want to find evidence against him," said Fisk. "If you're right, and you actually might be, I want to stay as far away from him as possible."

"I knew you'd agree," I said. "And think of—"

"No," Fisk said hastily. "I don't care about the reward. Besides, if everything is connected, then why is Burke trying to drive Makejoye away? He had a contract holding us here; if he was behind everything, surely he'd have canceled it."

'Twas my turn to frown. "Mayhap he feared 'twould draw suspicion on him. Or feared he might lose stature if he canceled the performance."

Fisk snorted. "He doesn't care what anyone thinks. Besides, he could have hired the Skydancers and paid Makejoye a cancellation fee. No one would have thought twice about it."

"Then I don't know. Mayhap the harassment isn't connected to the wrecking after all."

"Your theory has too many holes in it, Noble Sir."

"Do you think I'm wrong? About it being Burke?"

Fisk talks a great game about lying being the right thing to do, and he's willing to use indirection. But asked a direct question, he will seldom tell an out-and-out lie. At least not to me.

Now he sighed. "I don't know. You're right that Dawkins provides a connection to something, but there's still a lot of pieces missing. There's something about the way things have happened to the troupe . . .

Anyway, until we're certain, I'm not burgling his house."

"No one asked you . . ."

We worried at these questions on our way back to camp, and for once I was immune to the glory of the sunset. The birds started their evening chorus, the horses' hooves thumped rhythmically on the soft earth, and I could almost sense the storm hovering over the horizon. The wreckers liked to work in storms. I hoped the *Night Heron* was either early or very late.

I still thought 'twas Burke behind it; he fit too well, with his access to all the information the wreckers needed and his gang of toughs—not living wild in some hillside cave, but working in his household, right under the sheriff's nose. Who else could have ordered Dawkins to send that note? I wondered what excuse Burke had given him for not passing the note to me directly. Or mayhap Dawkins was in on the secret—'twould go far to explaining his nervousness, and why he dared not leave his master no matter how he was bullied. If what I suspected was true, the only escape from Burke's employ would be death. But what connection could all this have to Makejoye's troupe?

The players were gathered in the clearing when we walked in. Callista sat on the driver's bench of her wagon, sewing flashing glass gems onto a gown of blood red velvet, and Edith Barker and Rose were cooking.

Even up to her elbows in biscuit dough, she was so lovely 'twas like a knife in my heart. When I'd walked away from the severed tightrope, she had called for Fisk to go after me, but she hadn't come herself. The sight of her, laughing at Holly and Tuck's antics as they begged tidbits from Mistress Edith, made the wound bleed afresh.

Mayhap 'twas just as well that the prop wagon chose that moment to burst into flames—and I use the word burst advisedly, though 'twas not so mighty a thing as it should have been for the damage it caused.

The sound was more a *whuff,* like a great horse sighing; the flame crackle wasn't so loud as to disrupt conversation, but everyone in the clearing froze, as we gazed at one another and then sought the source of the sounds. 'Twas Edgar Barker who cried, "The props!"

Spinning as one, we saw the orange glow behind the windows and the yellow flame dance beneath the canvas roof. Wisps of smoke wound upward, and I was already running when Hector Makejoye exclaimed, "How could it start so fast?"

'Twas a good question, for the whole interior of the wagon appeared to be aflame, but at the moment I cared less for how it came to burn than stopping it. I snatched up a cook pot and ran for the stream.

The others had done the same, and they splashed into the water beside me, filling pails and kettles, the ladies' skirts drifting on the current. Cold water squished through my stockings as I ran back to the wagon, unbalanced by the heavy kettle. The dogs scampered about, getting in everyone's way, till a sharp gesture from Edith Barker sent them under their own wagon—even True went with them.

Flames were eating through the roof when I reached the wagon and saw Fisk kneeling before its closed door. A column of smoke rose above him.

"What are you doing?" I cried. "Get out of the way!"

"It won't do any good," said Fisk. "The doors are locked—both of them."

"Locked? But—"

Fisk shrugged and stood. "We'll do this the fast way."

The wagon's back step was barely wide enough to stand on, so he grasped the molding that ran down the corners, leaned out as far as he could, and kicked the door in.

I have to describe the result of his effort as a mixed success; though it enabled us to reach the fire, the sudden current of fresh air sent up a billow of flame and the roof began to burn in earnest. Fortunately the kick broke Fisk's grip on the wagon and sent him tumbling, or he'd have been singed. As it was, he rolled down the steps and then scrambled out of our way, as Falon and I stepped forward to cast water on the fire.

In all the chaos, no one noticed that the water from my pail did more good than that of the others. The power that dwelt within me had enhanced water before, to fight this ravenous red beast. It flowed more easily now, working almost without my consent. Which frightened me even more than the way the flames from the burning roof licked at the branches above.

"We should form a bucket line," Gwen Makejoye called, in a voice trained to carry.

"Wait," I shouted. "I've got a better idea." I ran to the front of the wagon, picked up the long wooden tongue, and pulled. I might as well have tried to pull a tree from the earth. Then the others came to grab the tongue, and Rudy leapt up onto the driver's seat, crouching below the flames, and pounded on the brake release.

With all of us pulling—and the brakes freed—the wagon rolled swiftly over the bumpy ground. We jogged into the stream, tripping on the water-smooth stones. 'Twas only three or four yards across, and knee deep, but there were no trees above it to catch fire.

We stood back a moment, panting. The flames worked their way down the outer walls now, and I was about to run for my bucket when Rudy said, "Tip it!" and grabbed one of the wheels.

'Twas harder than pulling the thing had been. I ended up crouching in the stream with my shoulder beneath the wagon's floor—I could feel the fire's heat through the wood—and then Makejoye cried, "Heave!" and I braced my feet among rounded, shifting stones and strained to lift it.

We got it up mayhap a foot before someone slipped and the wheels splashed back into the stream. The wagon rocked wildly, bits of flaming wood and canvas flying. One lit against my neck, stinging, burning, till I knelt and slapped a double handful of water over it.

"Again," Makejoye panted. "We almost got it." I heard the roughness of inhaled smoke in his trained voice. We hadn't succeeded, and we were tiring. Even as I braced my shoulder against the wagon and set my feet, I knew we'd soon be running for the pails, and that 'twould be in time to save very little—if there was anything left to save now.

Then a shout came from the bank, and three men ran into the stream to join us, jostling to find a place where they might help.

"All right now, heave!" Makejoye called again. Every muscle in my body locked in effort—but the wagon's wheels left the stream, dripping, spinning aimlessly. For a moment the wagon balanced, light on my aching shoulder, then it tipped over and a great billow of steam obscured my sight.

When it cleared, I saw Rosamund hurrying down the bank, her wet skirts flapping, her arms full of pans and pails. With the water so close, 'twas a simple matter to douse the remaining fire. Then, for the first time, we'd a moment to stand back, breathe, and think.

This couldn't be an accident.

"My sincere thanks to you, sirs," Hector Makejoye told the strangers. "We couldn't have managed without you. If there's anything to be salvaged, it's due to your efforts."

The strangers were countrymen by their clothes, and father and sons by their hooked noses and square jaws. The father shrugged. "Any man would do the same. We saw the smoke from the road. A forest fire does no one any good."

"You've our gratitude, nonetheless," said Makejoye. Well they deserved it; they also assisted us to right the wagon, hitch up our horses, and pull it back up the bank. Or mayhap I should say, what was left of the wagon. The roof, of course, was gone. The outer walls looked to be nearly intact, though their brave paint was cracked and peeling. But the inside was a charred ruin, and as for the contents . . .

"Ha," said Fisk. "Here it is." He burrowed into the wreckage like a rat and pulled out what was left of our bags. To my surprise, our medicine chest had survived more or less intact; we'd tucked it behind a set of flats, and the fire had burned more fiercely higher up—as if someone had poured lamp oil over the top of the stacked scenery, leaving the things on the floor out of range of the leaping flames. Most of our clothing, in packs on the floor, had survived. Our bedrolls, which had lain on top of the flats, were gone, and even the flats that hadn't burned were a smoke-stained ruin, along with the Barkers' hoops and platforms and the glittering fountain. The wagon itself . . .

"We're not going to worry about this tonight," said Gwen Makejoye firmly. Her teeth began to chatter, and her husband put his arm around her waist, pulling her close. "We'll go back to camp, get into clean, dry clothes, have some dinner, and face the mess in the morning."

It sounded sensible—especially the part about getting dry, for the sun had set while we coped with this latest catastrophe, and my wet clothes chilled my flesh. As for Fisk, digging our possessions out of the rubble had left him so smudged as to make a fair match for

Tipple. But 'twas impossible to keep from speculating, at least to myself. The players avoided each other's eyes, and when we returned to the clearing, Fisk wasn't the only one to look about sharply, as if the saboteur might have left some sign.

'Twas perfectly normal as far as I could see, but Fisk stiffened suddenly, as if someone had jabbed an elbow into his ribs—then a particularly bland, harmless expression swept over his countenance. I made my way unobtrusively to his side.

"What?"

"Michael, what don't you see?"

As foolish questions go, that one took a prize, even for Fisk. "What don't I see? Pink dragons for a start." But even as I spoke I looked around; the camp was as we had left it. A game of cards cast down by Falon's wagon, the half-peeled vegetables lying on a board beside the cook fire. The roasted pork shank that was to go into the pot with them was absent, but the conspicuously innocent expressions of the Barkers' dogs, and True's guilty look, accounted for that.

"What is it?" I asked again, but Fisk shook his head.

"Tell you later," he murmured. He refused to say another word even when we were alone changing into our borrowed clothes—Fisk's, lent by Rudy, a bit tight on his stockier form and Hector Makejoye's hanging loose on me.

The vegetables went into the pot with a bit of dried beef, and no one complained that the fare was lean, even though fighting the fire had put an edge on our appetites.

"In fact," said Hector Makejoye, "we'd better get used to tightening our belts. Until we can save enough to replace those flats, we're going to be on a very tight budget."

Rose made an inquiring sound, and Rudy took her small hand and tucked it into the crook of his elbow as Makejoye went on, "We're paid more for a play than any other act, lass. Unless we can erect a set, to give us someplace to change costumes and await our cues, we can't put on a play. And the less we make, the less we can save to replace our losses." His wasn't the only grim face in the circle of players.

"I have money," said Rose. "You can sell off the rest of my jewels—that will give you enough to make new flats, and repair your wagon too." She looked so happy at the chance to be of use that I couldn't have disappointed her, but Makejoye was made of sterner stuff.

"That's a fine offer, Mistress Rose, and I appreciate it. But when your uncle comes to claim you, he'll be expecting to take your jewels home too."

Rose's hand tightened on Rudy's arm and he laid

his over it protectively—a gesture that struck me as pathetic, despite my desire to punch him. They had chosen each other, but for all their courage and defiance they would never be able to withstand my father when he finally lost patience and came to fetch Rose himself. Rose was his ward; if she wed without his consent, he could have the marriage declared void, and he would no more consent to her marrying a vagabond player than he'd have allowed her to wed me. For a moment my heart ached, not just for myself, but for all of us.

"Since we need to start making money as soon as possible," Makejoye went on, "I think we have to leave. I'm going into town tomorrow, to tell the sheriff and Lord Fabian that we're pulling out as soon as we can get what's left of the prop wagon ready to travel. If they still want Rosamund to stay, then Rudy, Fisk, and Sir Michael can stay with her, and you can catch up to us later if that's your will. But whoever's been trying to drive us off has succeeded. We can't take another loss like that, and I can't afford to risk it."

Fisk's opened his mouth and then closed it; his expression was darkly baffled.

"But how could anyone set that fire with all of us here?" asked Edith Barker. Her husband clasped her hands in his.

"That's easy," said Falon. "They'd only to dump a

flask of lamp oil over the flats and leave a candle burning down to it. Soon as the flame hit the oil, poof!" His slim hands rose in a flyaway gesture. "Depending on the candle, it could have been set up hours ago. They could have been miles away when it happened." He didn't meet the others' eyes as he spoke, because the culprit could also have been cooking, or sewing, or playing cards—and that was far more likely.

I half expected Fisk to point this out, but he said nothing.

We washed the dishes by lantern light, then heated more water to wash our smoky clothes. And Fisk said nothing.

Makejoye's viol was so melancholy that night that it might have made any man mute. Indeed, most of the players were silent, for the seeds of suspicion had been sown. I wondered how long 'twould be before they sprouted into the petty backbiting and bickering that grow so well in the soil of fear and mistrust. It seemed to me that Master Makejoye stood to lose more than a few scenery flats if this went unsolved, for no one believed an outsider had played these "pranks." And how it connected to Master Burke or the murders I hadn't a notion.

But Fisk went right on saying nothing, and avoided all my attempts to get him alone. By the time we'd wrung out the last of our laundry and retired to the small tent Falon had pulled from his wagon, I was ready to strangle my squire if that was what it took to get some information.

"What didn't I see?" I whispered. Sound travels though tent walls as if they aren't even there.

"Pink dragons?" Fisk whispered back. "No, wait. I'll tell you as soon as Mistress Callista has gone to meet her lover."

"Her lover? What makes you think she'll go tonight?"

"You'll see," said Fisk, and rolled to turn his back to me. I considered grasping the edge of his blanket and rolling him right back over, but I refrained because a) Fisk can be unbelievably stubborn and b) when he gets this way, 'tis usually for good reason.

So I folded my hands beneath my head and thought about ways to prove that Burke was the chief wrecker—most of which, I must confess, involved burglary. The crickets, undisturbed by arson and stubborn squires, were giving a splendid concert, and the Green Moon cast shadow branches over the tent's roof. My eyelids were drooping when I heard soft footsteps approaching our tent. The door flap lifted.

"I just stopped to let you know I'm going out," said Callista mischievously. "You already know where."

She had to lean forward to look through the tent's door, a movement the bodice of that particular dress had not been designed to contain. My mouth was suddenly too dry to speak, even if I'd known what to say.

Fisk, however, had finally found his tongue. "We wish you a pleasant evening." He sounded so smoothly sincere that I choked on a laugh and began to cough.

Mistress Callista was not so inhibited. Her soft laughter made the fine hair on my arms prickle as she strolled off toward the road. Her lover had my respect.

Fisk rolled out of his blankets without a sound and parted the tent flap just enough to watch her go. His voice had been flippant, but his expression was so somber I sat up in alarm.

"Will she be all right? Should we follow her?"

"Yes and no, respectively," said Fisk softly. "Give it a moment. I want to make sure she's gone."

"Why?" I whispered. "How did you know she'd an assignation, tonight of all nights? What didn't I see?"

"Let's start with what you did see." Fisk let the tent flap fall and reached for his boots. "When we came into the clearing before the fire started, what was going on?"

"Nothing." I was dressing, too, as swift and silent

as my squire—who obviously had something planned, and would doubtless tell me about it in his own sweet time. "Rosamund and Mistress Barker were cooking dinner. The others were, uh, variously engaged."

Fisk opened his mouth to make some crack about love and blindness, but then thought better of it. "Hector and Falon were playing cards and Gloria was leaning over Hector's shoulder. Edgar Barker was oiling a horse collar, and Rudy should have been helping him but he was watching Rosa. Gwen Makejoye was sitting on her wagon bench darning stockings, and Callista was sitting on her wagon bench sewing gems onto the costumes."

He pulled on his doublet, and leaned forward to peek outside again before buttoning it up.

"Variously engaged, just as I said. Get to the point, Fisk."

"All right. What did you see when we came back into camp, after the fire?"

"The camp," I said impatiently, "just as we left it."

Fisk turned to me. Enough light soaked through the canvas for me to see one eyebrow lift.

"All right." I sighed. "I saw the cards, scattered where they'd been dropped. The cook table was set up; the roast was gone. The vegetables were only half peeled. True looked guilty." The scene came into my memory as I spoke, and my voice slowed. "Hector and Falon started looking over the wagon, despite what Gwen said about waiting. Gloria picked up the cards. Edith and Rosamund went back to their cooking, and Edith saw the roast gone and called all the dogs to be scolded . . ."

It had been amusing, even through the shock of loss and fear, but now my memory supplied a flash of white behind her. An apron and cap.

"Gwen Makejoye picked up her mending," I went on. "There were stockings all over the grass beside her wagon. Rudy was helping Rosamund with the vegetables. Callista and Edgar Barker picked up the horse collar, and the rags and oil he was using, and took them back to the tree where the tack is piled. I remember being glad they hadn't stored it in the prop wagon, or they'd have lost their horse tack too. That's all."

"Exactly," murmured Fisk.

"I think I should warn you, I'm about three seconds from swearing loud enough to wake the whole camp."

"Don't do that. You've almost got it."

"The whole camp, Fisk. One—"

"All right." He let the flap fall, turning to face me in the dimness. "What you didn't see was the gown Callista was working on. It was red, too. Very noticeable."

I frowned, trying to summon up a memory of Callista's wagon, of a red dress thrown carelessly over the seat or onto the ground. "I don't remember it," I admitted.

"That's because you didn't see it," said Fisk. "She put it away." He pushed the tent flap aside and crawled out. I followed, fighting my seething impatience. 'Twould serve him right if I did wake the camp.

The Creature Moon was down but the Green Moon was near full tonight, laying sharp-edged shadows across the grass. The charred corpse of the prop wagon stood off to one side. No one else seemed to be stirring, but I was surprised when Fisk walked right across the clearing, stopping at the remains of the fire to light a small twig.

I wasn't surprised to see him go to Callista's wagon and enter as if he owned the place. Indeed, at this point I was so filled with frustrated curiosity that I followed him right up the steps and closed the door behind us.

The tiny flame shed enough light to show Callista's bed, with a number of shadowy boxes stacked beneath it. On the other side hung the long row of costumes, which were Callista's charge—everything from beggar's rags to a queen's glittering finery. A crate beneath the shirts held a jumble of shoes and boots.

"What do you mean she put it away?" I demanded softly. Sound didn't carry as well through the wagon's wooden sides, but even a small flame would show through the windows. I was taken utterly aback when Fisk lit the lamp and turned it up.

"Don't worry. If anyone sees the light, they'll assume Callista couldn't sleep. And she won't be back for at least an hour—probably more."

"No one takes the time to put away their mending when they're running to fight a fire." Yet a chill crept over my skin as I spoke. I remembered the red velvet spread over Callista's lap—the flash of glass, even in the wagon's shade. But when we came back, she went to help Edgar Barker. He picked up the heavy horse collar, and she gathered up the oil flask and rags and put them away in the tack chest.

"That's right," said Fisk. "No one would take the time to tuck their mending out of sight—unless they had a compelling reason to hide it." He sorted through the rack and pulled out a red velvet gown. Ruby sparks flickered at collar and cuffs.

"You're not serious," I said, as Fisk held one of the larger gems close to the lamp. "Makejoye's people have never been in this town before. And no one trying to

hide stolen jewels would stitch them onto a costume,
to wear on stage in front of hundreds of people."

"But they're not performing in this town anymore,"
said Fisk. "Can you think of anything a deputy would
be less likely to inspect than an actor's costume, hanging in plain sight? Assuming they bothered to search
the troupe's wagons at all. As far as I know, they're
only checking the outbound ships."

"You think Callista hasn't got a lover?" I demanded.
"That she's been meeting . . ."

I remembered the men who'd chased me in the
moonlight, the hiss of a crossbow bolt past my ear,
and fell silent.

"Her contact with the wreckers," said Fisk. "Maybe
her boss, depending on whether she works for the
wreckers or their fence. If these are glass, it's good
glass, but I can't be certain in this light. Maybe not
even by daylight, without a magnifying lens."

"But we have to know!" I said. "If Callista is carrying away the wreckers' loot—"

"It explains why someone might encourage Makejoye
to move on, doesn't it?" Fisk hung the gown back in
the exact place it had come from. "I bet the wreckers
were dealing with someone in that other troupe—Red
Mask?—that used to come here regularly. I remember Makejoye talking about how they'd changed

their route. How inconvenient for Master Burke. Although . . ."

"What?" I was already searching Callista's boxes. "Everything you've said makes perfect sense, so far."

"It's nothing." Fisk's shrug looked more like a shiver in the dim light. "I just—"

"Here it is." I pulled out the chest that held the jewelry-making kit that Fisk had found so admirably complete. The tools were wrapped in the neatly stitched felt pouches Fisk had borrowed to keep them from clanking.

"Does everyone keep their tools wrapped for burglary?" I asked.

"Jewelers do," said Fisk. "To keep them from damaging any stones that might come loose." He pulled out a small kid bag and poured a pile of sparkling gems into his palm.

"Glass?" I asked. They were appallingly valuable if they weren't.

"I don't know," Fisk admitted. "If they're not, they'd be a very distinctive cargo."

"And one you'd be reluctant to dump into the bay," I agreed. "Especially if you had a way to smuggle them out of town. If only you could force the troupe to defy Lord Fabian and go. Fisk, these people are in danger."

"Now there you're wrong." Fisk spread his fingers, measuring the outside of the box with his hand. "The last thing the wreckers want is a murder investigation focused on Makejoye's troupe. . . ." He laid his outstretched hand inside the box—it was at least two inches shallower.

Even knowing what we were looking for, it took several attempts to find the catch that released the false bottom. The compartment beneath it was padded, and fit tightly enough to keep the dismembered settings of several necklaces, half a dozen rings, and a handful of earrings and bracelets from rattling. Several smooth gold ovals showed that some of the settings had already been melted down, but a few bracelets and earrings still held their gems. Callista wasn't quite ready to leave, but she would be by the time the prop wagon could travel.

"Here's our connection," said Fisk, eyeing the flaring stones. "You think this"—he held up a sapphire earring—"will get the sheriff's attention?"

"I think it will get Callista's if she sees it's missing," I said. "And there's still nothing to connect her to Burke."

"Who do you think she's reporting to right now? She doesn't strike me as the type to sacrifice herself to avoid incriminating her accomplices."

"No, but suppose she only met Burke's field commander?" I countered. "Look how carefully he distanced himself from the note—do you think he's dealing with Callista in person?"

Fisk eyed me with extreme misgivings. "Why don't I like the sound of this?"

"You never like any of my plans," I complained. "Get a gem off that dress, Fisk. Someplace she probably won't notice. I hate to disturb anything, but we have to get the sheriff's cooperation somehow."

"We could take him the whole chest," said Fisk. "And turn this over to the people who are supposed—no, the people who are *paid* to handle it." But he extracted a small pair of pliers and rose to pull the red dress from its hanger.

"We'll be paid," I said mischievously. "When we get the reward. Don't moan like that—you'll wake someone. Besides, I really do have a plan."

## CHAPTER 11

# Fisk

Michael got his revenge for my previous silence by refusing to tell me anything about his plan—he said he'd rather sleep than argue all night, a statement that didn't reassure me. Especially given the way he'd been acting since he got his "clue" to the wreckers' identity. A clue that seemed pretty shaky to me, but that lit up his face like a lamp, because . . . ?

He did sleep, curse him, while I lay awake and tried to devise some plan for getting him out of camp before one look at his open face sent Callista flying to her cohorts. Whoever they were, the wreckers killed.

Ordinarily I have little faith in the law, but I'd far rather have them handling this than Michael, and especially me. It was their job, curse it, and anyone else would have left it to them. Anyone but a self-appointed knight errant.

Not for the first time, I wondered how I'd gotten myself into this—but I knew the answer. Jack Bannister would have disowned me for being so foolish, if he could have stopped laughing long enough. *Caring about people will get you killed faster than anything I know,* he'd said, slapping my shoulder so briskly, the glass in my hand had spilled. I was trying to recover, in the time-honored way, from losing Lucy—a sentimental weakness Jack had no patience with. *You're sharp enough, Fisk, but you've got to do something about that soft streak of yours.* Jack had taken care of my soft streak himself, so effectively I'd thought it wholly eradicated until Michael came along.

I stayed awake worrying so long that I overslept—which wrecked my plan to bundle Michael out of camp on one of his hunting trips before Callista could see him. But my scheming and worrying proved unnecessary, for morning brought its own distraction in the form of a visit from the Skydancers—indeed, it was the rattle of their wagon pulling into camp that woke me.

Michael's bed was empty, so whatever catastrophe was going to happen probably already had. That didn't stop me from rolling forward to look through the tent flap before I'd even gotten my eyes properly open.

"We heard about your fire." Out of his paint, Master

Skydancer had a lined face, and his voice was as deep and rich as molasses. "We've just put some money into new stage sets—that's why I was so glad when this contract popped up. But it leaves us with a number of bits and pieces cluttering up our wagons."

The wagon whose arrival had awakened me was disgorging players and an astonishing number of items, including a near life-size statue that looked for all the world like marble, but couldn't weigh more than ten pounds by the way Gloria lifted it.

Michael, like the rest of Makejoye's troupe, had abandoned breakfast to help unload and exclaim over the treasures. Callista's well-schooled face was alight with pleasure as she pulled out numerous kegs of paint—partly used, by the spills down the sides, but very helpful for creating new flats. If Michael had given away our suspicions, nothing in her manner showed it.

I ducked back into the tent and dressed hastily, but in the bustle of unloading and heartfelt thanks, Michael's dealings with Callista were casual enough. The Skydancers didn't have enough spare canvas to replace more than a few of the damaged flats, but . . .

". . . but not all sets have to be two stories high," Makejoye pronounced. "We shall manage, indeed we shall."

Our escape was absurdly easy—Michael simply offered to go into town and tell the sheriff that Makejoye planned to leave soon. "'Twas Fisk and me he wanted to keep as witnesses, so it makes sense for us to talk to him."

Makejoye, caught up in replanning his plays around a smaller set and new props, was quite happy to foist the errand off on us.

As we turned Chant and Tipple onto the Wide Road that led into town, Michael commented, "That worked out well."

He looked content—happier, in fact, than he had since Rosamund had announced she was in love. What was going on in that twisted, honorable mind?

"Easy for you to say," I grumbled. "You got breakfast."

"I told you to take some biscuits before we left. If you didn't, that's—"

"Forget breakfast," I said, hoping he wouldn't remember that I'd brought it up. "Michael, what are you going to do?"

"Go to the sheriff, just as I said." Michael's smile was smug in the clear sunlight. It was already getting hot, but there was a breeze blowing off the sea for the first time in days. "It ill becomes a knight errant to lie."

"You did pretty well with Callista," I admitted. "I'm impressed."

Michael grinned. "It must be the company I keep." Then his grin faded—he turned and looked over his shoulder, searching the road behind us.

"Is someone following us?" I turned to look, too, and saw nothing but the dusty road and rustling trees. I wished I could dismiss it as nerves, but there was something pricking in the back of my mind, a sense of something running beneath the surface.

"I doubt 'tis anything," Michael murmured. "Who could be following us?"

"Every murderous thug in the fief, most likely. What are you up to, Noble Sir?"

"I'm going to report a crime to the local authorities," said Michael. "Which is the duty of any honest man."

And that made him look cheerful for the first time in days? But nothing we'd found had implicated Rudy . . .

"Nothing we found implicates Rudy in anything," I said.

"I'm not seeking to implicate Rudy," said Michael sharply. "You should know me better than that."

"I do," I said. "That's why I'm so worried. As your squire, don't I have a right to know what you're planning? Before you drag me into it?"

"Hmm." Lunatic logic always appeals to Michael. "I suppose you do." So he told me. I was glad I hadn't eaten breakfast.

"Where did you get this?"

The ruby I'd taken from the red gown glinted in Sheriff Todd's hand—and judging by his expression, it was neither glass nor irrelevant to the wreckers. Sometimes I hate being right.

Its existence got us an instant, and private, interview with the sheriff. Not that there was room for many deputies in this austere office—there was hardly room on the other side of his desk for the unpadded chairs in which Michael and I sat.

"From Callista Boniface," Michael replied. "Though she doesn't know we have it." He told the story of last night's fire, and how we'd discovered the gems and traced the note, while I sat in gloomy silence. What were the odds that Todd would be sane enough to veto Michael's plan? Not high. Whether Lord Fabian kept the town charter or the guilds succeeded in taking it from him, everyone wanted the wreckers caught. If Todd supported any plan that resulted in their capture, he'd keep his job no matter what happened to the town—and if we failed, it cost him nothing. But for Michael and me . . . This exceeded even his usual standard of suicidal insanity, and for what? Michael was the last person to care about the reward. I knew he wanted to stop the wreckers—so did I, though not enough to lay down my life for it—but this . . . He was too cheerful about it, too.

"This explains everything that's happened to the players," Michael finished. "Burke, trying to force them to move on. But we've no proof of his involvement, except that 'twas his clerk who gave Master Sanders that note."

He'd also been too cheerful tracking down the note. More cheerful than he'd been since he'd acknowledged Rosamund's choice.

"And on that basis you believe Lionel Burke is behind the wreckers?" Todd didn't sound as incredulous as I'd hoped. He'd regarded Michael throughout with the reserve any sheriff shows an unredeemed man, but the intensity of his gaze betrayed his interest, and Michael has learned to ignore being despised by respectable folk.

"Who had better access to the ships' manifests?" Michael demanded.

"Any other banker who insured them," I said, without much hope. "Anyone who gossiped with the clerk who filled out the forms. Or bribed a clerk for the information, or—"

"But none of them would send Dawkins as his errand boy," said Michael.

"That's assuming there's a link between Dorn's death and the wreckers, which we also haven't prove—"

"Dorn was acquainted with Master Quidge," Todd put in quietly. His brows knit with concentration, tacking what we knew onto what he knew. "They were seen together by several witnesses. I think Ebb was the 'old friend T' Quidge mentioned in his journal."

"T?" Michael asked.

"Ebb had a nickname," said Todd. "He didn't like it, so it wasn't used much, but folk sometimes called him—"

"Tippy," I said, suddenly remembering Potter's comment. The memory of Dorn's body, sprawled open-eyed on the steps, came with it, and my neck tingled as if brushed by a noose. Michael must be getting something out of this, but what? All he cared about was—

"But if Quidge told Dorn that he recognized a criminal, someone who might be one of the wreckers, why didn't Dorn come to you the moment he learned of Quidge's death?" Michael asked

"I don't know," said Todd. "But now that you've told me about Mistress Boniface, I may be able to find out.

If you'll excuse me?" He rose as he spoke, reaching for the sword belt hanging on the rack behind him.

"Wait," said Michael urgently. "You're assuming she knows who it is. Think how careful these men have been to cover their tracks. What makes you think their leader would show himself to Callista, instead of sending an underling?"

Todd's hands didn't even pause on the buckle he was fastening. "If she doesn't know, I'll trace the bastard back from whoever she dealt with. I assure you they'll tell me—in exchange for a quick death, if nothing else."

His expression was grim enough to convince me he meant it. It might even convince Callista. Michael looked quite startled, as if the thought that the authorities could torture information out of criminals had never occurred to him. It's rare enough, since there are legions of laws proscribing the judicial use of torture except in very extreme and unusual circumstances. But I'd bet the wreckers fit those circumstances. Good. Maybe Michael would leave it to—

"The wreckers probably know that," he said urgently.

"I don't care." Todd walked around his desk toward the door, and Michael rose to his feet.

"The moment you seize Callista, they'll know you

know," he said. "And the men she can identify will die!"

Todd stopped, his hand on the doorknob. He turned slowly. "Why do I get the feeling that you want something?"

"'Tis the same thing you want," said Michael. "To capture those villains before they kill again. I've an idea that might accomplish that, if you'll listen."

Instead of returning to his chair, Todd leaned against the door. His eyes were hard. "Why?"

I didn't like the man, but he wasn't a fool.

"Why what?" asked Michael blankly.

"Why do you care about catching the wreckers? You're already up for the reward. Why should I trust any plan you put forward? In fact, why shouldn't I believe that you're in league with the wreckers yourselves, and trying to put the blame on Mistress Boniface because you're about to be caught?"

I took it back—he was a fool. "Maybe because you aren't anywhere near catching anyone. Maybe because you couldn't find your own—"

Michael's upraised hand cut me off. "You were there, Sheriff, when we found that girl's body. Did you ever learn her name?"

"Of course," said Todd. "Rebecca Chase. She was a maidservant. The family she worked for was moving to another town, but her master got seasick, so they traveled overland, sending only their possessions by sea."

"Including their jewels," I said, the picture taking shape. "And their other valuables."

"And the money to open a new branch of their fur-importing business," said Todd. "But money's not easily identified, unlike a ruby necklace with numerous small stones, six round-cut stones, and one large oval stone, pendant, centered. We have good descriptions of the other jewels as well. Good enough to convict anyone who's caught with them."

But he didn't really believe it was us. At least I hoped he didn't.

"So Rebecca Chase was in charge of her mistress's valuables?" Michael asked.

"No, those were in the keeping of a company clerk and two guards," said Todd. "Along with the money. Mistress Chase's charge was the family's clothing and household goods. She was only a maid, after all."

"Lord Fabian might think that," said Michael. "I might even believe you felt that way, if I hadn't seen your face when we brought her body in."

Todd's gaze fell. He'd seen Michael's face then, too. "All right, Sevenson. What's this plan of yours?"

Michael's explanation sounded convincing. It was convincing, but it wasn't quite enough. Not that

Michael wasn't capable of the lunacy he was proposing simply on moral grounds. But he was too . . . eager? As if he thought success would not only prevent more tragedy, and avenge the dead, but actually right some wrong. As if it would . . .

He couldn't think that, could he?

"Are you thinking that if you catch the wreckers, Rosamund will fall in love with you?" I demanded.

I had waited till we left Todd's office—the sheriff already thought we were mad, and I'd no desire to confirm it. Though perhaps I should have. He might not have agreed to help us, and Michael might have given this up. Or he might have gone ahead on his own. I was glad I'd waited.

We were on our way out of town. The streets were busy, but a breathless silence lurked behind the bustle.

Michael sighed. "Not fall in love with me. I know 'tis not so simple. But she might at least see me as something other than her foolish cousin. Without that, I have no chan— Um, I'd like her to see more in me than she does now."

"Michael, my sisters still call me Nonny."

It made him laugh. "Rosamund isn't my sister."

*She thinks she is.* But I didn't say it aloud.

"Besides," he went on, "'tis not as if we sought to capture them single-handed. We need only befool Burke into confessing his part; then we can signal the deputies."

He turned in the saddle, looking over his shoulder. A street sweeper leaned on his broom, gossiping with a woman who'd set down her yoked pails to chat with him. An older woman and a young girl held a rug between them, while a young boy beat dust from it with a stick.

"We are being followed," I said. "I knew it. Michael, there's something wrong here."

"If we're being followed, 'tis probably just that the deputies picked us up early," said Michael. "They're supposed to follow us."

"Not this morning when we left camp."

"Fisk, you know how little these feelings can mean. It could simply be that someone's thinking of me. It could be naught but my own nerves."

"I wish you had the sense to be nervous," I grumbled.

Michael pulled Chant to a stop. "Our plan is sound, and we act on it with the sheriff's support. What harm can Burke do us in his own house, among his own servants, with dozens of deputies only a cry for help away? I'd have thought you'd approve of this. What troubles you so?"

"Nothing," I said, urging Tipple onward. Todd and Michael had decided it would be less conspicuous if we left the city and came back later, instead of going straight from the sheriff's office to Burke's bank. "Do you realize that this plan depends on you being able to *lie*? To a very clever and desperate killer? Convincingly? And you wonder why I'm worried?"

"For this," said Michael, "I can and will lie. You know I can do so if I must."

I did, too. When it absolutely mattered, Michael could lie almost as convincingly as I could. As long as he didn't have to keep it up too long.

"You're the one who keeps looking behind us," Michael went on. "More often than I am. And starting at sudden movements. And generally acting like a boy who's put a snake in his tutor's bed and not yet had time to dispose of the sack. What's wrong, Fisk?"

"Nothing!"

Michael lifted his brows. "Which is why you haven't asked about the reward? Todd said we'd earned it, and you didn't even ask how much it was. You can't tell me nothing is wrong."

We rode in silence till the tall brick arc of the town gate came into view.

"I don't know," I admitted finally. "I just feel . . .

This plan isn't half as safe as you seem to think, but it's not that. There's something . . . familiar about this."

Familiar, and deeply disturbing.

"Familiar about what?"

"The pattern of events. It's something Jack taught me, but it's more than that. I've been trying to put my finger on it for days, but I just can't."

"Mayhap 'tis similar to a dream you've forgotten," said Michael.

The clop of the horses' hooves on cobbles gave way to the thud of hooves on earth as we passed through the city's protective wall. It was unlike most towns, in that only a handful of buildings had moved outside the gate, and orchards and fields commenced in a few hundred yards. The sea was to our left, but I couldn't see it from here—just fields, rolling away. Soon, we'd find a farmhouse and buy something for mid-meal. And then turn around and go back.

"I don't have any Gifts. I don't have prophetic dreams."

"Then mayhap 'tis similar to something that happened in your past. Something that frightened you." Michael's voice held only sympathy, but a chill shivered over me.

"I never did anything like this before," I said. "I'm not that crazy. Maybe it's just the storm."

I gestured toward the unseen sea. Dark clouds were gathering on the horizon.

Michael's eyes narrowed. "Nutter prophesied 'twould come in tonight, didn't he? And I don't think the *Night Heron* has made port. We have to do this, Fisk. Or at least I have to."

"Don't be ridiculous. You couldn't possibly pass yourself off as a criminal without my help." Though I was half tempted to take him up on it. It wasn't the storm. It wasn't a dream, or a premonition, or any such foolishness. There was something wrong. Something that was right in front of me, but I couldn't see it. Something . . .

Or maybe there was nothing, and being with Michael so long really had driven me mad. Be hanged to it.

"Let's get a meal," I said. "Unlike some people, I missed breakfast."

The storm was coming in. The sun still beat down, but the morning's pleasant breeze had risen to a wind that tossed the horses' manes and blew Michael's hair into his eyes. The people in the streets hurried about their errands.

Michael and I drew our horses to a stop before Lionel Burke's bank. It was a medium-size building, brick of course, with the windows covered by wrought-iron grills, in a finely made pattern of vines and leaves with the Bankers' Guild's crest in the center. This, not his mansion, was the heart of Burke's power. I'd bet most of Burke's magica hounds spent their nights here, and probably most of his guardsmen as well—when they weren't out wrecking.

I took a deep, panic-stilling breath and summoned up a confident smile.

"Can you still see the deputies?" I murmured, sliding from Tipple's saddle and tying the reins to the hitching post.

"The three we spotted," Michael confirmed. "And I think I've identified two more, though I'm not certain."

For once, I found being followed by a large number of deputies reassuring.

"And you remember that I'm going to do most of the talking?"

"Yes, Fisk." Michael sounded amused, curse him. "You can do the talking."

But he was the one who walked up the steps to the dark wood door, leaving me no choice but to drag my reluctant feet after him. I told the bank clerk, at his desk near the entry, that we wished to see Master Burke, no we hadn't an appointment, but we'd wait.

I hoped the deputies would wait too.

The suspense told more on Michael than on me. Now that the scam was on, the clerk's attentive eyes upon us, I found my heart beating steadily, the discipline of the act relaxing my tight shoulders so no signs of nervousness should pass themselves on to my mark.

*If you're tense, they'll tense up too,* Jack had taught me. *Without even knowing why. And then they'll start to wonder why.*

Michael's tension wasn't obvious, but he was too quiet, his eyes darting to follow the men who came and went from the bank's inner offices.

Then a boy, in a sailor's rough britches and soft shoes, rushed in to cancel his captain's appointment— they were battening down for the storm—and Master Burke could see us now.

His office was opulent, the brocade of the drapes alone worth enough to make a burglar a goodish haul. The chairs before his desk were padded, and I relaxed into one and gave him a confident smile. I ignored the bored-looking guard who stood behind him.

Burke's doublet today was a deep green linen, cheaper than velvet but much cooler. Though there was no lace at his cuffs—bankers have to sign the contracts their clerks write—the finery dripping from his wide white collar made up for it.

"Good day, gentlemen. I understand this is an unscheduled— Wait a minute." His small eyes narrowed. "Don't I know . . . You two are from that player, Makejoye. I thought I told him to settle everything with Dawkins."

"You did, Master Burke." I put enough assurance into it to stop his gesture for the guard to show us out. "We're not here on Master Makejoye's business. We're here on yours."

He looked from Michael to me, interest replacing indignation. "Very well, Master . . . Fisk is it?" He glanced at the door clerk's note on the desk before him. "And Sevenson. I've had profitable tips from less likely sources. But I warn you, I've no patience with rogues who waste my time."

"I suppose this counts as profit," I said. "You get to keep your life."

Burke's shrewd face tightened. The guard, suddenly alert, stepped forward, but I smiled and waved him back.

"No, no, nothing like that. All we're offering you is silence. And our services. Callista got sloppy. We think you could use better couriers, Master Burke. Such as Michael and myself."

"Callista," said Burke slowly. "That remarkable puppeteer?"

"We found the jewels," said Michael. "We could have gone to the sheriff, but we didn't. We came to you."

"Jewels?" Burke drawled. His expression was very contained. "In Callista's possession, I take it?"

"You should know," I said. "And it should be profitable for both of us if the sheriff doesn't. Know, that is. Isn't that reasonable?"

"Hmm," said Burke. "This is blackmail, then."

"No, no," I said. "This is the beginning of a long and rewarding partnership. We're not blackmailing you—we're offering to take Callista's place. For a slightly larger cut, but that's only fair because we won't get caught. And she did."

Burke's eyes were on his pudgy hands, clasped on his desk. "I see. But Master Fisk, what makes you think these jewels have anything to do with an honest banker like me?"

"I believe that kind of candor is only given to partners. Don't you?" My smile was wide, and the nervous sweat wetting my shirt didn't show.

"And you, Sevenson." Burke turned to Michael. I'd hoped he wouldn't do that. "What's your part in this?"

"An equal cut," said Michael coolly. "But I can also offer proof of our . . . good character." With a somewhat bitter smile, he unbuttoned his cuffs and held out his wrists, the broken circles dark on his pale skin.

Burke drew back as far as his heavy chair would let him. "Very well, gentlemen," he said. "You've convinced me."

Triumph flashed in Michael's eyes as they met mine.

Burke opened his desk drawer, pulled out a small bell, and rang it briskly. "I'll send for—"

The door behind him burst open and his guards raced in. The guard behind Burke dragged his master's chair back—no small feat—and leapt in front of Burke, drawing his sword.

"Master Burke, no need for this." I kept my voice as calm as my pounding heart allowed. The tip of a sword came to rest just above my collarbone. I heard more guards coming, in response to the clerk's urgent shouts. "You're far too clever not to realize that we'd have, ah, obtained some insurance before we came here."

"Since the two of you are obviously deranged," said Burke, rising to his feet, "I don't much care. Rogers, take them to Sheriff Todd. They've got some bizarre idea that they can blackmail me over something or other—well, they've been babbling about jewels, so it may be related to those cursed wreckers. And this one"—he gestured to Michael—"is unredeemed. Barrow here heard the whole conversation—he can tell Todd what they said."

My confident smile vanished. I sat up, despite the sword pricking my throat. "You want them to take us to the *sheriff*? But that's . . ." Insane, impossible, some sort of trick . . .

"That's right," said Burke. "Now, if you please, Rogers."

Michael's jaw had dropped, but no words emerged. It was up to me.

"Wait," I sputtered. Firm hands pulled me from the comfortable chair. "I don't . . . You can't . . ."

He could. The guardsmen dragged us down the corridor, through the outer office, and into the street.

"What's going on here?" I cried.

"We're taking you to the sheriff," said Rogers. He looked to be in his late forties, with a soldier's scarred hands and hard-muscled arms. "Shut up about it. Or we'll make you."

I shut up, not resisting as they pulled us down the street to the town hall, ignoring the startled, interested stares of the people they passed. They passed a lot of people, I was glad to see—enough to provide plenty of witnesses if our bodies should turn up unexpectedly. Not to mention the deputies, who followed, wide-eyed, behind our procession. So they probably didn't intend to kill us, but that made it all the more confusing. Unless, of course . . .

They led us up the town hall's steps, and then down to Lester Todd's office.

Todd listened patiently to Barrow's account of our conversation with Burke—perfectly accurate, allowing for the difference in point of view, though I rather objected to hearing myself described as "this slimy fellow."

Michael stood, his gaze on the floor. He bit his lip once, when the testimony was particularly damning. Eventually Todd dismissed Burke's men, with thanks to them and their master, whom he promised to thank in person "when this strange affair is settled."

Then he dismissed his deputies, came back, and sat down at his desk. "So, gentlemen," he said mildly. "You were wrong."

"So it seems." Michael's voice quivered . . . with laughter. "As wrong as it gets. He'd never have reacted thus if he'd anything to do with the wreckers."

Todd was grinning too.

"But we weren't wrong about Callista." Michael sobered. "Nor Dawkins. . . . Or some man who wears spectacles."

"Some man who wears spectacles," said Todd, "about sums it up. But it was worth a try. Now I'll have a talk with your Mistress Callista, she'll tell me who hired her, and we'll arrest them before they kill again. The reward's still yours—you did well. But I'd rather capture Mistress Callista without your . . . assistance. If you don't mind."

He then departed, detailing a brace of deputies to keep us for at least an hour, so he had a clear shot at Callista whether we minded or not.

It was an hour and a half before they let us go, and I was delighted to be out of it.

"That was embarrassing," I remarked. I took Tipple's reins from the deputy who'd fetched the horses from Burke's at Michael's request. Michael had grown quieter, his original humor fading as my heart lightened.

Swinging into the saddle now, he looked downright glum. Thunder rumbled in the distance.

"Cheer up," I said. "They'll have Callista arrested and out of the way before we even get back. We'll probably pass them on the road."

"'Twill be hard on Makejoye and the others, to lose a troupe member in such a terrible way." Michael set Chant toward the town gate at a trot. The streets were almost empty now. Shops had closed, or at least looked closed, with stout shutters fastened over their windows.

"Rosamund won't blame you once she knows who

Callista was working for," I said. "None of them will."

It's hard to converse on a trotting horse, but Michael said shortly, "I should have been there."

I didn't see why, but he was obviously determined to get there now, so I bit back my sensible suggestion that we get a room for the night and weather the storm there, instead of in a small, and probably leaky, tent.

Michael pressed on rapidly till we passed through the town gate. The wind, no longer blunted by the buildings, felt strong enough to make the horses stagger, though they didn't. The dark wall of advancing clouds looked ominous to me, but Michael pulled Chant to a walk, so he must have thought we could make it to camp before the storm hit.

"None of them would tolerate her helping the wreckers," I went on now. "And you're responsible for catching them. I wonder how much that reward is."

It made his lips twitch, but he sobered immediately. "I wonder if Callista's crimes will get Makejoye's troupe in trouble with the Players' Guild."

"Oh." That was a legitimate worry, but . . . "Probably not, if the local authorities clear them. Which makes me glad we reported all the harassment they suffered to Todd. It should be perfectly clear that the wreckers regarded the rest of the troupe as enemies—or at least expendable—and that Callista was their only cohort. Though I wonder . . ."

The insight niggled at the edges of my mind. "I don't think the wreckers planned the things that happened to Makejoye's people." My voice was almost lost in the tearing wind. "The harassment, the two murders, were a lot subtler than bashing people over the head. I think there was another hand, another mind, behind it."

"Callista herself?" said Michael. "She has a subtle mind."

"Um." That was true, but it didn't quite account—

"I just hope that Ro— they don't feel I blundered too badly, sending the sheriff in on them like this," Michael fretted. "I meant to have the mastermind in custody, the taking of Callista all but unnoticed by the authorities. And the guild."

"It's not your fault it wasn't Burke," I told him. "Frankly, I'm glad it wasn't. If he was the chief wrecker, all the deputies in the world hiding outside wouldn't have made much difference to what happened in that room."

"Um," said Michael, turning to look over his shoulder.

"What?" I looked back too—nothing but empty road, for its bends had taken us out of sight of the walls, and all sensible people were holed up to weather out the storm. Aside from a coach coming rapidly toward us, hoping to reach the town before it hit, we'd seen no one on the road at all.

"'Tis likely nothing," said Michael. "Just nerves. I've been feeling it on and off all day, and that's cursed foolish."

It was, but I've seen Michael's Gifts at work too often to dismiss them. It might be something harmless, or trivial, but it wasn't nothing.

"You felt it this morning, didn't you?" I asked, pulling Tipple off the road so the coach could pass.

"Yes, but no one would have followed us then, and no one would want to follow—"

The coach pulled up beside us and stopped. I gazed at it in surprise; surely no one needed directions this close to town. Then, in the brush behind me, I heard the creak of a crossbow being spanned. And then three others.

I turned slowly, lifting my empty hands away from my sides. I'd seen enough of Master Burke's guardsmen to recognize two of the four, though I didn't know their names. But if it wasn't Burke, who—

"Hello, my boy. You're keeping strange company these days."

My heart contracted so powerfully that I hunched in

the saddle. Then it began to pound sickly: fool, fool, fool.

I turned back to face the owner of that sardonic, *familiar* voice. "Hello, Jack."

He looked the same; only a little taller than me, of indeterminate age. I had seen him pass for as young as twenty-four and as old as fifty-four. I had seen him pass for merchants, miners, clerks, and, on one memorable occasion, a sheriff. He had even passed for my friend, but I'd learned better than that.

"You're keeping strange company as well." I let my gaze sweep contemptuously over the guardsmen, the wreckers. Two of them pulled Michael from Chant's saddle, binding his wrists, taking the dagger from his belt and his sword from the sheath he'd strapped to the saddle. I prayed he'd show some sense for once in his life. Crossbow beats fists every time.

"I thought you never got involved in hanging crimes," I added, gazing into Jack's eyes, which were hazel, or gray, or brown, depending on the light. He kept his medium brown hair at medium length like an actor's, and for the same reason.

"I haven't committed any murders," he said. "Though a judicar might argue the point. I'm only an expediter, if you will. Not part of this organization at all."

"I grant you, none of the players were killed," I said. "I recognized your touch there, though I was too cursed dense to realize it." Fool, fool, no wonder our tormentor's style had seemed familiar. "But what about Quidge and Dorn? You can't tell me you'd nothing to do with that."

The guards finished with Michael and shoved him into the coach; then it was my turn. I paid little heed to the rough hands that pulled me from the saddle and tied my wrists with painful, competent tightness. There was no chance they'd miss my boot dagger. Jack was the one who'd taught me to carry it, and he smirked when they handed it over to him.

"Ah, the bounty hunter and his weaselly cohort." Jack waited till they hauled me into the coach and pushed me down on the seat beside Michael. Two of the guards sat opposite us, bows at ready. Jack sat between them, looking relaxed despite the crowded quarters. As well he might—at this range no one could miss. And the other two would bring the horses, so there was no chance they'd wander back to camp and alert the players that something had gone wrong.

"I didn't kill either of them," Jack went on. "I just pointed out that if Quidge was obviously murdered, his blackmailing friend might go to the sheriff before we had a chance to learn his identity. But if it looked like an accident . . ."

"Dorn was fool enough to blackmail the *wreckers*?"

"Amazing, isn't it?" Jack agreed. "Beyond mentioning

that a subtle approach would draw less attention, I didn't have anything to do with his death, either. Well, I gave them a few pointers. Subtlety isn't what you'd call their strong suit. Though their approach is quite efficient, all in all."

Thunder rumbled over his last words. The sky was darkening rapidly.

"Efficient," said Michael contemptuously. "And I suppose you've nothing to do with the slaughter or drowning of the dozens of sailors and passengers aboard those ships."

"Nothing at all," said Jack. "I've been in town for only a few months—sent by my employer to see why certain deliveries had been delayed. Fortunately, I'd worked with the fair Callista some years ago, and we were able to maneuver Lord Fabian into sending for her troupe without his ever realizing that he was help-ing us get our shipments back on schedule."

"Your employer?" I was so startled, I almost for-got the sharp-barbed crossbow bolts. "I thought you worked alone, or with just one partner. To lower the risk"—my voice went cool—"that someone might set you up to take the fall."

"Now, now," said Jack cheerfully. "You can't say I didn't warn you."

Michael followed this with interest, though his face

was rather pale. "You two were partners. And you set Fisk up to take the blame for something you did?"

"Something we did," said Jack. "I was sorry for it—best apprentice I ever had, young Fisk. But the attention that particular scheme generated was far too intense."

"So it was." I'd nearly died twice, eluding the law.

"And he needed that final lesson," Jack finished. "I'd been telling him for over two years to trust no one, but he just couldn't seem to take it in."

"You bastard," Michael hissed.

Jack eyed him with amused tolerance. "Fisk understood."

I had. I couldn't say he hadn't warned me.

"But I don't understand your working for someone else," I said. "For just that reason. How can you trust him? Assuming that you aren't inventing him, so you can finger someone else if the judicars come down on you."

Jack grinned. "It's a good idea. I'd forgotten how sharp you are. But no, I really do have an employer. He's a respected cargo broker—"

"A fence," I supplied.

"A fence," Jack admitted. "Among other things. But fencing stolen goods isn't a hanging crime unless the fence is the one who instigates the scheme. The wreckers' organizer came to my employer, not the other way around. Though if the judicar was feeling particular, the fact that my employer . . . assisted him to find the right men might be a problem. But in Tallowsport the judicars are as far from particular as it's possible to get. My employer's a pillar of the community. A winner, Fisk." Jack sorted everyone into winners and losers.

The carriage turned toward the sea. This road was rougher, and the horses' pace fell to a walk.

"You'll like Tallowsport," Jack went on. "And my employer will appreciate you. He can always find a place for talent."

Michael's jaw dropped. "You're offering Fisk a job? After what you did before? He'd have to be mad—"

"He'd be foolish to turn me down," said Jack softly. "He isn't a fool."

My pulse beat thickly. "Michael too," I said.

"My dear boy, I'll be lucky to convince them to let you live," said Jack. "My employer has influence, and I've gained some small respect on my own account—though our pretty Callista's failure may have diminished that."

"The sheriff has gone to arrest Callista," said Michael. "You're the one who should be bargaining for your life."

At least he realized the stakes.

The guards snickered. Jack was smiling. "Yes, he's going for Callista. But fortunately, your little farce with Burke gave us some warning. The sheriff will find all the players in camp and no sign of the jewels. Or if she can't get rid of the evidence without her fellows seeing it, he'll simply find our poor Callista. In no shape to tell anyone anything. Ever."

Michael's skin went a shade paler. "They've killed Callista?"

"Only if she doesn't have time to hide the evidence. She may be happily lying to them, even as we speak."

I hoped she was, but remembering the number of gems that had flashed on the costume rack . . . The others would be readying the camp to face the storm—what excuse could she give for carrying off an armload of costumes? I hoped Callista was the only one in danger. At least Todd and his men were there now, whatever had gone on before. Which was good. On the other hand, if he was there, he couldn't be here, which was very bad indeed. The coach rolled down a small hill and lurched to a stop. I caught Jack's gaze with all the intensity I could summon. "Michael too."

"Please don't be a fool," he said, and opened the door and jumped down.

The guardsmen dragged us out. The storm was

close now. Standing as we were, in a clearing on the edge of the sea cliffs, it drew the eye like a charging panther. Claws of lightning arced down to the water, and thunder grumbled. The wind made me stagger. But for all its ferocity, it wasn't the storm that was going to kill us.

There must have been thirty of them, Burke's men all, I thought. No masks hid their faces, but that hardly mattered since a low rise concealed us from the road— necessary, since the trees this close to the cliff were sparse and stunted. To our right was a tall mound, the remains of something man-made, for its slopes, covered with rocks and tufted grass, were too steep to be natural. Too steep to climb easily, so the wreckers had laid a ladder against it to carry their pitch-covered logs up to the top.

They were going to bring in a ship.

Michael made a choked sound of protest, twisting in his captors' hands. One of them knotted his fist in Michael's hair and hooked a foot from under him, and he fell to his knees.

A slim man in a long dark coat turned from the edge of the cliff, folded a spyglass, and put on a pair of flashing spectacles. He didn't look nervous at all.

"Willy Dawkins," said Michael. "I was expecting him."

"You were?" I said.

"Think about it, Fisk. Who else could have arranged to hire those men as Burke's guards? And arrange their schedules so that they wouldn't be gone when Burke needed them? Who had access to the same information as his master? A clerk can spend hours in the files."

One of the guardsmen carried our weapons to Dawkins, then went on to the cliff and pitched them over the edge—if the wreckers kept them, someone might recognize them. Another man took the spyglass, and Dawkins strolled forward and looked down at Michael. The guard's hand twisted in his hair, forcing his head back. It must have hurt, but Michael's face didn't show it. His eyes, meeting Dawkins', were calm.

"The sheriff knows you sent me that note," he said. "He knows everything we know. He'll put it together eventually, no matter who Callista's contact was."

"That was Master Markham here." Dawkins waved a casual hand toward Jack, who'd gotten a lot quieter after we arrived. "Not that it matters. She won't be telling anyone."

My mouth went dry. I hoped Callista's death had been quick, but I was too terrified for myself to worry about it much.

"What I'm more concerned about," Dawkins went on, "is how you linked this to good, fat Lionel."

There was no doubt in his voice that he'd find out—no trace of the nervous, pathetic clerk. The man must have spent most of his adult life acting, but if this was an act, it convinced me. I glanced at the hard-faced killers who surrounded us. Some of them were grinning, some looked on with an indifference I found even more frightening. No, this wasn't an act, and Michael's only hope was to hold back the information as long as—

"We traced the note back to you," said Michael, "through the boy and the farmer."

I made a stifled sound. One of my guards wrapped his hand in my hair and shoved me down. I hardly noticed the pain, as Michael went on, "The farmer didn't know your name, but he gave us a very good description. Good enough that Sheriff Todd will realize you must be the one who killed Callista—only the men at Burke's bank knew she'd been discovered. With your tie to that, your tie to the note, and Burke having proved his own innocence, you're the only one who could have done it. It will all have been for nothing, and if you light those fires, it will only be the worse for you."

He said nothing about it being worse for them if they killed us. He wasn't thinking about anything but that ship out there. An idiot to the last. Noble Sir.

Dawkins opened his mouth to speak, but the thunder crashed, drowning him out. He waited till the echoes died. "So now I'm supposed to . . . what? Surrender to you? Drop everything and flee for my life?" He turned to his men. "Throw them over."

"Wait!" I said urgently. I had no idea what to say next, and they ignored me anyway. The hand gripping my hair hauled me to my feet. It hurt a lot.

"Not that one," said Jack calmly. "We have an agreement, remember."

My guards shoved me to my knees again, but the guards—three of them—hauling Michael toward the edge didn't stop. Michael's boots skidded on the stony ground.

"Don't do this," I shouted. "Don't!"

"You really think he'd go with you?" Dawkins asked Jack. "And not turn on us later?"

Jack went on speaking, but I paid no attention. Michael was fighting now, throwing his weight from side to side. A gust of wind sent all of them staggering, and he almost broke free.

I must have tried to stand; the grip on my hair forced me down so hard that tears blurred my vision. I strained against the ropes.

The three men struggling with Michael called for another to help them. They picked him up, one grasping each kicking leg, one at each shoulder. They moved more rapidly, carrying him.

"Wait!" Two guards were holding me now. Fighting wasn't going to work. "Jack, stop this! I'll do it. I'll do whatever you want!"

Michael got in a good kick as they drew near the edge and sent one of them sprawling. The man almost went over, and rolled away from the drop swearing with fright. The other three stepped up to the cliff and pitched Michael over. I don't know if he screamed, because I did, raw and wordless. Useless.

My heart was trying to pound its way out of my rib cage. My throat had locked tight. My blank, no-it-can't-be shock was edged with knives. It could be. It was.

I doubled over, despite the drag on my scalp, a strangled whimper escaping my choked throat.

"All done, sir," the guard reported to Dawkins, who was arguing, low voiced, with Jack.

"Did you watch to be sure he got to the bottom?" Dawkins asked. "You ass! You know the cliff's not sheer. He could have hung up on the path, or a bush or something. Look over and make sure."

It's hard to get good help these days.

I knew I should pay attention to the discussion between Jack and Dawkins—it was my execution, after all—but I couldn't bring myself to care. Maybe Michael had hung up on a bush, or the path, or some such thing. Maybe . . . I watched the guard grumble his way to the cliff edge, glance over, and come back.

"He went all the way down," he reported.

"Well, make sure of him when you get down," said Dawkins. "No point—"

The storm interrupted him. Thunder boomed and heavy drops pelted down, just a handful at first, leaving wet circles on the rocks, wetting my shoulders. Then they thickened to a downpour. Cold water trickled down my scalp, down my face, down my back beneath my vest. It would hide any tears I might have shed, and that was good, because I had to lie in order to survive. To survive, come back, and see these bastards hang to the last man.

I owed Michael that. I took a deep breath, struggling for calm. The cold helped, but my throat still felt like an iron shackle was clamped around it—my voice would give me away. Well, let it. At this point, it was useless to pretend I hadn't cared. But Michael was dead now—I had to look out for myself. Jack would believe that. It was what he'd do.

I would use that blindness. Use it to destroy him.

The first fury of the storm dwindled from a torrent to a hard, steady fall, but one that men could speak through. And more to the point, see through.

The man with the spyglass called, "Ship!" and Dawkins turned abruptly.

"Can you make out her name?"

"Not at this distance. She's coming from the west, though."

"Then she's probably the *Night Heron*. We'll try for her." Dawkins stepped forward and took the glass. "You, up the ladder, but wait till you see a man on the other high point before you light it. Markham . . ." He turned to Jack, a thoughtful gleam in his eyes. "Why don't you light the other signal. I don't trust a man whose hands are too clean."

Jack glanced at me. "No problem, as long as you promise not to . . . make our debate academic, shall we say, in my absence. My employer can make use of this man, and he hates it when people waste things he can use."

Dawkins's lips compressed. "Very well, I won't kill him till you get back. But hurry."

"Jack, don't," I murmured as he passed me.

He stopped, looking down. "Don't what?"

"Don't light the other signal. If they see only one, they won't know where the harbor is. They won't come in."

Jack shook his head. "You've changed, Fisk. Must be that loser you've been traveling with. Maybe . . ."

He shrugged and went to the horses, riding out at a gallop a few seconds later. He was going to do it. My shoulders sagged. But I had to try. Michael would have haunted me forever if I hadn't.

On the other hand, if Jack wrote me off as a loser, I'd be in no position to do anyone any good. And I really wanted to see these bastards hang.

No, what I really wanted was Michael, alive. But I'd settle for what I could get.

It didn't take Jack long to reach the other signal. I couldn't see him, but the guard who'd scuttled up the ladder with a torch called down that he was there and bent to kindle the logs. Even in the rain, the pitch-soaked logs weren't hard to light. Soon the fire crackled and leapt—high enough for me to see the flames.

The minutes crawled past. Through the leaden numbness that filled my heart, a precarious hope began to sprout. Maybe the sailors wouldn't spot the fires till they were too far past to turn in. Maybe the captain would be too alert, too wary.

Then Dawkins turned away from the sea, folding the glass with a snap. "They're coming." He ignored the others' hungry cheer and went on crisply. "We'd better get into position. Rogers, take everyone down. I want the boats ready to launch the moment she hits the rocks—take no chances on this one breaking up."

The men were already moving down the cliff path, which started at one side of the clearing. No wonder Dawkins had feared Michael might hit it. If only he had. Grief flooded in, but I'd learned the futility of wishing the dead back to life before I met Jack.

One of my guards followed his comrades, and the man who was gripping my hair called, "What about me?"

Dawkins, who'd just put on his spectacles, regarded me thoughtfully. "You come over here and keep an eye on the ship." He passed his man the spyglass and drew his sword. "I'll watch this one. If he tries to run"—he shrugged—"that ends the debate."

Suddenly my head was free. I started to rise, instinctively, but desisted at a gesture of Dawkins's sword. We both knew that if I ran for it, he could catch me and cut me down, probably before I made it out of the clearing. Unless he was really distracted—by a ship, say, striking the rocks. I settled back, letting my shoulders sag, faking defeat.

I had to wait, bide my time. But my heart ached, and it was for more than Michael's loss. I didn't want that ship to strike the rocks. My all-too-excellent imagination painted the picture clearly. The biting crunch as the hull struck, the lurch of the ship, sending the crew tumbling, injured, disoriented. Easy prey for the wreckers slipping alongside in their slim, dark boats.

My stomach knotted. I was bound, under guard, and Michael was dead. If there was anything I could do to save them, I didn't see it. The only thing I could do for the people on that ship was survive to avenge them. And revenge was already foremost in my plans.

The ship continued to sail in, slowed by the rough seas. My clammy clothes stuck to my skin and I shivered. I lowered my eyes, hoping to lull Dawkins into ignoring me, but two muddy boots appeared in my field of vision and I looked up to meet Dawkins's gaze. His spectacles were speckled with raindrops, despite the wide brim of his hat.

"So, Master Fisk, Markham says you'll come over to us. Not turn us in. Not try to avenge your friend. Is that true? Are you such a spineless bastard you'd trade your friend's life for your own and a bit of gold?"

He was bored, curse him. I hate being "entertainment" for a multiple murderer.

"Why not?" I asked. "You've killed dozens of people, some of them your own townsfolk, for a bit of gold."

"And here I thought you liked him." He reached out with the tip of his sword, tracing a line from one eye down my cheek, where a tear would fall. If he cut the skin, I was too numb with cold to feel it, but it was hard not to flinch.

"He's dead," I said. "All the revenge in the world won't change that. And it puts no food on my plate. Let's just say I'd listen to an offer."

"An—"

"Coming in, steady as she goes," the guard called. But he'd lowered the spyglass to watch the little drama Dawkins was playing out, with only occasional glances seaward.

"An offer?" Dawkins's sword whispered up the side of my throat, claiming my undivided attention. The sharp edge came to rest under one ear, then bit, just a little.

I wasn't as cold as I'd thought. The trickle of blood down my neck felt like fire.

"If I have ears, of course." It was hard to keep my voice steady. "It's difficult to listen to an offer without ears."

"You're interested in my money?"

"Why not?" I asked again. "You must have a lot of it, by this time."

"Ah, but it takes a lot of money," said Dawkins, "to start your own bank."

I choked. "You want to be a *banker*? That's what this is about? There are easier . . . Oh. Planning on competing with Burke, are you?"

"Planning on killing Burke."

The sword scraped across my throat, not cutting this time.

"Then planning on surpassing him, and all the stupid bastards who've been pitying me. They pitied my father, too. By the time I'm finished, this town will be bankrupt, and I . . ."

The sword waltzed slowly downward, a direction I really hated to see it go, past my madly thumping heart, past my quivering belly. My genitals were retracting when it withdrew.

". . . I will be a rich banker in Tallowsport. What do you think of that, Master Fisk?"

"Sounds fine to me." My voice shook now, despite my best efforts. "But it also sounds like you'll be needing the services of a good fence for some time. Do you want to anger your friend Markham's employer over a trivial matter like—"

Michael's head appeared over the edge of the cliff. He had a bruise on one cheekbone, and his lips were pressed tight with determination.

Michael.

Reality seemed to shiver around me, then shift back into its proper place. The guard was looking at me, his back to the cliff. Dawkins began to laugh. "Oh, well done. The sudden stop, the wide, fixed stare. The oldest trick in the book. Do you really expect me to turn around and give you a chance to run for it?"

"I rather hope you won't," I said truthfully, watching Michael stride softly toward the guard, lifting the rock clenched in his fist. My heart was singing.

The thud of stone striking flesh, the clatter of the guard's fall, sent Dawkins spinning. I seized the moment to wobble to my feet and stagger away, lest it occur to Dawkins to take me out of the equation before he went for Michael.

Michael reached down, steel shrieking as he drew the fallen guard's sword. "Get that fire out, Fisk. The ship's coming in."

"How? There's a guard up there."

But looking up, I saw the guard stepping onto the ladder, coming to add his sword to the fray. However Michael had survived, two-on-one odds are too much for anyone. I tried to ignore the clash of swords behind me as I ran for the ladder and wiggled into the small space behind it.

I hooked one foot outside the first rung, so as not to bring the thing crashing down on my head, and leaned all my weight against the rung that was level with my shoulders. The wood bit into my flesh and didn't budge an inch.

My leverage was rotten with a man's full weight

on the top steps—though he was getting lower far too rapidly. I twisted around, braced my other foot against the hillside, and tried again, and this time the ladder quivered and began to shift. If the descending guard had had any sense, he'd have climbed up again, and the ladder would have fallen back, squashing me in the process. But he tried to come down faster, and the ladder swung slowly out, away from the hill, and then crashed.

Hopping wildly, I managed not to fall when the lowest rung caught my foot. The guard lay on his back, half under the ladder, one hand wavering toward his head.

I ran and kicked his temple with my boot heel, hard enough to keep him from rising for a good long time—maybe forever, but I didn't care.

Dawkins and Michael were still fighting, the clash and rasp of their swords echoing through the pattering rain. I prayed it couldn't be heard on the beach below. Dawkins was surprisingly good for a banker's clerk—I supposed he'd learned from his men over the years. But Michael was holding his own, despite cold, bruises, and an unfamiliar sword.

The ship was coming in to the rocks, with thirty wreckers waiting for it. If Michael could survive a three-hundred-foot fall, he could look after himself for a few more minutes. I had to put that fire out now.

The fallen guard's sword was beneath his body, but the hilt was clear. I knelt, then sat with my back to him, my numb fingers groping for the hilt. I could barely feel it, but finally I succeeded in wrapping my hands around something hard. I pulled, and my grip slipped off.

A flurry of swords rang out behind me, and Dawkins swore breathlessly. I grinned and tried again. Same result.

I turned on my knees and bent to look more closely—the leather strap that held the sword in its scabbard was twisted firmly over the hilt. I couldn't see the end of it, and with numb hands I could be fumbling for hours.

And that ship would hit the rocks.

I looked at the rough slope where the ladder had lain, more rock than grass and almost vertical. With my hands bound there was no way to put the ladder back. I started around the tall mound looking for another way up. The clatter of swords quickened my pace, but I didn't dare look back. If I looked, I might not leave, the ship would sink, and Michael would never forgive me whether he lived or not.

The mound's west side was the most gradual, which wasn't to say it was an easy climb for a man with both hands tied behind his back. A third of the way up my boot skidded on a clump of wet grass and almost pitched me over backward. I leaned in and slithered up the rest of the slope on my belly. It wasn't as if I could get any wetter.

I was panting by the time I crawled onto the shelf the wreckers had dug for their fire pit. The fire crackled, big enough to send welcome heat through my damp clothes. I staggered to my feet.

Michael was still holding his own, but the battle looked more even than I liked. His doublet sagged away from a slash over his stomach, but if that cut had been deep, he'd be dead by now and I saw no blood. They circled like tomcats in an alley.

I turned and looked out to sea, and my heart sank. I could see the ship, even through the curtains of falling rain. Its masts were bare as winter trees, with only the small front sails unfurled, but it still moved forward, seeking the lying safety of the wreckers' trap.

I had to get that fire out *now*. I dashed to the neat pile of blazing logs, suddenly glad for my soaked clothing. They were large—it took several tries, long enough for my eyebrows to feel scorched, to kick one of the lower logs from under the stack. Half a dozen of the logs on top rolled with it, still burning, making me skip and swear.

Blessing the stout protection of my boots I started kicking logs down the hillside in whatever direction they were inclined to roll. One hurtled into the duel below and came within inches of knocking Michael off his feet.

He jumped as the guttering monster lurched past, and Dawkins took advantage of his distraction to launch a sweeping stroke that would have eviscerated him if he hadn't leapt aside.

"Sorry," I shouted.

A string of breathless curses drifted back. I thought perhaps I'd better hurry, but I didn't roll any more logs down that side of the mound even though I had to turn several in different directions.

I gave the last log a final shove. At least my feet were warm. I turned toward the sea, blinking rain out of my eyes.

The ship was turning. It had probably started shortly after the fire began to sink, for it was half around now—not quite headed away from the treacherous rocks but soon it would be.

I was smiling, a wide, ridiculous grin. It faded as I turned my attention to the fight below. Dawkins was pushing Michael—only a quick parry and a desperate scramble kept him free of the tangling junipers. But now his back was to the cliff, and thrust by thrust,

Dawkins forced him toward it. I'd better get down there.

Down was faster than up, since I skidded down the slope on my butt, like a toddler on a staircase. I lost control about halfway down and hit the ground so fast, I almost fell flat on my face.

Instead I turned the momentum into a staggering run, around the hill and behind Dawkins, who had Michael nearly backed over the cliff. One of Michael's sleeves was stained with red. He was no longer holding his own. In fact, he was about to lose.

I ran toward the fight. All I had to do was tackle Dawkins from behind—roll under his feet like a log—and Michael could step forward and skewer the bastard. A sound, simple plan.

Until Dawkins spun like a dancer and lifted his sword, and I realized I was not only weaponless, but had my hands tied behind my back. What in the world was I thinking of?

My feet scrabbled on the muddy ground as I struggled to reverse direction before that blade fell. I fell instead, rolling, slithering, drawing breath for my final scream—

Then Michael leapt forward, his sword sweeping in from behind, and Dawkins screamed instead, dropping his blade, blood dripping through the fingers of his left hand as he clutched the wrist Michael had all but severed. Both the sword and the blood fell on me.

Dawkins took a step to run, but I swung my legs and knocked his feet from under him. He fell to his knees, the tip of Michael's sword coming to rest against his back.

"Stay!" Michael was breathing so hard he barely got the word out. But the pressure of his sword tip, which pierced Dawkins's coat, made the point—so to speak.

Breathing almost as hard, I rolled to my knees and then stood, still bound, with an exhausted comrade, a prisoner, and thirty wreckers no doubt hurrying up the path to report that their prey had escaped.

"Now what?"

Michael, still gasping for breath, glanced at the cliff path and then at his prisoner. "Hanged . . . if I know."

"Well, he's one problem we could solve." I nodded to Dawkins since I couldn't point. "If you'd only consider—"

"No!"

"He did it to you." I would have gone on to make an eloquent argument for dropping enemies over cliffs, if not for the sudden rumble I heard behind us. Not thunder, which I'd long since tuned out, but something like—

Sheriff Todd and twenty deputies galloped over the rise and into the clearing, which grew very crowded, though they left a clear circle around Michael, Dawkins, and me. The horses' wet coats steamed. I could warm my hands on one of them, if anyone ever untied me.

Todd swung out of the saddle, practically on top of us. His expression was grimly appreciative, and not at all surprised. How had he found us? And what under two moons was Rudy Foster doing with them?

Michael stepped back, his sword point dropping—less in the manner of surrendering his prisoner than as if he couldn't hold it up much longer. He drew the sleeve of his free arm across his sweaty, rain-wet face and grinned.

"I'm very glad to see you, Sheriff. It seems my plan worked—after a fashion."

## CHAPTER 12
# Michael

Fisk was still sputtering when they let him come to seek shelter under the dense juniper where I crouched. With my soaked doublet cast off, and someone's nearly dry coat wrapped tight around me, I was nearly warm.

The man the sheriff set to watch the path had seen half a dozen wreckers start up it shortly after I'd borrowed a dagger and cut Fisk free. The sheriff then asked Fisk to kneel in the clearing with his hands behind him, under the guard of a deputy in Dawkins's coat and hat. The ambush worked, the wreckers rushing into the clearing without a thought for self-defense, until the deputies swarmed out of the trees and surrounded them.

Three laid down their swords in surrender, but two fought, one to the death. The last broke free and ran for the cliff, hurtling himself into space as if he might take wing. I covered my ears not to hear him strike the earth, and if that was cowardice, then so be it.

You might think all this would have distracted Fisk, but the first words from his mouth were "You think this plan succeeded? I hope I'm never around you when one fails, because your idea of success is evidently just short of suicide!"

He'd acquired a raw-looking scrape on one side of his jaw, probably climbing up to put out the fire, an act which earned him the right to sputter all he wished. But if he could be diverted . . .

"Have you spoken to Rudy?" I asked, handing him the dry coat I'd borrowed. "He's the one who truly saved us. He realized we were up to more than we confessed, so he followed when we left camp this morning." He'd probably thought we were up to no good, though he hadn't admitted it. I understood that all too well. "He was following us all day."

As I'd hoped, it caught Fisk's attention. "He's the one you kept sensing?"

"Most likely. When he saw the wreckers, he realized what was going on and rode for the sheriff. He found them returning from Makejoye's camp and brought them here."

Fisk wrapped himself up and sat beside me, bringing

down a cold shower when the branches shook. "Have they found Callista's body?"

"Not yet." The cold I felt had little to do with the weather. "I'm glad I'll not be here for the executions."

Fisk snorted. "Not long ago, I'd have been happy to slaughter them with my own hands. Michael, what happened? It's three hundred feet to the bottom of that cliff."

I sought for words and failed to find them.

"Dawkins said the cliff wasn't sheer," Fisk went on. "That you might have struck the path, or hung up on a bush."

He knew it wasn't true. He was giving me an excuse, and his generosity unlocked my frozen tongue.

"I made the air thicker." My voice was harsh.

"With magic?" Fisk prompted gently.

"I didn't mean to—it just happened. I was falling. I hit the path, other things too, but they didn't stop me. Then the power flared up and . . . and I started falling slower."

Not much slower at first, but the next outcrop I slammed into didn't hurt so badly. I could feel the air on my skin like thick cream—then thicker, though it had no texture. I fell slower and slower till the protruding rocks and ledges left no bruises as I bumped past them.

"When I slowed down enough to think, realized

what I was doing, I panicked and stopped it," I said. "Fortunately, by then I was about ten feet from the ground. It knocked the wind out of me. I was lying there when I saw them look down to confirm I was dead, so I waited awhile, and when they didn't check again, I cut my hands loose. I was doing that when I heard the lot of them coming down the cliff, so I played dead. The foot of the path comes out several hundred yards from where I'd fallen. I was afraid they'd come back to make sure of me, but they didn't."

"They were supposed to." Fisk eyed me with interest, but without a trace of the queasy horror such strangeness made me feel. "How did you cut yourself loose?"

"They threw our weapons over, remember? I couldn't find the daggers, and my sword was broken—that's why I brought a rock up with me instead—but I found a piece of the blade to sever the rope. Fisk, this . . . this power that I seem to have, I can't control it. It does things before I can stop it, or even think about it."

"I suppose that is a bit unnerving," said Fisk. "But all it's done so far is to save your skin, so I wouldn't complain too much. As for the lack of control—train it."

"No," I said with a shiver. "I may be stuck with it, but I'll not use it unless I absolutely have to. Only if the alternative is death."

Fisk shrugged. "It's your life. Speaking of life and death, what are we going to do about Nutter?"

That was something I hadn't considered. "We can't prove he did anything," I said at last.

"But we know he helped them kill Quidge. They couldn't have handled the magic without a Savant's assistance. The earth voices probably told Nutter the wreckers would drive everyone off the sea. What will they tell him to do next? He's crazy, Michael."

"Yet we all answer to voices," I said slowly. "Mine impel me to knight errantry, which most folk think as mad as anything Nutter does. As for you—"

"I don't hear voices," said Fisk.

I knew that to be a lie; his heart's voice was as strong as any man's, and the voice of his conscience growing louder all the time. But I know better than to say such things to Fisk.

"We'll tell the other Savant what we've learned," I said. "I believe she cares enough, for both him and the townsfolk, to keep him from harming anyone else. Will that do?"

Fisk frowned but he nodded, just as a second batch of wreckers bustled up the cliff path. We left them to the deputies.

They captured almost all the wreckers, eventually.

When the wreckers realized the law awaited them at the cliff top, the last of them rowed out in their two small boats. They were badly overladen and the rough seas capsized one—a fitting end, given all they'd had a hand in drowning. The other boat made it to the harbor, and the deputies hunted them down. Only two escaped, along with Fisk's old . . . acquaintance, whom no one had seen after he lit the other fire. From that vantage point, he probably saw the sheriff's men coming down the road. Fisk said he'd never been caught, and that it would take a better man than Todd to do it now. 'Twas hard to tell what he felt, except glad that it was over—a sentiment I heartily endorsed.

"Of course you're free to go," Todd assured us. "This town owes you both a great debt."

He'd sent for a doctor as part of his reinforcements, and the man was dressing the shallow cut on my forearm. He politely ignored the tattoo on my wrist, saying he was honored to assist the men who'd caught the wreckers . . . and would send his bill to the sheriff's office.

"What's the difference between a healer and a bandit?" Fisk whispered, as the doctor went to tend others.

"I'm sure you're about to tell me." I sighed.

"A bandit doesn't charge extra for house calls."

I winced. "That hurts worse than the cut."

But not so badly as what was to come.

Sheriff Todd, along with Rudy and two deputies, accompanied us back to Makejoye's camp, since he was more concerned with recovering the jewels than tracking down the wreckers whose boat had survived.

We rode between the bright wagons and into the clearing in weary, sodden silence, though the storm was finally dripping to an end. The players, wrapped against the chill, peered through open doors, their faces wary and grieved. Except for Rose. She ran down the wagon's steps, frightened eyes flashing from face to face, over Fisk, over me . . .

"Rudy, you're drenched! You'd better change into dry clothes right now. I've been so worried . . ."

Rudy swung out of the saddle, and Rose embraced him and led him off, clutching his arm and chattering about how fearful she'd been when he vanished, without a word, for a *whole day.*

I looked down at my blood-spattered clothes. A white strip of bandage showed beneath the too short sleeve of my borrowed coat. And surely the sore stiffness where my face had struck the rocks indicated a bruise?

I looked at Fisk—with his scraped jaw, and mud and grass stains from collar to boots, he looked almost as battered and bedraggled as I felt. Though more sardonic.

We were wet, too.

The weight of defeat descended on my shoulders, so heavy I almost expected Chant's legs to buckle. "I suppose this is where the best man wins." It came out more bitter than I'd intended, and I bit my lip wishing I hadn't spoken. Wishing . . .

Fisk snorted. "Or loses. I think you're well rid of the lovely ninny."

"Rosamund isn't a ninny," I said hotly. "She's just . . . just . . ." *In love. And not with me.* "Ah, be hanged to it."

Fisk fought back a grin, successfully, which was a good thing. I'd probably have punched him if he'd failed.

I took Chant and Rudy's horse back to the picket lines and brushed them down, since I knew the distracted lover wouldn't and there was no point letting the poor beast suffer. Then I made my way to the wagons. Fisk had already cared for Tipple and gone. "Cheer up," he'd remarked. "Your father will separate them, anyway."

I felt strange, aching, and out of balance—and I

don't mean physically, though 'twas as true of my body as of my heart. I had lost.

But so would Rudy when my father caught up with them. Rose would be miserable, and I'd not be able to console her. She'd probably be married off to some rich old man, who might or might not love her, and then what?

Win, lose, or draw, I never wanted Rose to feel like I did now. But what could I do about it?

The sheriff and Gwen were in Callista's wagon going over the costumes, trying to tell which stones were real and which were fake. They'd probably have to send for a jeweler. Sometimes real and fake are all but indistinguishable. Sometimes . . .

My heart began to pound. It would work. I knew my father, and I'd swear it would work. Rose would be happy, and Rudy too, though I couldn't bring myself to be glad about that even if he had saved my life. It was the best I could do for the woman I loved. The proper, knightly thing to do.

I turned and strode toward the costume wagon, my steps shaking droplets from the wet grass. "Sheriff, you say this town owes me a favor. I wish to claim it."

He thought I was crazy. It made me feel better, for the first time since I'd realized Rose's choice was irrevocable. My heart still ached, but my balance was returning. Fisk would think I was crazy too. Yes, I was doing the right thing.

So the adventure that started with us taking Rose to her lover ended beside her grave . . . after a fashion.

Huckerston's burying grove was on a ridge north of town, with a splendid view of the tawny hills and sparkling sea. Blood oak leaves, red all year round except for a few brief months in spring, rustled in the breeze. The rasp of shovels in stony ground was oddly soothing.

The players had come to plant a blood oak on Callista's grave. Her body had been found, finally, hidden beneath an undercut bank of the stream. Her neck was broken; quick at least. I felt sorry, despite all she'd done.

Fisk pointed out that a public execution would have been worse.

And I had to admit, being able to write to Father that Rose went looking for Callista and fell into the wreckers' hands as well made a plausible tale. Lord Fabian was enchanted with the whole idea.

"Do you think she'd mind?" I asked Fisk, looking down at Rebecca Chase's grave. "Having Rose officially buried here, instead of her?"

"She's dead," said Fisk. "She won't mind anything.

But if you're feeling guilty, consider it payment for catching the bastards who killed her. And Fabian's right—if your father sends someone to check, there should be a body in that grave."

A girl of about the right age, with reddish hair. Her hair had been so dark with seawater, I'd not known its color. No one else would die thus. Fisk was right—that was worth something. I was still glad we were leaving tomorrow, before the executions.

"Father won't send anyone," I told Fisk. "This gives him both excuse and reason to stop—that's all he needs."

Fisk frowned. "An excuse, yes, but what reason?"

"Who do you think inherits Rosamund's money?"

"Ah. Now that makes sense."

"In fairness to Father, had she married properly, he'd have been perfectly willing to give it to her. And if she turns up in six years with a handful of toddlers clinging to her skirt, he'll still give it up—though he'd be angry about that. In fact, I expect he'll be quite distressed about her death . . . until he notices Kathy's not grieving. Then he'll figure it out, but he still won't send anyone. Excuse and reason."

Fisk had written to Kathy and sent the letter off first thing; it should reach her before the news of Rose's "death."

"Well, it's a fine scam," said Fisk. "I'm impressed. I didn't think you had it in you."

I grinned. "'Tis the company I keep."

The troupe was leaving, and Fisk and I turned to follow them. The sapling on Callista's grave looked fragile and alive.

Rosamund, now Rose Foster, had set sail on the morning's tide with her husband, bound for a troupe owned by a friend of Makejoye's who worked on the eastern coast. Far enough away she'd be unlikely to meet anyone who'd recognize her, especially under an actress's paint. Before they left, I told Rudy about Quidge's warrant, so he'd be alert for other bounty hunters. He thanked me. I called it a wedding present. My throat was tight. My heart ached.

"Rudy . . . take care of her."

"Count on it." His smile had held nothing but grave sympathy. I tried not to hate him for it.

Callista's death and their departure left the troupe shorthanded, so Fisk and I had agreed to travel with them, at least till they picked up a few more acts. Besides, Hector was threatening to write a play about Fisk's and my adventures, and we'd yet to come up with a threat severe enough to stop him in our absence.

"She may have to claim her money someday," said Fisk, returning to the subject of Rosamund. "Since she gave Makejoye the rest of her jewels. They're going to be short of cash, especially when they start having kids."

"No, they won't." The thought of Rose bearing children that weren't mine still had the power to hurt. And to distract, or I'd have remembered that I'd planned to put off telling Fisk about this aspect of my scheme.

"What do you mean?" His brows drew down as he observed my guilty expression. "Michael, what have you done?"

"I gave the reward for capturing the wreckers to Rosamund," I admitted. "As a dowry. I'm her family, and since she and Rudy insisted on helping Makejoye make up his losses, it seemed the least I could do."

Fisk's mouth opened and closed like a landed fish. "You gave the money away?"

"You said you didn't care about the reward. Time after time. You didn't even want to know how much it was."

"That was when I thought we'd have to die to get it. Which we cursed near did! And you *gave the money away?*"

I tried to think of some further defense, but there wasn't any. "Yes. I gave the money away."

Fisk closed his eyes in pain. "How much was it?"

"You don't want to know."

I set off down the sunlit hill; our friends were getting ahead of us. It had been a while since we'd had friends. I was looking forward to it.

"Yes, I do," said Fisk, scrambling after me. "How much?"

"Trust me, you really don't want to know."

"That much? You might as well tell me, since it's gone. I can't believe you gave the money . . ."

I'd a feeling we'd be having this discussion for a long time to come. The future beckoned, adventure in the offing and my squire beside me. Who needs gold when you have friends? I would try that argument on Fisk sometime. When he was calmer. And duck. I looked forward to that, too.